"Did the kidnapper give you a deadline?"

Matt's voice was calm, as if he dealt with this sort of thing every day. For a second, Emma allowed herself to believe he could fix things. That he could find her baby before anything bad happened. And perhaps he could. Weren't park rangers good at tracking?

"Three days," she said, a lump forming in her throat. "He wants half a million dollars in three days."

"And you don't have it."

"No." She jerked her head up, glaring at Matt. "My God, do you think I'd be here if I did? Do you think I care about money? I'd give him ten times that amount if it meant getting Christina back safely! I'd do anything to hold her again." Her arms ached with the memory of her baby, warm and soft against her body. Would she ever feel that sweet weight again? Christina was her life. She'd never stop looking for her daughter, never rest until she found her.

* * *

If you're on Twitter, tell us what you think of Harlequin Romantic Suspense! #harlequinromsuspense

Dear Reader,

Welcome to the second book in my Rangers of Big Bend series! This is one of those stories that grabbed me by the throat and demanded to be written. I started with the image of Emma standing next to an empty crib and the book unfolded from there.

Emma is a woman facing every mother's worst nightmare—her baby has been taken. Desperate to find her daughter, she's forced to turn to a stranger for help.

Matt isn't sure what to think about Emma. But when he realizes she's telling the truth about her baby's kidnapping, he's determined to do whatever he can to help her.

Emma and Matt are complicated people, with their fair share of past heartbreaks. I enjoyed getting to know them both, and discovering how they put loss and betrayal behind them to move forward in their lives. I hope you'll like their story, too.

Happy reading!

Lara

RANGER'S BABY RESCUE

Lara Lacombe

HARLEQUIN® ROMANTIC SUSPENSE

Recycling programs
for this product may
not exist in your area.

ISBN-13: 978-1-335-66196-8

Ranger's Baby Rescue

Printed in U.S.A.

www.Harlequin.com

Lara Lacombe earned a PhD in microbiology and immunology and worked in several labs across the country before moving into the classroom. Her day job as a college science professor gives her time to pursue her other love—writing fast-paced romantic suspense with smart, nerdy heroines and dangerously attractive heroes. She loves to hear from readers! Find her on the web or contact her at laralacombewriter@gmail.com.

This one is for Erin, the sister of my heart.

Chapter 1

Emma Foster opened her eyes in the darkness, filled with the sudden knowledge that something was terribly wrong. She listened hard, straining her ears for any noise that was out of place. Nothing sounded amiss—the refrigerator hummed quietly in the kitchen; the ceiling fan ticked softly over her head. But despite the absence of obvious issues, the house didn't *feel* right.

She slipped out of bed, stepping lightly to avoid making too much noise. She'd had a devil of a time getting Christina to sleep tonight—her normally cheerful and good-natured ten-month-old daughter was teething and grumpy with it, which made for long nights. The baby had finally surrendered to exhaustion about an hour ago, and Emma had slipped off to her own bed for a few stolen moments of sleep. Everything had seemed fine at the time, but now she couldn't shake the feeling that something wasn't right.

She headed for the front door, knowing that it was locked but needing to check it again for her own peace of mind. Sure enough, the dead bolt was secure, just as she'd left it earlier in the evening. The windows were all shut, the blinds lowered into place. There was no sign of any trouble, nothing to explain the sense of dread that weighed on her.

Moments like this made her miss Chris all the more. He wouldn't have hesitated to wake up with her, to double-check all the locks and peek into the closets and under the beds until she was certain they were safe. He'd been a perfect boyfriend and fiancé—Emma had no doubt he would have been a wonderful husband to her and a fantastic father to their little girl.

For the millionth time, she cursed the driver who had decided sending a text message was more important than paying attention to the road. Chris had stopped at a red light when he'd been hit from behind and pushed into cross traffic, where he'd been hit again by a bus and a garbage truck. Chris had died at the scene before the firemen could even get him out of the mangled wreck of his car.

Emma hadn't known she was pregnant at the time. She'd been so busy working and wrapping up the plans for their wedding that she'd assumed the fatigue and upset stomach were due to stress. After the accident, she'd been so consumed with grief she hadn't paid attention to her symptoms. It had been her mother who put two and two together and suggested she take a pregnancy test.

She could still remember the feeling of shock that had washed over her when she'd realized the test was positive. She and Chris had talked about starting a family soon after they got married, but Emma had figured that dream died along with him. Finding out she was pregnant with Chris's baby had eased her grief a bit and had brought a spot of joy back into her life.

Chris had been gone a year and a half now, but Emma saw his face every time she looked at their daughter. Christina had her father's blue eyes, impish smile and love of avocados. Emma had never gotten over losing Chris, but she comforted herself with the knowledge that a small part of him lived on.

She paused in the hallway outside Christina's door, silently debating. Should she try to slip into her daughter's room to check on her, even though there was a very real possibility of waking her up? Or should she leave well enough alone and go back to bed?

Better not risk it, Emma decided. Christina had had a hard enough time going to bed earlier—if she woke her up, it might take hours to get her back down again.

Emma headed in the direction of her bedroom but stopped after a few steps. The sense of wrongness returned, as sudden and intense as before. The urge to see her daughter built with every heartbeat until she felt her chest might burst with it. She turned and walked back toward the nursery, forcing herself to move as quietly as possible so as not to wake the baby.

Panic lapped at the edges of her worry as she twisted

the knob and pushed against the door. The dim glow of the night-light provided just enough illumination to see the crib and the still form lying on the mattress.

She's fine, Emma told herself. But she crept closer, wanting to see her baby's face and hear the soft sighs of her breathing.

She reached the edge of the crib and looked down, expecting to see Christina's chubby cheeks and rosebud mouth relaxed in sleep. But all she found was a crumpled blanket lying in the spot where she had placed her daughter only an hour before.

Emma gripped the edge of the crib, her mind refusing to comprehend what she was seeing. "No," she whispered numbly. "It's not possible."

The roar of blood filled her ears, drowning out the sound of her screams.

Her baby—her world, her life—was gone.

Three days later

Park Ranger Matthew Thompson knew the moment the woman walked into the station that something was wrong. She stood just inside the lobby, clutching her purse, shoulders rounded as if she were expecting a blow. She glanced around uncertainly, her gaze flickering past the educational posters on the walls and the interactive displays scattered throughout the room. She looked out of place, lost even, and Matt took a step forward to greet her. As soon as she saw him move, her eyes locked on his, and he saw a glint of determination that made him realize his first impression was wrong—

she wasn't as fragile as she seemed. This woman was on a mission.

"Can I help you?" he asked, meeting her in the middle of the room. She stopped and eyed him up and down, her expression assessing as she took his measure. It had been a long time since someone had sized him up, and Matt felt the absurd urge to fall into a parade-rest stance. Army habits died hard.

Apparently, the woman liked what she saw; she nodded slightly before looking up to meet his gaze. This close, he could see she was younger than he'd originally thought. The lines of strain around her mouth and eyes made her look prematurely old, but her skin was otherwise smooth and youthful. Her eyes were brown, lit from within by a fire that burned bright. She wore her dark hair pulled back in a messy ponytail, and given the slightly wrinkled look of her clothes, Matt guessed her appearance was the last thing on her mind.

"I'm looking for my baby," she said.

"Ah, okay," he said, stalling as his mind raced. Whoever she was, it was clear this lady was confused. Now he had to figure out if she needed professional help, or if he should just try to send her on her way with a minimum of fuss.

"My brother took her," she continued, her tone low but intense. "I think he brought her here and is hiding out in Big Bend."

Matt arched one eyebrow at her absurd story. "I see," he said noncommittally. He glanced around the lobby, hoping another ranger would show up so he could pass this woman off to them, or at least get some backup in case she turned violent. She only came up to his shoulder and she was slender enough, but he knew better than to underestimate a woman in the grip of strong emotion.

She pressed her lips together at his reaction. "I'm telling the truth," she said, a hint of anger in her voice. "Three days ago I went to check on my baby in her crib, only to find her missing. My brother has her—he told me that when I called him to let him know she was gone. The police are searching for the two of them in El Paso. But I think my brother ran to the park."

Matt decided to entertain this crazy story, if only for the moment. "Why would he bring an infant here?"

"We used to camp a lot with my dad," she said. "This was one of his favorite places. I think Joseph came here because it's familiar and he can hide."

Her story sounded plausible, at least on a superficial level. Matt studied her face but saw no signs of deception. She appeared to truly believe what she was telling him, but he wasn't quite ready to buy into her tale. A missing baby would be big news, and he hadn't heard or read anything about a kidnapping.

"Where did you say you're from again?"

"El Paso," she replied, sounding a little impatient now. The city was hours away from the park, which meant it was possible the news hadn't trickled down to them just yet. Still, it sounded quite far-fetched.

"And your name?"

"Emma Foster." She dug into her purse and withdrew a card, which she extended to him. Matt took it and glanced down. It was the business card of a detective in El Paso, assuming it was legitimate and not something she'd forged to lend credence to her story.

But why would she lie about something like this? He knew some parents hurt their own children to get attention. Was she the kind of woman to fake a kidnapping for the same reasons? A small stone of worry formed in the pit of his stomach. Had she hurt her baby?

"That's the contact information for the detective in charge of the case," she said. "Call him and he'll confirm everything I've just told you."

Matt nodded but didn't reply. Emma's story was quite compelling, the kind of thing that would make a great movie plot. And she certainly seemed earnest. But Matt wasn't willing to suspend his disbelief just yet. He'd been lied to before, and he wasn't about to let Emma's pretty face short-circuit his skepticism.

"I'll call in just a moment," he said. "In the meantime, why are you here?"

Emma swallowed hard. "The police said they didn't have the man power to comb through Big Bend and still follow up on other leads. So I'm here to look for myself. I need a park ranger to go with me."

His first reaction was denial. "That's not really the kind of thing we—"

"Please," she said, cutting him off. "I know I'm asking for a lot. But I have to do something. I can't just sit at home while my baby is missing. I have to try to find her." A look of desperation crossed her face as she stared up at him. Matt felt his initial resistance softening as his curiosity grew. What would it hurt to check out her story? A few quick phone calls, and he'd have some answers.

"Stay here," he said. Emma sucked in a breath, and he held up a hand. "I'm not promising anything. But let me make a few calls and if you're telling the truth, I'll see what kind of assistance we can offer you."

She nodded vigorously. "Thank you," she said. Her shoulders relaxed a bit. Matt wanted to warn her not to get her hopes up, but he feared it was too late for that.

He left her in the lobby and headed for his desk, tossing the business card next to his keyboard. Typing quickly, he pulled up the number for the El Paso police department and dialed. When the call was answered, he asked for the name on the card and was put on hold while the call was transferred.

So far, so good, he thought to himself. Apparently this detective really did exist. Now to find out if he knew Ms. Foster, or if she was simply delusional.

"Doug Randall," said the voice on the other end of the line.

"Detective Randall, this is Matt Thompson. I'm a park ranger down at Big Bend." He quickly explained Emma's appearance in the ranger station and summarized her story. "I'm calling to verify the details."

"It's true," Randall said shortly. "All of it. Her baby was kidnapped three nights ago, and her brother, Joseph Foster, admitted to taking the child when she spoke to him over the phone. We're currently searching for him."

"What about the FBI?" Matt asked. "I thought they were involved in kidnapping cases."

"They are," Randall confirmed. "But we're focusing our efforts in El Paso and the surrounding areas. Most of the evidence suggests Joseph hasn't gone far, despite what Ms. Foster thinks."

"I see," Matt said. So Emma was telling the truth, but it seemed the police and FBI didn't agree with her conviction that her brother and baby were in Big Bend. "What would you like me to do? I don't want to interfere with your investigation. I can try to send her home if you think that would be best."

"That would be ideal, but I don't think she'll cooperate. She's got a bee in her bonnet about her brother and that park. I explained to her we simply don't have the man power to mount a thorough search of that area. In fact, I was just about to reach out to you guys, ask y'all to keep a lookout for anything suspicious. I doubt you'll find anything, though—our evidence suggests her brother and the baby might still be in El Paso. One of his associates swears on a stack of Bibles he saw the pair two days ago. I just can't see him taking a baby out into the wilderness, away from any kind of supplies or support."

"It does seem a bit unrealistic." Matt sympathized with the detective—searching for one man and a baby in a large city like El Paso was probably a lot like trying to find a needle in a haystack.

"I asked Ms. Foster to stay close," Randall continued, exasperated. "I guess our definitions of the term vary widely."

"I'll tell her we can't do anything and that her best bet is to go home." Now that he knew she was telling the truth, Matt felt sorry for Emma. But he didn't know the first thing about searching for a missing baby, and it was important she cooperate with the police.

"Actually," Randall said, sounding thoughtful, "maybe you could help me out."

"How's that?" Matt replied. He had a sneaking suspicion the bottom was about to drop out of his day.

"Keep her there," Randall said, confirming Matt's premonition. "You can keep tabs on her while she goes on this wild-goose chase. Based on our preliminary findings, she's not a suspect in her baby's disappearance. But I still need to know where she is. If you stay with her, you can let me know if her brother tries to contact her or if she does actually find something relevant to the investigation."

"Do you really think that's a possibility?" Babysitting a stubborn, misguided woman wasn't exactly high on Matt's list of desirable activities, nor did it fit his job description.

"It's worth considering, especially since she's already there. Can you do it?"

"I suppose," Matt said. "I'll have to clear it with my supervisor, though." It wasn't unheard of for park rangers to assist law enforcement investigations, but the rangers in question usually worked directly with the officers involved. There had been such a case recently, when a ranger had teamed up with an FBI profiler to catch a serial killer who had been using the park as his hunting ground. In this situation however, he'd be working with the victim, with no clear search plans in place. How long was he supposed to help her? Unless he missed his guess, Emma was determined to comb every inch of this park. She probably wouldn't be willing to leave until her baby was found, either here or in El Paso. He couldn't help her indefinitely, that much was certain.

"Patch me through to him and I'll put in the formal request," Randall said. "I really appreciate you helping out like this," he added.

Matt sighed, wondering how in the hell he'd gotten into this situation. *I never should have made eye contact*, he told himself. *I should have turned around and let another ranger handle her.* But it was too late for that now.

"All right," he agreed. "I'll be in touch, but don't expect us to find anything."

Randall let out a short laugh. "I don't, but at least now I know we're truly covering all the bases. One of us is bound to get lucky."

It won't be me, Matt thought sourly. He didn't have the greatest track record where babies were involved.

Jennifer's face flashed in his mind, the image of her accompanied by the familiar feelings of betrayal and pain. Three years ago, he'd shipped out with his army unit for a quick overseas tour and had come back to find his fiancée holding a baby. She'd sworn it was his, but even though the math just barely worked out, Matt had taken one look at the infant and known in his soul he wasn't the father. The child was adorable, though, and he'd felt a tugging at his heart like he'd never experienced before. It would have been so easy to fall in love with the little one, even though the boy wasn't his flesh and blood. But while he might have been willing to raise another man's child, Matt wasn't willing to forgive Jennifer for her deception. She'd cheated on him and spun a web of lies, trying to trick him into staying with her. He simply couldn't spend the rest of his life with someone he couldn't trust. After a paternity test confirmed his suspicions, Matt had packed his things and moved out.

He'd been worried about the baby, but Jennifer hadn't wasted any time. The door had barely shut behind him before she started seeing the baby's real father again. Last he'd heard, they were a cozy family of three, living the American dream in the suburbs. Matt felt a pang of jealousy every time he thought about them. That should have been his life; he'd signed up for the wife, the child, the dog, the house. Hell, he'd even looked forward to driving the standard-issue minivan. It was a vision that had kept him going throughout his time in the army, and coming home to find out Jennifer had lied to him had ripped the rug right out from under his feet. Seeing her holding a baby had been like a dream come true. Realizing the boy wasn't his child had been a kick in the gut. It had shaken him to the core, and he was still trying to recover.

Matt ran a hand through his hair and sighed, trying to brush off the shadow of his memories. He heard the faint sounds of his supervisor speaking, and based on the snatches of conversation he was able to make out, Paul Anderson, the chief ranger in the office, was only too happy to have Matt cooperate with the police. It seemed he was going to have a new focus, at least for the foreseeable future.

Time to go give Ms. Foster the good news.

Chapter 2

Emma wandered over to a poster mounted on the wall and stopped, staring at the glossy pictures of animals without really registering what she was seeing. *He has to help me.* The thought circled round in her brain, drowning out everything else. If she kept repeating it to herself, it would have to be true, right? There simply wasn't another possibility. She couldn't search the park alone, and she didn't have the money to hire a private guide. The ranger was her only hope, and if he refused, she didn't know what she was going to do.

He didn't believe her story, that much was clear. She'd seen the skepticism in his eyes and known he was writing her off as crazy. But Detective Randall would vouch for her, and then the ranger would have to understand. After discovering she was the real deal, surely he couldn't refuse to help her find Christina, even though that wasn't something a park ranger normally did.

She still couldn't believe Joseph had taken her baby. He'd called a few weeks ago, asking for money to pay off some debts. When Emma had told him she didn't have any cash to spare, he'd simply said, "Okay." She figured that had been the end of it.

But when she'd found Christina's empty crib, she'd called the police and then her brother. She'd wanted him to tell their mother what was going on—Emma hadn't had the emotional energy to break the news to anyone else.

Joseph had sounded unconcerned at hearing his niece was missing. "She's fine, Em."

"How can you say that? You don't know where she is!"

"Actually, I do. She's with me."

Joe's confession had turned Emma's blood to ice. She'd begged and pleaded with him to return her daughter, but her brother had refused.

"I told you, I need money." He'd sounded exasperated, as if he was tired of repeating himself.

"And I told you, I don't have it."

"We both know that's not true. You got a fat settlement after Chris's death."

"It wasn't a lump sum," she'd protested. "I don't have a pile of money gathering dust in my bank account."

"Anyway," he'd said, ignoring her. "Christina and

I will be fine. You can have her back once you get me what I need."

He'd hung up then, leaving Emma feeling even more distraught. The police had tried to trace his phone, but to no avail.

"He probably dumped it already," one of the detectives had told her.

The police and the FBI thought Joseph would stay in El Paso, figuring it was his home base and he wouldn't want to stray far from the familiar. But Emma wasn't so sure. The two of them had spent a lot of time in Big Bend as children, camping with their parents. Joseph had used the park as an escape before, when he'd needed to clear his head or take a break. It was a long shot, but Emma thought he might have run here again.

The thought of her baby girl out there in the wilderness sent a shiver down her spine. Big Bend was a huge park; God only knew where Joe had taken her. But the little one *was* here. Emma felt it in her bones, a tingling of her mother's intuition that gave her a sense of certainty despite everyone else's overwhelming doubt. And even though she was looking for the proverbial needle in a haystack, Emma wasn't leaving until she had her daughter in her arms once again.

Fortunately, the hospital had been understanding about her need for a leave of absence. There was a pool of nurses happy to step in and take her ER shifts while she focused on finding Christina.

"Take as long as you need," her supervisor had said.

With that worry taken care of, Emma had been free to focus solely on the search for her baby.

She wouldn't have picked this ranger had there been another option. But he'd been the only one in the lobby when she'd walked in, so she hadn't had much of a choice. He seemed competent enough—tall, with broad shoulders and lean, muscled arms. She had no doubts he could handle the physical aspects of the search with ease. But there was a hardness about him that gave her pause. It was as if he wore an invisible suit of armor. She'd seen a glimmer of wariness in his blue eyes, even before she'd told him about Christina. Maybe she was mistaken, but he seemed to regard the world with a hint of suspicion. It was this air of reserve that worried her now. Would he be sensitive to the dangers facing her little girl, or would he decide she was too much trouble and send her back home?

"He can try," she muttered. But if he thought she'd simply turn around and walk away, he was sorely mistaken.

Resolve stiffened her spine. If he refused to help, she'd ask another ranger. And another and another, if need be. She'd go through the whole damn roster of them until she found one who would search with her. And if that didn't work, she'd call a reporter. Not that she knew anyone in the media, but it couldn't be that hard to find somebody who worked at a news station or wrote for a paper. She'd raise holy hell until she got the help she needed. Beg, borrow or steal—Emma didn't care what she had to do at this point. She had no pride left. All that mattered was bringing Christina home safely.

Indignation bubbled in her chest, the leash on her

temper growing shorter with every passing minute. What was taking so long? It shouldn't be that difficult for him to call Detective Randall. He wouldn't be happy to learn she was here—he'd encouraged her to stay in El Paso while they searched for Christina, but Emma couldn't sit in her empty apartment twiddling her thumbs while her baby was missing. Despite what the detective thought, Joseph would feel comfortable in Big Bend, and more importantly, he probably figured no one would think to look for him so far from home.

"But I know," she whispered to herself. "And I will find you."

The clop of boot heels on tile sounded in the otherwise quiet lobby. She turned to find the ranger emerging from the back offices, his expression inscrutable. As he approached, she saw that a hint of worry had replaced the skeptical glint in his blue eyes.

Good, she noted with satisfaction. *He believes me now.*

"Ms. Foster," he said, his deep voice reminding her of tires on gravel. "I spoke with Detective Randall. I'm so sorry for your situation."

She nodded, appreciating the comment. Under normal circumstances she would have let her manners dictate her response, but she had little patience for the expected niceties at the moment. "Will you help me?"

He hesitated, sending her heart plummeting to her toes. Her fear must have shown on her face, for he reached out and placed a hand on her arm. "It's okay," he said kindly. "I'm going to do my best, but I can't promise anything."

A wave of relief washed over her, making her feel a little light-headed. "I know," she said. "But I need to try."

He nodded as if he understood. "Why don't we start from the beginning? Detective Randall told me some of the details, but I'd like to hear your side of the story."

"That's fine," Emma said. It suddenly occurred to her that she didn't know his name. "Uh, we haven't actually been introduced yet. You know my name. What's yours?"

Twin pink spots appeared high on his cheeks, making him look suddenly boyish. "Matt," he said. "Matt Thompson. I'm sorry I failed to introduce myself before."

She shrugged off the apology. "Is there someplace we can talk?" The lobby of the ranger station was nice enough, but she'd prefer to sit for this conversation.

Matt ushered her past the desk into the back room, which housed several desks and chairs. The far wall sported a large map of the park and a whiteboard full of text, but Emma didn't bother to read any of it. He led her to a counter that ran under the board and gestured to the coffee maker. "Need a cup?"

"Yes, please." Emma normally didn't drink coffee, but she'd learned over the last few days that it helped to have something to hold on to while she told her story over and over again.

Matt poured two cups, adding cream and sugar at her nod. Then he guided her to a desk and chair and sat, gesturing for her to do the same. He pushed the mug across the desk and looked at her expectantly.

Emma wrapped her hands around the cup, appreciating the warmth leaching through the porcelain. A familiar heavy weight settled over her as she gathered her thoughts. Talking about the night she had discovered Christina was missing never got any easier. She'd lost count of the number of times she'd repeated the story to the police and the FBI. Unfortunately, the repetition didn't dull her emotions or help her process what had happened. Her heart still pounded the way it had when she'd realized the crib was empty; her stomach still cramped as she relived the horror, as fresh as the first time.

Matt nudged a box of tissues toward her, as if sensing she might need them. She sent him a grateful smile and took a deep breath. "Three nights ago, I woke up at one thirty in the morning because I felt like something was wrong." She told him about searching the apartment but finding no signs of anything amiss, and how she'd nearly gone back to bed. "But I had to check on Christina. I knew I wouldn't be able to go back to sleep until I made sure she was okay."

He nodded, his blue eyes full of understanding. Emma appreciated the fact that he was simply listening and not bombarding her the way the police and FBI had done. She'd barely been able to get a sentence out before an officer had fired another question at her, which had made it difficult to get through the telling. But Matt remained quiet, apparently content to hear what she had to say before talking himself.

His silence was oddly encouraging, and she felt her shoulders relax. "That's when I discovered my baby was gone." Her throat tightened on the last word, and she felt the familiar prickle of tears. She blinked hard, dismissing them before they had a chance to fall.

"I called the police immediately," she continued. "They thought that since there were no signs of forced entry into the apartment, whoever took her must have a key. My brother, Joseph, is the only one with a spare, but I didn't think he would ever take Christina." Disappointment and anger swirled in her chest as she recalled her naive assertion that her brother would never kidnap her child. How wrong she'd been!

"Then I called Joseph, and he actually answered. At first, I was relieved. I figured if he had taken Christina, he wouldn't have answered the phone."

Matt lifted one eyebrow. "He didn't try to hide the fact that he'd kidnapped your daughter?"

Emma shook her head. "I think he was preparing to call me himself, to let me know she was safe."

"Why did he take her?"

"Money," she said simply. "Joseph has a gambling problem. It's something that developed over the last several years. I'd helped him once before with a small debt, but told him never again. He agreed, and for a while I thought he had stopped gambling. But he'd just been hiding it. Now he owes some bad people a lot of money, and he'd come to me about a week ago asking for help. I told him I didn't have anything, but he didn't believe me."

Matt tilted his head to the side, his eyes narrowing a bit. "Why would he think you're lying?"

The question hit close to home. Emma shifted in her

chair, not really wanting to get into the details of Chris's death and the subsequent lawsuit. "I was involved in a lawsuit about two years ago that resulted in a settlement. Joseph thinks I have a lot of money. He doesn't understand I haven't seen a dime. He accused me of holding out on him, of deliberately abandoning him."

"So he took your baby to try to force your hand," Matt said. The words dripped with disgust, as if he couldn't believe anyone would stoop so low.

Emma nodded. "Exactly. But I still don't have the money. And I don't know what he's going to do once he realizes that." Fear bubbled up in her chest as she wondered again how her brother would respond when he discovered there was no ransom coming his way. Joseph wasn't normally a violent person, but Emma felt like she no longer knew her own brother. Three days ago, she would have sworn he'd never kidnap a baby. Now she had no idea what he was capable of doing. He was plainly desperate, and she could only hope that desperation didn't override his basic humanity where her daughter was concerned.

"Did he give you a deadline?" Matt's voice was calm, as if he dealt with this sort of thing every day. For a second, Emma allowed herself to believe he could fix things. That he could find her baby before anything bad happened. And perhaps he could. Weren't park rangers good at tracking?

"Three days," she said, a lump forming in her throat. She glanced down, swirling the mug a bit to stir the coffee within. "He wants half a million dollars three days from now to pay off his debts."

"And you don't have it."

"No." She jerked her head up, glaring at Matt. "My God, do you think I'd be here if I did? Do you think I care about money? I'd give him ten times that amount if it meant getting Christina back safely! I'd do anything to hold her again." Her arms ached with the memory of her baby, warm and soft against her body. Would she ever feel that sweet weight again?

Matt held up his hands. "I didn't mean to imply otherwise. I'm sorry."

Her temper cooled quickly, leaving despair in its wake. "I don't have the money. The only way I can get that kind of money is by robbing a bank. And even then, I doubt they keep half a million in cash on hand these days."

"Probably not," Matt said. His voice was soothing now, as if he were trying to calm a wounded animal.

"This is my only option," she said. Her shoulders dropped, her energy starting to flag as the hopelessness of the situation took hold once again. The past few days she'd vacillated between a burning sense of urgency and a feeling of total defeat. It was growing more and more difficult to beat back the darkness trying to claim her spirit, but she had to keep trying. The police and FBI were doing all they could to find Christina, but at the end of the day, this was just another job to them. Christina was her life. She'd never stop looking for her daughter, never rest until she found her.

"If this doesn't work…" She trailed off, unwilling to give voice to her fears. What if she was wrong, and Joseph hadn't taken her baby to the park? Was she

wasting her time and efforts, time that would be better spent looking elsewhere?

But what other choice did she have? Emma couldn't
rest while her baby was gone. She had to trust that Detective Randall and his team were doing their best in El
Paso. They thought it unlikely Joseph had fled to Big
Bend, which meant they weren't going to spend time
looking here. Even though they figured it was a long
shot, Emma refused to leave any stone unturned in the
hunt for Christina. If that meant spending the rest of
her life wandering the desert, then so be it.

"Let's not get ahead of ourselves," Matt said. He
reached across the table and placed his hand over hers.
His palm was warm against her skin. Even though he
was a stranger, Emma drew comfort from his touch.
She hadn't been with anyone since Chris's death, and a
frisson shot up her arm as she realized how much she'd
missed the touch of a man. Her body cried out for more
contact, but not in a sexual way. She simply wanted to
be held by someone bigger and stronger, someone who
could fold her into his arms and make her feel safe.
She wanted to lay her head against Matt's chest and
surrender her worries and fears. For one brief, aching
moment, she wanted a man to take care of her, to fix
her problems and give her the gift of rest.

It was a lovely fantasy, but that's all it would ever
be. In reality, there was no knight in shining armor
waiting in the wings, ready to swoop in and rescue her
from the nightmare her life had become. And while
Emma prided herself on her accomplishments as a
single mother, she wasn't too proud to admit that she

missed having a partner, someone to share things with and lean on for support when the going got tough. She'd had that once with Chris. Would she ever find it again?

Doesn't matter, she told herself. Her loneliness wasn't important, not right now. She couldn't allow self-pity to distract her from her search. She'd never forgive herself if she missed a clue because of pointless navel-gazing.

"I'm trying to stay positive," she said, forcing herself to return to the conversation. "But it's hard. Every minute that passes without her feels like an eternity."

"I can imagine." Matt's eyes were full of sympathy and a hint of understanding, as if he had some idea of what she was going through.

"Do you have children?" *He's probably a great dad*, she figured. She imagined him playing catch with a towheaded boy, a smaller version of himself. She felt a pang in her heart as she pictured him hugging his son, burying his nose in the little boy's hair. *Does he take it for granted, the way I used to?*

To her surprise, the light left his eyes and a wall shot up between them. "No," he said shortly. "I'm not a father." His tone was curt; it was clear she had inadvertently touched a nerve.

"Oh," she said dumbly. "I'm sorry. I didn't mean to pry."

He ignored her apology, changing the subject. "You said you and your brother camped here a lot as kids. I'm going to grab a map of the park so you can mark where you think he'd go." He pushed back from the desk and stepped away, leaving Emma alone with her cold cup of coffee.

She gripped the mug, staring into the dark liquid. For the first time in days, she felt like she could catch her breath. And as she watched Matt walk back toward the desk, moving with an easy confidence she envied, a strange sensation took root in her chest. It took her a few seconds, but she finally identified the feeling.

Hope.

This was shaping up to be a lot harder than he'd thought.

Joseph frowned as he watched his niece play with a small cloth ball, rolling it across the surface of the sleeping bag. She was all smiles now, but he'd learned quickly that her mood could change on a dime. Not even ten minutes ago she wailed loudly after he'd removed a rock from her mouth. Her quicksilver temper was enough to give him whiplash. How did Emma handle this? He was only three days in and ready to throw in the towel.

"Not much longer," he said quietly, not wanting to disturb the baby's play. He'd given Emma a deadline for the money—he'd been quite generous with the amount of time he'd granted her to get the funds.

It didn't have to be this way. Bitterness rose in his chest as he pictured his sister. He'd come to her in good faith, asking for help to pay his gambling debts. She hadn't been his first choice. He'd much rather take care of his own problems—he had his pride, after all. But the debt was out of control, and there was no way he could scrape together that kind of cash in time to keep the enforcers at bay.

Karnov was not a patient man. Whispers swirled that he was in with the Russian mafia. Joseph had dismissed them as mere rumors, but now he realized what a mistake that had been.

Even now, he broke into a cold sweat at the memory of Karnov's warning. Joseph had literally been plucked off the street and thrown into the back of a van, a cloth bag jerked down over his head. When they'd stopped, he'd been manhandled into a warehouse. Someone had pulled the bag away to reveal an unsmiling Karnov and a gun, inches away from Joseph's nose.

"It doesn't have to be like this," Karnov had said.

"Please, I'll do anything." Joseph had nearly soiled himself, and only the two men gripping his arms had kept him from falling to his knees. "I just need a little time to get the money together. A month, that's all."

"Two weeks." Karnov uncocked the pistol and let his arm hang by his side. "And I'm charging you interest. Now it's five hundred thousand."

The figure had taken Joseph's breath away, but he couldn't exactly protest. "Thank you," he'd said, swallowing hard. Not for the first time, he cursed his bad luck. First, he'd backed the wrong football teams. Then, he'd tried to buy himself out of the hole by betting on ponies. That had only made things worse.

And so, out of options, he'd come to his sister, tail between his legs.

"I'll pay you back," he'd promised. And he'd meant

it. He had no intention of mooching off his baby sister; it was more like he'd asked her for a loan.

But Emma hadn't seen it that way. "Joseph," she'd said, perfectly replicating the note of disappointment their mother had mastered over the years. "How could you do this to yourself again? You're smarter than that."

He was smart, that much was true. But neither the football teams nor the ponies respected intelligence. It was all a game of chance, and Lady Luck hadn't smiled on him in far too long. He certainly hadn't meant for things to get so out of hand, but life was a cruel bitch sometimes.

The downturn in his fortunes had stung, but not nearly as much as his sister's denial. Emma's refusal to help him was a betrayal of their relationship, and it cut him to the quick. She had the money—he knew she'd gotten a fat settlement from the other driver after Chris's death. But she lied to his face, acting like she had nothing to give.

"I don't have the money." She'd said that several times, as if repetition would convince him to believe her lies. "The other driver doesn't have money, so I'm not getting any."

Yeah, right. Did she think he was stupid? The guy who was responsible for killing Chris might not be Mr. Moneybags, but Joseph knew he was paying. Maybe not all at once, but a monthly sum had to add up quick, and it had been over a year since the judgment. By his reckoning, Emma was sitting on a nice lump of cash. It might not be enough to pay his debt in full, but it would definitely buy him some breathing room. He'd heard through the grapevine that Karnov's enforcers were brutal, going so far as to remove body parts from debtors.

But no matter how clearly he explained the situation, she clung stubbornly to her lies.

"I know you want to use the money for Christina's education," he'd said. "And I'll have plenty of time to pay you back. You won't even miss the funds."

"No, Joseph. I can't help you."

More like won't, he'd realized as he left her apartment. If he'd had more time, he probably could have come up with a way to persuade her to lend him the money. But a few hours after his conversation with Emma, Karnov's thugs had found him and administered a painful beating. His ribs still ached from the blows.

"Next time, we take things," the square-jawed enforcer had made a scissoring motion with his fingers as he and his partner left Joseph in a heap on the floor.

With his time running out, Joseph had resorted to desperate measures to secure his sister's help. He felt bad about taking the baby, but really, Emma had only herself to blame. If she had simply agreed to help him instead of being stingy, he never would have had to take Christina.

The baby in question was apparently bored with her ball. She began to crawl, her gaze focused on the open backpack lying a few feet away.

"Oh, no you don't," Joseph muttered. He reached out to snatch the bag from her grasp, depositing it on the other side of the tent.

Deprived of her goal, Christina opened her mouth
and let out a piercing wail. Fat tears began to roll down
her chubby cheeks, and her face turned pink with distress.

"It's okay," Joseph said, scrambling to find some
kind of distraction to stop the crying. The sound of
her voice was like nails on a chalkboard, and he felt
his hackles continue to rise with every passing second.

"Are you hungry?" In desperation, he twisted the
top off a pouch of baby food and stuck it in her mouth.
Christina blinked in surprise at this unexpected devel-
opment. She gummed the nozzle for a moment, testing the plastic. Apparently deciding the offering was
acceptable, she began to suck on the pouch, restoring
a peaceful quiet to the tent.

Joseph let out his breath, grateful for the reprieve
but knowing it wouldn't last long.

Bringing the baby to Big Bend hadn't been one of
his smarter decisions, but there was no other place he
could think of to hide while Emma got the money together. He'd camped here so much as a kid, but now
that he was responsible for a child, he realized how
difficult those trips must have been for his own father.
There weren't a lot of creature comforts out here in the
wilderness. But fortunately Christina was too young to
notice that. He'd grabbed diapers and baby food before
taking her, figuring that was all he'd need. Camping
with an infant was not exactly fun, but at least they
were isolated enough that her cries wouldn't bother
anyone else. A single man with a baby would raise

suspicion; all he had to do was lie low for a few more days, and his problems would be solved.

He knew Emma had called the police. They were probably searching for him now, thinking he was a danger to his niece. It wasn't true—he had no intention of hurting the baby. As soon as he got the money, he'd make sure Emma got her daughter back. But he wasn't going to stick around for the reunion. He was going to have Emma leave the money at a public location. Then he was going to tell Karnov where to find it. Let the Russian deal with the police when he sent his goons to retrieve the funds. Joseph smiled at the thought, imagining the square-jawed thug taking a few on the chin as he was arrested. Karnov would be pissed to learn he'd been double-crossed, but Joseph didn't care. He'd be long gone by the time it all got sorted out. Besides, he was technically paying his debt. It wasn't his fault Karnov wasn't going to get to keep the money.

Joseph retrieved the ball and set it in front of Christina. She eyed it with interest, the now-empty pouch dropping from her mouth.

"Ba, ba, ba," she babbled. She rocked forward to grab the ball, treating Joseph to an eye-watering whiff of her diaper.

"Didn't I just change you?" he grumbled. He reached for a fresh diaper and the wipes as the baby cooed happily to her toy.

"Almost done," he told himself as he set about the unpleasant task. "Just a few more days."

They couldn't pass quickly enough.

Chapter 3

"Is this going to take much longer?"

Matt glanced up from the computer screen to offer Emma what he hoped was a reassuring smile. She'd been pacing in front of his desk for the past twenty minutes, clearly on edge. She was obviously anxious to start the search, but there were things they needed to deal with before heading out into the park. He sympathized with her desire to do something, but he wasn't about to head into an unknown situation without doing a little prep work first.

"I'm almost done," he said. "Do you have a photo I can add?" He was putting together a flyer to print, a sort of wanted poster that showed the baby and briefly explained the situation. He wanted his fellow rangers to know what was going on, so they too could be on the lookout.

"A picture of Christina?" Emma asked. "Or Joseph?" Matt could tell by the way she practically spat her brother's name that there would be no forgiveness for her sibling. Not that he blamed her—kidnapping wasn't exactly something a mother could forget.

"I'll take both, if you have them," Matt said. It would be good to show Joseph's face as well, especially since he might have the baby in a tent or otherwise have her face obscured when people were around.

Emma pulled out her phone and tapped the screen. After a moment, she flipped it around so he could look at it.

"That's my love," she said, choking up a bit.

Matt had to admit her daughter was a beautiful child. She had her mother's curly dark hair and heart-shaped face. But her eyes were startlingly blue, like a cloudless summer sky. Deep dimples reminded him of a cherub, and her toothless smile held such joy Matt couldn't help but smile back.

Seeing her made his heart ache for the child he'd lost. Even though he hadn't been the father of Jennifer's child, he'd been well on his way to falling in love with the little guy.

"How old is she?" he asked, unable to take his eyes off the picture.

"Ten months," Emma replied.

Almost a year, he thought. A little older than Fisher had been when the DNA test results had proved Matt wasn't his father. Did babies that young have memories? It broke his heart to think that Fisher, now three years old, might remember him or feel abandoned because he'd left.

Matt cleared his throat, trying to cast off his melancholy. "Too young to be away from you for long," he said.

Emma nodded. "She's eating solids now, so as long as Joseph has baby food she won't starve. But she still likes a bottle, and he won't know that."

"We'll find her," Matt said. The thought of that innocent baby crying from hunger made his own stomach twist with anxiety. He hadn't considered all the logistical reasons why Christina needed her mother—he'd just assumed maternal love was driving Emma's sense of urgency. But now he realized all the practical issues involved—the diaper changes, feeding, dressing, rocking. All tasks that could technically be completed by anyone with half a brain, but from the baby's perspective, her needs had only ever been met by her mother. To have a stranger caring for her now had to be stressful and frightening.

All the more reason to get out there and start looking.

"Send me that photo, please." He rattled off his email address. "And send me any pictures you have of your brother."

Her fingers flew across the screen of her phone. "Done."

A moment later he heard the chime indicating a

new email. He inserted the photos into the flyer and hit Print.

The printer across the room hummed to life and began spitting out pages. He walked over and grabbed the stack, bringing it back to his desk.

Emma reached for a sheet. She studied it carefully, her gaze lingering on the page. Her scrutiny made Matt self-conscious; hopefully he hadn't made any spelling errors or other glaring mistakes.

It was a simple flyer, showing both Christina and Joseph and asking visitors to report any sightings to the park rangers or the police. He'd distribute some among his coworkers as well, so they all knew to keep their eyes open. The more people aware of the situation, the better the chance of finding Emma's daughter.

"This looks good." Emma returned the page to the top of the stack and swiped at her eyes with the back of her hands.

Sympathy welled in Matt's chest at the sight of her obvious pain. "I can change things if you want," he offered, unsure of how to comfort her. Had it been a mistake to create the flyers? But how else could they spread the word?

She shook her head. "No, they look great. I just never imagined I'd see my baby's face on a missing person poster, you know?"

"I can't imagine how hard this must be for you," Matt said. Walking away from Fisher was the hardest thing Matt had ever done, and he'd only known the little guy for a few weeks. Emma was functioning amazingly well for a mother whose child had been kidnapped—he didn't think he would be so tough if he were in her shoes.

"She's my world," Emma said, sniffing. "I'll never stop looking for her."

But why are you searching alone? he wondered. Based on the little he knew, he didn't think Christina's father was in the picture. Why not? Emma didn't look like the anonymous one-night stand type; being deployed while in the army had made him an expert of sorts at spotting the women who hung around base, only wanting a quick roll in the hay. No, he could tell Emma was the kind of woman who did relationships. She had a girl-next-door appeal that screamed "wife and family." She was the type he and his army buddies had talked about settling down with after they'd had their adventures.

Of course, Jennifer had been like that, too. That hadn't exactly turned out well for him. Maybe something similar had happened between Emma and the father of her baby?

It really wasn't any of his business, but curiosity got the better of him. "Where is Christina's dad?" Not the most delicate way to ask the question, but since Matt was going to be spending the foreseeable future with Emma, he wanted to know why the father of her child wasn't out beating the bushes, as well.

Her lips tightened, and for a second, he thought she wasn't going to answer the question. Then she spoke, her voice low. "He's dead."

"Oh." It wasn't the answer he'd been expecting, and

Matt felt like a world-class idiot for pressing the issue. "I'm so sorry."

Emma jerked one shoulder in a dismissive shrug. "You couldn't have known."

No, but he could have been a bit more sensitive. He had to stop thinking the worst of people; not every woman was a liar like Jennifer.

He cleared his throat, needing to change the subject. "I'll leave these out front, so people will see them. Let's start getting supplies together, and then I can hit the trails."

"You mean *we* can hit the trails," she said.

Matt bit his bottom lip, cursing silently. Did the woman ever miss anything? "I don't know if it's such a good idea for you to accompany me—" he tried, but she cut him off.

"I have to go with you. I can't stay here doing nothing."

Matt took a deep breath and tried a different tack. "I know you're frustrated and feeling helpless, but it's best if you stay behind. What if your brother tries to call? Cell service in the more remote areas of the park is patchy at best."

Emma frowned, as if she hadn't considered that possibility before. Matt began to relax, thinking she'd accepted reason.

But she shook her head again. "It's a chance I'll have to take."

Okay, he was clearly going to have to be a little rude to get her to listen. "Look, I can't take you with me. You'll slow me down and limit how much ground I can cover at a time."

"No, I won't." She sounded supremely confident. He ran his eyes over her body, looking for clues as to her fitness. Her oversize T-shirt didn't reveal much—from this angle, he couldn't tell if she was all softness and curves or lean, toned muscle.

Did it matter? At this point, he knew she would follow him whether he wanted her to or not. Perhaps he should give in. If it turned out she couldn't keep up with him, he could send her back to the ranger station. But if he remained stubborn and refused to let her join him, he'd be distracted by worries that she was out there wandering the park alone and with no one to help her should she find trouble.

"All right," he said finally. "I guess we'll find out if that's the truth." It shouldn't take long for her to realize she was out of her depth, and by that time, she'd likely be all too happy to return to the refuge of the ranger station. "We can start as soon as I get my bag packed. Do you have supplies?" Maybe he'd get lucky and she'd say no.

"Yes," she replied. "I'm all set in that area."

He nodded. "I'd like to look at what you brought, make sure you have the essentials." Experience had taught him that hikers didn't always bring the necessities when packing for a trip. People tended to skimp on some of the supplies, filled with misplaced confidence that their journey would be free from accidents.

"That's fine. I'll go grab my bag."

Matt nodded. She returned a moment later with a

pack that looked broken in, and his impression of her capabilities inched a little higher. This was not the bag of a novice—she'd clearly done some kind of camping in her life.

Emma placed the bag on his desk and unzipped it, pulling it open with a little flourish. "Search away," she said, the barest edge to her voice.

He met her eyes and could tell she knew he was looking for a way to discredit her. But he wasn't going to apologize for his resistance. He'd been roped into this investigation without warning, and he wasn't about to take her on a search without first knowing she could handle herself on the trails.

He combed through her bag, feeling a little self-conscious under the weight of her gaze. A sense of grudging admiration built as he realized she'd brought all the essentials, plus a few extra small conveniences. She was definitely prepared, at least from a packing perspective.

Matt zipped her bag closed and pushed it toward her. "Okay," he said. "Let me get my stuff and we'll set out."

Emma nodded, relief flashing across her face. "That sounds great." He could tell she was anxious to get started, and truth be told, he was eager to begin, as well.

"Have you ever done anything like this before?"

"Not exactly," Matt hedged. He'd never mounted a search like this in his time as a park ranger, but it reminded him of one of the missions his squad had been sent on overseas. They'd been tasked with providing extra man power to a small group of Special Operations soldiers as they hunted for a well-known terrorist operative. They'd spent days combing the desert and beating down doors, but ultimately their search had proved unsuccessful. It wasn't exactly the kind of encouraging story Emma needed to hear right now.

Hopefully this time, he'd have better luck.

The sun was high in the sky, a fiery ball that made her eyes water from its brightness. Emma was grateful for her hat, and hoped that Joseph was keeping Christina in the shade. Her baby skin was sensitive to the sun, her blue eyes even more so.

For the millionth time, she wondered what her brother had been thinking. He'd always been impetuous, acting on emotion rather than reason. And after their dad's death a few years ago, Joseph's self-control had practically disappeared. That's when his gambling had gone from a hobby to a problem. But kidnapping was beyond the pale, even for him. She'd never thought him capable of endangering a child, especially one he'd held and played with before. Had she simply missed the signs, or was this a new, dangerous aspect of his personality? Joseph was a stranger to her now, and Emma knew that later, after she had Christina back safely in her arms, she'd mourn the brother she'd lost.

She glanced over at Matt, walking alongside her. It was clear he'd been reluctant to let her join the search, but he wasn't being an ass about it now. With his long legs, he could easily have set a pace designed to make her quit. Instead, he'd kept them moving at a steady, sustainable clip. She appreciated the consideration, more determined than ever to prove she could keep up with him for as long as it took.

"How long have you been a park ranger?" She normally wasn't a chatty person, but the silence was getting to her. She needed a distraction from her own thoughts, or else fear and panic would take over, leaving her unable to function.

"A little over a year," Matt replied.

"What did you do before then?"

He slid her a glance. "I was in the army," he said neutrally.

It was clear Matt wasn't a big talker, but Emma didn't care. Anything was better than being trapped in her head at the moment. "Joseph was in the military, too," she commented. "He joined right out of high school, except he signed on with the navy."

"Really?" Interest sharpened Matt's tone, and he looked at her fully now. "How long did he serve?"

"Only a few years. He got into some trouble and was dishonorably discharged."

"Ah." Matt nodded as if that made perfect sense. She got the impression he didn't think much of her brother. Why would he, though? Any man who kidnapped a baby was no better than pond scum.

"He's always been impulsive," she said, stepping around a large rock in the path. "Loves to gamble. It used to be under control, but after my dad died a few years ago, Joseph couldn't be bothered with moderation anymore. And since he was a single man, he didn't need to worry about sending money home to a wife."

Emma wasn't sure why she was telling Matt all this, but it was something to talk about. "He set up a gambling ring on his ship. Got caught eventually. The navy didn't take too kindly to his actions, so they kicked him out."

"The military is tough like that," Matt said. "It's not a perfect institution, but the service does hold its members to a high standard."

"Yeah." Emma was quiet for a moment, remembering her mother's distress when they found out what had happened. "He came home, tail between his legs. We hoped he would learn from the situation, get some help for his addiction. But he refused." She shook her head, the sound of their arguments still fresh in her mind. She and her family had tried everything to convince Joseph he had a problem and needed to take action, but his denial was too strong to overcome.

"That must have been hard."

"It was. On my mother, especially. Joseph swore he was in control and didn't need help, and for a while, he kept his nose clean. But I guess the lure of gambling was too strong to resist."

"What kind of gambling?" A fallen tree trunk bisected the trail in front of them. Matt stepped over it, then reached back to help her. Emma slipped her hand into his, grateful for his assistance.

"Horse races," she replied. She stepped carefully onto the trunk, trying to maintain her balance. But the bark was smooth and worn, and her boots lost traction. She began to slide forward, her heart leaping to her throat as she lurched toward the ground.

Suddenly, Matt was there. He stepped in front of her,

stopping her fall with his body. His arms slid around her waist, his broad chest absorbing her forward motion. Emma had a split second to register the feel of his strength surrounding her before her head jerked from the sudden stop, her nose smashing into his shoulder. A starburst of pain filled her head, making her cry out.

Matt loosened his grip. "Are you okay? I didn't mean to hurt you."

Emma stared up at him through watery eyes. "Not your fault," she said, holding her nose. "I appreciate you catching me."

"It's the least I could do." He reached out and gently pulled her hand away from her nose. "Let me take a look at that."

She felt wetness on her skin and figured she was bleeding. Matt's look of horror confirmed it.

"Here, sit down." He helped her sink onto the log and quickly wriggled the pack off his back. He dug through it and withdrew a small plastic box, from which he extracted a few squares of gauze.

"Let me," he said softly. He gently applied the gauze to her nose, then moved her hand into place to keep it from falling. "Here's an ice pack." She heard a crunching sound, and he handed her a small pouch that was rapidly growing cold to the touch.

"Thanks," Emma said, gingerly applying the pouch to her nose. It hurt, but after a moment, the cold seeped into the tissue and numbed it.

"May I see?" At her nod, Matt reached out and gently lifted the cold pack to examine her nose. He frowned.

"That bad, huh?" she asked.

He shook his head. "It's not pretty, but I don't think it's broken."

"That's good, then."

"Yeah," he replied. But his tone made it sound like the news was anything but.

"Don't sound so happy," she joked.

Matt winced. "I'm sorry. I just feel bad. I've never made a woman bleed before. It's not one of my finer moments."

"It's not your fault," Emma said. "If anything, you saved me from much worse. If you hadn't caught me, I would have fallen flat on my face, and that would have done more damage than a busted nose."

"I suppose you're right," he said.

"Trust me, I've had worse," she said.

"Oh?" His gaze sharpened on her face, his brows drawing together in a slight frown. "Who hurt you?"

Emma realized he had misinterpreted her statement. "It wasn't deliberate," she said, wanting to clarify that from the beginning. "But my fiancé and I were moving furniture together once and had a bit of an accident. I thought he was going one way, he thought I was going the other, and we wound up dropping the couch. Onto my foot." She crinkled her nose at the memory, wincing as a fresh bolt of pain zinged into her brain. "I fell and hit my face on the corner of the table and wound up with a broken foot and two black eyes."

"Ouch."

"Yeah, it was like a comedy of errors. Would have been funny if it hadn't hurt so bad."

Matt dug two water bottles out of his bag and passed her one. "What happened to him?" he asked softly. "If you don't mind my asking."

Emma took a swig from the bottle, stalling for a second as she debated how to answer his question. She didn't talk about Chris very often, and especially not to people she'd just met. But Matt was different. He was helping her search for Christina, and while they hadn't been looking very long, she already felt like they were a team. It was a sensation she hadn't had since Chris was alive, and it made her heart ache a bit.

"He was killed in a car accident," she said. "We were a week away from the wedding, and he was stopped at a red light. The driver behind him was texting and didn't see." Emma took another swallow, trying to dislodge the lump that always formed in her throat whenever she thought of the accident. "His car plowed into the back of Chris's, sending him into the intersection. He was hit by a bus and then a garbage truck."

"My God," Matt said softly.

Emma shook her head and blinked away tears. "The firemen couldn't even get him out of the car."

"I'm so sorry." His big hand covered hers, his skin warm.

She sniffed, immediately regretting it as pain spiked through her nose. "Thanks. I found out I was pregnant a couple weeks later. It was a shock, but I figured it was Chris's last gift to me."

"So he didn't know about the baby?"

"No." Emma shook her head. It was one of the most painful aspects of his death for her—the fact that he'd been killed before knowing he was going to be a father. Chris would have been over the moon at hearing the news. Another moment she'd never get to share with him, all because someone figured that texting their friend was more important than paying attention to the road.

"Damn," Matt said softly. "That makes it even worse."

She nodded, a little pleased to know he saw things the same way.

"What happened to the other driver?"

"Physically? Not more than a few bumps and bruises. There was some legal loophole that he used to keep from going to jail, so I sued him in civil court. Wrongful death. It didn't seem right that he would get to go on with his life like nothing had ever happened while my life had been shattered into a million pieces."

"Can't say I blame you for that," Matt said. "I'm surprised he was able to get out of a criminal conviction."

"He had a fancy lawyer," Emma said. A bitter taste formed in her mouth at the memory of the man in his expensive suit and perfectly cut hair. He'd waltzed into the courtroom like he owned the place, and a few moments later, after spewing a bunch of incomprehensible legalese Emma hadn't been able to follow, he'd gotten the charges against the other driver dropped. The district attorney's office hadn't been able to give her a satisfactory explanation, and so she'd been left feeling enraged and helpless to do anything about it.

"But you won the civil suit?"

"Oh, yes," she said, smiling. "His attorney couldn't

get him out of that one." She still recalled the look of shock on both of their faces—driver and lawyer— when the verdict had been handed down. It was almost enough to ease the pain of her loss.

"I was awarded a pretty hefty sum, which is why Joseph thinks I have the money to bail him out of his gambling debts."

"But you don't?"

Emma shook her head. "The settlement is awarded in a series of payouts and, to be honest, the other driver used up most of his money paying for his hotshot attorney. I'm getting a little bit here and there, but nothing like I should be and nothing that would help Joseph."

Matt frowned. "Does your brother know that?"

She shrugged. "I tried to explain it to him several times. He came to me before taking Christina, begging for funds. I told him I couldn't help, but I know he didn't believe me. A few days later, Christina was gone." Her throat tightened around the words, as if she could change her reality by leaving them unspoken. If only it were that easy...

Matt was quiet a moment, studying her face thoughtfully. His blue eyes reminded her of a wolf, intelligent and assessing. She tried to figure out what he was thinking, but he kept his emotions close to the chest. He was a puzzle, that much was clear. In another time, she would have been intrigued enough to want to get to know him. What secrets hid behind his handsome face? What made this man tick?

But now was not the time for distractions. Not while her baby was still in danger.

She took the gauze from her nose and inspected it for fresh blood. She didn't find any, so she crumpled it and stood, grabbing her backpack off the ground and slipping it back on. "We should go," she said. "We've lost too much time already."

Matt nodded, getting to his feet and shouldering his own pack. "All right," he said agreeably. "Lead the way."

Emma started down the trail, determination driving her on. Matt had proved to be a good listener, and he was dangerously easy to talk to. It had been a long time since she'd had a conversation with a man that went beyond the polite, superficial level. But she couldn't allow her loneliness and selfish desire for comfort interfere with her search. Finding Christina was her sole focus—nothing else mattered as long as her daughter was missing.

Matt had to hand it to Emma—she was one tough woman.

She set a brisk pace, even though he knew her nose had to be throbbing with every heartbeat. But she wasn't letting her pain slow her down; if anything, it seemed to make her even more determined.

Once again, he marveled at her strength. Not a lot of people would be able to function in the wake of their child's kidnapping, much less drive several hours alone and strong-arm someone into mounting a search.

He felt a twinge of guilt at the way he'd initially treated her. At least he'd kept the worst of his doubts to himself. He might have thought she was crazy at first, but he was glad he hadn't shown it. The more he got to know Emma, the more convinced he became that she was someone special.

He was a bit surprised to find himself wanting to get to know a woman better. It wasn't just sexual attraction driving him, though he had to admit she was quite pretty. He let his gaze drift across her body to land on her rear, and for a split second, he wondered what it would feel like to cup her there. She'd been a tangle of heat and curves in his arms when he'd caught her earlier, but he hadn't really registered the contact between their bodies until after it was over. And while he certainly hadn't meant to cop a feel, he wouldn't object to getting his hands on her again.

Not gonna happen, he told himself silently. Emma was searching for her lost baby—no way in hell was she going to be interested in anything but finding her daughter. He felt a little skeevy for even considering it, but he'd never been good at controlling his imagination.

He cleared his throat. If they kept talking, he wouldn't have to worry about his fantasies taking over his thoughts.

"I just realized," he said as they rounded a bend in the trail, "I don't know what you do for a living."

"Oh." Emma sounded surprised, as if she hadn't realized she hadn't shared that information with him yet. "I'm a nurse."

Her answer didn't surprise him. She had a no-nonsense vibe that likely served her well in the job. But he knew underneath her tough exterior she had a caring heart.

"What kind of nurse?"

"Emergency room," she replied.

No wonder she was so calm under these trying circumstances. That explained her stamina, too—she probably spent her entire shift on her feet or running from one place to another. It was no mystery why she was in such good shape.

"I bet you've seen some interesting stuff," he said.

She smiled briefly. "I've had my share of entertaining patients. It's the funny or strange cases that help get me through the tragic ones, you know?"

"Kind of," Matt said. "I saw some pretty messed up things while I was deployed, but there were also a few absurd situations where I just had to laugh or I'd go crazy."

Emma nodded. "That's exactly it. You take the humor where you can find it, even if it's pretty dark at times." She smiled at him, and he felt a moment of true understanding pass between them. For the first time in years, he felt like someone else got him on a visceral, soul-deep level. It was a kinship he'd found in the army but had missed after returning home. Even the park rangers, while a close-knit community, were missing that vital spark he'd shared with his fellow soldiers. He was a little surprised to feel that connection now, of all times, but he wasn't about to dismiss it.

The question was, did Emma feel it, too?

It was on the tip of his tongue to ask her, but how could he phrase it so he didn't sound creepy? He didn't want to give the impression he was trying to hit on her. He just wanted to know if this sensation was all one-sided, or if she shared it.

But before he could find the right words, she darted off the trail like a bloodhound who'd found a scent. Matt hurried after her, pushing past bushes and wading through a bit of tall grass until she stopped in a small clearing a few feet away.

She stood in the middle, eyeing the ground intently. He followed her line of sight, but saw nothing. Why had she suddenly veered off to this spot? Was this one of the places she'd camped as a child?

"Emma?"

She ignored him and began to slowly turn in a circle, her gaze locked on the grass and dirt as she moved. It was clear she was looking for something, but what?

After a moment, her shoulders relaxed and she frowned. "Sorry," she said. "I could have sworn I saw a glint of something from the trail." She sounded dejected, and he could tell she was getting discouraged.

He glanced around, hoping to see something she had missed. But all he saw was dirt and gravel and a bit of grass—nothing that would have gleamed in the light of the afternoon sun.

"I'm sorry," he said, stepping forward. "Is this close to where you camped a lot as a child? Is that why you thought to look here?"

She shrugged. "We did camp nearby once, but it wasn't one of our regular spots. I really did think I had seen something, though. That's why I left the trail."

"We can stay and search if you want," he said. It was getting too late in the day to go much farther. Might as well go through this spot carefully so they could mark it off their list.

"That's fine," she said. But she didn't sound enthusiastic.

"I bet you did see something," he said, trying to boost her spirits. "People leave trash behind a lot."

"Yeah, but it's probably just an empty chip bag or something equally generic," she said. "That won't help us."

"No." He began to walk in an ever-widening circle, scanning the area near his feet for debris of a manmade variety. "But at least we'll know."

They were quiet a moment as they worked, moving in opposite directions so as not to step on each other's toes. He'd just about completed his circuit when he heard Emma suck in a breath.

"Matt," she said, her voice tight. "Look at this."

He turned to find her holding up what looked like an empty foil pouch. A plastic nozzle stuck out of one end and as he moved closer, he realized it was a squeezable yogurt that had been left behind.

Emma's brown eyes sparkled with excitement. "This is what I saw—the light reflecting off the foil."

He nodded. "Probably so. You look like you recognize it?"

She grinned, bouncing on the balls of her feet a little as she held it up for his inspection. "Yes, I do. I give them to Christina all the time. She loves them—can't get enough."

And you think your brother left this trash behind. It was clear Emma had made that assumption, and Matt's heart ached a bit for her. While it was technically possible her brother and baby had camped here, it was a lot more likely the wrapper had been left behind by a random innocent hiker. Who knew how long the trash had been here?

"It might not be from your brother," he said, trying to manage her expectations. He understood her need to believe they were on the right track, but he didn't want to see her get her hopes too high. Even if the wrapper *did* turn out to be from Joseph and Christina, there was no way of knowing where they had gone after leaving this site. Assuming he had brought the baby here in the first place, he might be long gone by now. Perhaps he'd crossed into Mexico and had disappeared in one of the border towns? It was a possibility he didn't dare bring up to Emma, but one he had to consider nonetheless.

"It is," she said with certainty. "I'm sure of it."

"How do you know?" He was curious to hear her logic, to assess if she was merely engaging in wishful thinking, or if she had a solid reason for believing this particular piece of trash had been left by her brother.

"This is Christina's favorite flavor," she said.

Matt smiled sadly. "How would your brother know that?" he asked gently.

Emma's confident expression faltered a bit, but then she shook her head. "He took some food from me when he kidnapped her. I didn't notice it until later, after the police had left. But there were several baby food and yogurt pouches missing. This was one of them." She shook the wrapper slightly in emphasis.

Matt held up a hand. "Okay," he said, conceding the point. He knew no matter what he said, Emma believed the trash in her hand had been left behind by Joseph.

And maybe that was the truth. But her brother wasn't around now, and that was the most important point.

He decided to give her the benefit of the doubt. "Any idea where he might have gone now?"

Emma shook her head, a troubled light chasing away the gleam of excitement in her eyes. "No. But I have to think we're getting close."

Maybe, Matt thought.

For her sake, he hoped she was right.

Chapter 4

"We need to stop soon."

Matt's words filled Emma with dismay. "But we just got started—we can't quit now!"

"It's getting late in the day," he said.

She glanced at the sky. The sun was sinking lower, but there was still plenty of daylight left. Enough to suit her, anyway.

Matt followed her gaze. "There's maybe two hours of full light left," he said. "That gives us enough time to get back to the station before night sets in."

She couldn't argue with him on that point, but a sense of desperation rose in her chest at the thought of stopping. She couldn't shake the feeling they were getting close to finding Christina and Joseph. If they went back to the ranger station, it would give her brother even more time to take her baby farther into the park. She hated the thought of losing his trail when they might be over the very next ridge.

"Can't we make camp somewhere?" She sounded desperate, even to her own ears. But she had no pride when it came to finding Christina. "It'll save us having to retrace our steps in the morning."

Matt looked reluctant. "We can..." He trailed off, let out a sigh. "But my tent isn't very big. It'll be cramped quarters."

"I don't care," she said reflexively. Matt didn't look thrilled at the thought of sharing a small space with her, but she truly didn't mind. She'd sleep with the devil himself if it meant getting her baby back.

"I was afraid you'd say that," he muttered.

"If you don't want to camp with me, just leave the tent and come back for me tomorrow." It wouldn't bother Emma to stay out here alone. She'd continue to hike until dark, then settle in for a sleepless night of worrying. Neither activity required company.

"I will not." Matt looked mildly scandalized at her suggestion. "I told you I'd search with you, and part of that job involves keeping you safe while we look. I'm a park ranger—I'm not going to leave you out here by yourself. Besides, you'd probably spend all night looking, and wind up getting into trouble because you stepped on a snake you didn't see until it was too late."

She had to smile at his imagination. "It's a distinct possibility," she admitted.

"Okay," he said. "We can make camp tonight, but

we need to head back to base tomorrow to restock our supplies."

"After we spend the morning searching," Emma said quickly.

Matt nodded. "Yes. After we spend some time looking for your baby."

It was a fair compromise, even though Emma would prefer to stay on the trails until they had success. But logically she knew they had to be careful. She'd be no good to her daughter if she let herself go hungry and get dehydrated.

"There's a flat stretch not far ahead," Matt said. "It'll be a good spot to set up the tent for the night."

"Sounds good," she replied.

They hiked in silence for a few more minutes, rounding a bend that skirted the bottom of a large hill. As Matt had promised, the ground leveled out, and she spotted a clear expanse bordered by a line of cactus and scrub.

"This looks like a nice spot," he said.

"Sure." Emma knew she didn't sound enthusiastic, but it was hard to switch gears from actively searching for Christina to settling down for the night.

Matt knelt and placed his pack on the ground. Emma stood nearby, feeling out of place as he began to unstrap the tent from his bag.

"I'll go gather some kindling for a fire," she said, needing something to occupy her hands and mind.

"Don't bother," Matt said. "There's a burn ban in effect in the park."

"Oh." Now she felt even more useless.

Matt glanced up, his gaze assessing. "Here." He rummaged in his pack and tossed something at her. Emma reflexively caught it and looked down to find it was a jar of peanut butter.

She held it up. "What am I supposed to do with this?"

He fished out a sleeve of bread and a bottle of honey. "I figured you could start on dinner."

"I see." It was something to do, but the thought of making sandwiches in the dirt was less than appealing.

Matt picked up on her hesitation. "Would you rather set up the tent?" He placed the supports in a pile and began to unroll the fabric.

"No, I'll make sandwiches." She slipped off her pack and placed it on the ground to use as a sort of table. She plopped down and reached for the food, then grabbed a knife from her own bag.

They were quiet for the next few minutes, each focusing on their respective task. Emma tried to push her worries to the back of her mind, but Christina dominated her thoughts. They should have gone farther, walked a bit longer before stopping for the night.

A gust of wind rustled the bushes nearby, and for a second, Emma swore she heard the faint cry of a baby. "That's her!" She jumped to her feet, the sandwiches forgotten. She started down the trail, determined to find her baby.

She didn't make it more than twenty feet before Matt dashed past her and stopped, forcing her to either halt or run into him. She skidded on the loose gravel, hitting his chest as she came to a stop.

Matt's arms wrapped around her before she could change direction. "Let me go!" She struggled to break free from his hold, but he didn't release her.

"It's not her," he said.

"It is," Emma insisted. Panic clawed up her throat, and she redoubled her efforts. Her baby was crying nearby—she had to get to her!

Matt drew her closer, pressing her against his chest. "That wasn't a baby," he said. His voice was calm, his hold firm but gentle. "It's not Christina. You have to believe me."

She heard the sound again and tensed her muscles, preparing to kick her way free. Matt's arms tightened around her. "Listen closer," he urged. "That's a mountain lion."

Emma stilled, straining to listen. The cry reached her ears once more, and this time, she heard a strange note that sounded more animal than human.

All the fight left her, and her muscles went limp. If it weren't for Matt's grip, she would have fallen to the ground. He adjusted his hold, taking her weight as she dropped her head to his shoulder.

Sobs rose in her chest, breaking free with great, heaving bellows. Tears flowed freely down her cheeks, soaking into the fabric of his shirt. She hadn't meant to cry, but once she started she wasn't able to stop. Emotions poured out of her—all the stress, anger, worry and terror she'd been holding inside finally breaking free. She sobbed until her lungs ached and her eyes were swollen and gritty.

She wasn't sure how long she cried. Matt held her

through it all, his chest absorbing the sound of her sobs along with the flow of her tears. Gradually, she became aware of his hand stroking up and down her back in a comforting caress. His touch was gentle and unobtrusive; she focused on the feel of his hands on her body, using the sensation as an anchor in her emotional hurricane.

"I'm so sorry," he murmured, his voice close to her ear. "I should have warned you."

Emma leaned back to wipe her cheeks and found the skin clammy from her tears. "It's not your fault," she said dully. She felt empty now, like a hollowed-out log left to rot. "I've heard mountain lions before. I just forgot how much they sound like a baby."

"Especially when you're searching for your own." His tone was gentle, understanding even.

Matt loosened his grip and Emma stepped back, putting some space between them. She looked up to meet his face, her gaze catching on some red marks marring the skin of his arms.

Her lips parted as shame filled her. "Did I do that to you?"

Matt tilted his head to the side. "Do what?"

She pointed at his forearms, and he looked down. "Oh." He blinked at the scratches, apparently noticing them for the first time. "It's no big deal."

"It is to me," she said. Guilt filled her as she studied the evidence of her struggles. "I'm so sorry. I shouldn't have fought you."

"Don't worry about it," Matt said, brushing aside her apology. "I understand why you did it."

She appreciated his quick forgiveness, but still felt bad. "At least let me take care of those scratches. I'd hate for them to get infected."

"That sounds a bit dramatic," he said.

"I insist," Emma said. "Take it from me—fingernails are filthy. You'd be surprised how many people wind up in the ER with an infected scrape because they didn't clean it properly."

He nodded. "I'll defer to your expertise then." He held up his arm, indicating she should precede him back to the campsite.

Emma started down the trail, embarrassed over her actions but oddly grateful to have something to do. Once back at the bags, she knelt and began to rummage through her pack for her first aid kit.

Matt stopped nearby, waiting patiently while she gathered her supplies. She dressed his scratches quickly and competently, relieved to find they weren't too deep. She felt his gaze on her the whole time, watching her hands as she worked.

She considered stalling so she wouldn't have to meet his eyes yet. The last time she had cried like that was after getting the news that Chris had died. It felt cleansing in a way, the release of all those pent-up emotions. But she also felt a little uncertain and insecure. She hadn't meant to break down in front of Matt. He'd handled it well, though. If her tears had bothered him, he showed no sign of it.

Knowing she couldn't drag this out any longer, she placed a bandage over one of the deeper scratches and crumpled up the trash. "All set," she said, lifting her head to look at his face.

His smile was kind and understanding. "Thank you," he said simply.

Emma nodded. "I'm just sorry I hurt you in the first place. You've been so great about helping me look for Christina, and this is how I repay you?"

"No need to wear a hair shirt," he said easily. "But if you're feeling that bad about it, I'll let you help me set up the tent."

"Deal." They walked over to the pile of fabric, the supports knocked askew by Matt's hasty chase. Working in tandem, it didn't take long to put everything together.

Emma took a step back, surveying the scene. Matt was right; the tent was small. But it was better than nothing.

Sunset was in full swing when she returned to the peanut butter and bread, now scattered in the dirt. Fortunately, only a few slices were ruined—there was still more than enough left to make some sandwiches for their dinner and next morning's breakfast.

Matt picked up the dusty bread and headed down the trail while she made dinner. He returned a few minutes later, empty-handed.

"Bears," he said, noticing her slight frown. "Don't want them to smell the ruined food and get any ideas."

Emma nodded. "I feel like I've forgotten everything I used to know about camping."

"Hopefully we won't be out here long enough for you to need it," he said.

She passed him a plate of food and they ate quietly for a few minutes. Emma watched the sun sink below the horizon. Objectively, she recognized that it was a beautiful sight. The sky was bathed in a tapestry of pink and orange, the last rays of the sun casting a golden glow across the land. But she couldn't appreciate the view. The knowledge that her baby was going to sleep without her again weighed heavily on her soul.

"We made good progress today," Matt said. "I know it might not feel that way, but I think we're getting close."

Emma glanced over. She could still see his face in the fading light, the subtle glint of his eyes. His expression was earnest; he seemed to truly believe what he was saying. She took some comfort from his confidence and hoped he wasn't simply trying to make her feel better.

"Why a park ranger?" She didn't know what made her ask the question, but she wanted to talk about something different, to get out of her own head, if only for a few minutes.

"I've always loved being outside," he said, accepting her change of subject without argument. "Ever since I was a kid, I've felt more comfortable outdoors."

"Is that why you joined the army?"

"That's part of it. Park ranger was always on my list of dream jobs, so when I left the army I decided to go for it."

"Was Big Bend your first choice of location?" It was a beautiful park, but it wasn't as popular as some of the other spots like Yellowstone or Yosemite.

"Actually, it was." He stretched his legs out, crossing his feet at the ankles. "I grew up in Houston, and we'd drive out here for our annual family camping trip. When it came time to state my preferences, Big Bend was at the top of my list."

"Maybe we crossed paths during one of your summer trips," Emma said jokingly. "My dad brought Joseph and me out here a lot. Of course, living in El Paso, we didn't have as far to drive."

"It's possible," Matt said.

"I think I would have remembered you if that was the case, though," said Emma.

"Oh? What makes you say that?"

"Your eyes." She replied automatically, before the filter in her brain could engage. "I've never seen blue like that before."

Matt didn't respond, and after a second, Emma realized she must have embarrassed him. "I'm sorry," she said. "I didn't mean to make you uncomfortable."

"You didn't," he said. "Flattered, more like."

That didn't seem so bad. But Emma still felt like she'd revealed too much. They were about to share a very small tent for the night—the last thing she wanted was for Matt to feel like she was hitting on him.

They both fell quiet again, but the air around them was far from silent. The park was alive with the sounds of night, as all manner of creatures woke up and started their shifts. It was lovely music, a serenade that Emma had enjoyed in the past. But now she was just counting the minutes until sunrise, when she could pick up the search for her baby.

"Ready to turn in?" Matt asked. "I laid out some blankets in the tent. Feel free to take as many as you want."

"Thanks." Emma got to her feet, dusting off her butt before bending to grab some toilet paper from her bag. "I'm going to make a quick pit stop and then I'll head inside. Are you ready for bed?"

"Not quite yet," Matt replied. "You go ahead and get to sleep. I'll take the first watch and turn in a bit later."

"First watch?" Emma echoed. She felt mildly alarmed at his words. "Do we need to keep an eye out for something?"

His teeth gleamed in the starlight. "No. But old habits die hard."

"Got it. I'll be right back." She headed off to find a bit of privacy. In truth, she felt better knowing Matt was going to stay awake for a while. Now that it was time to occupy the tent, she was feeling a little shy about the prospect of sharing such close quarters with him.

Especially after her earlier breakdown.

Despite the emotional intensity of the moment, her body had registered how good it felt to be held by a strong man. Knowing that, it was going to be a lot more difficult to keep distracting thoughts at bay as they continued to search for Christina.

The moon was barely a sliver of silver in the sky, more of a decoration than a source of light. Was Christina having trouble sleeping? Joseph didn't know the lullaby she always sang as she rocked her baby, or the way Christina liked to start out sleeping on her side with her hands curled under her chin.

Her eyes stung with fresh tears, and her heart felt too big for her chest as she pictured her baby girl, too scared to sleep. Would Joseph be patient with her? Impotent rage bubbled in her chest at the thought of her brother yelling at the baby, or worse, laying hands on her.

She took a moment to compose herself before heading back to the tent. She'd already displayed enough emotion in front of Matt today. Any more, and he might want to cut the search short because he was afraid she couldn't handle it.

It didn't take long to reach the campsite. Matt sat with his back to the tent, elbows planted in the dirt and head tilted up to look at the stars. In that moment, he looked like a sleeping panther, the lean lines of his body a study in leashed power.

"Good night," she said.

"Sleep well," he replied.

She stood there, knowing she should slip into the tent, but unwilling to go quite yet. The silence stretched between them as she tried to figure out how to show her gratitude for his earlier help without reminding him of the way she'd broken down in his arms.

"Did you need something?"

She startled at the sound of his voice. "No. I mean— yes. Well, not yes, but—"

"Emma." She stopped, grateful for the darkness so he couldn't see her cheeks flush.

"Yes?"

"If you're trying to thank me, it's not necessary." His tone was kind, almost like a caress. "Get some rest. We'll find your baby tomorrow."

"Okay," she whispered. "I hope you're right."

She slipped past him, kneeling to crawl inside the tent. The ground was a little bumpy, but she didn't care. Her muscles twinged from the day's efforts; it had been a long time since she'd hiked all day, and she was feeling it now. It was nice to stretch out and stop moving, despite the pebbles digging into her back.

Another faint cry of a mountain lion sounded through the thin walls of the tent. Her heart began to pound, even as her brain recognized it wasn't her daughter. The big cat yelped a few more times, singing to some unknown audience. The wails made Emma's skin crawl, but she couldn't escape the sound. She clapped her hands over her ears, then curled up in a ball and sobbed quietly into the blanket.

Matt sat outside, forcing himself to remain put even though every cell in his body wanted to crawl inside the tent and hold Emma. He could hear her crying despite her attempts to remain quiet. The sound of her muffled sobs tore through him like shrapnel, and he wished there were something he could do to help her.

But as much as he wanted to take action, he knew in this moment discretion was the better choice. Emma was a proud woman; it was easy to see she was upset over the way she'd cried in his arms earlier. The kindest thing he could do for her right now was nothing, even though it went against all his instincts to ignore a woman in distress.

He quietly got to his feet, unable to sit any longer. He wasn't going to bother her now, but he felt like a voyeur, eavesdropping on her private pain.

There was a large, low rock a few feet down the trail. He headed for it now, stepping as lightly as possible so as not to make too much noise. After a quick check for critters on the surface, he sat down and stretched his legs.

His thoughts swirled as he stared up at the stars. Had it really been only a day since Emma had walked into the ranger station that morning and upended his life? The events of the day had been so emotionally intense, it was hard to believe they hadn't known each other for years.

Never before had he felt such a strong connection to a woman he'd just met. He felt drawn to her, and not just because he wanted to protect her and help her find her baby. Her personal plight was compelling—he hated the thought of a baby in danger—but he wasn't attracted to her simply because he needed to feed a knight-in-shining-armor complex. No, it was more complicated than that, though he couldn't explain it to himself.

Part of the problem was he was out of practice when it came to acknowledging his emotions. After leaving Jennifer and Fisher, he'd sworn off personal relationships for a while. By the time the acute heartache had dulled, he wasn't terribly excited by the prospect of starting over again with someone new. But he'd forced himself to go out on a few dates, thinking his attitude would improve after he rejoined the dating world.

It hadn't.

Nothing against the women he'd seen—they'd been lovely, saying all the right things at the right times. On paper, they'd seemed like perfect matches. In person, things had been less ideal.

None had made him feel that spark of interest. He was enough of an adult to know that developing relationships took time, and he hadn't expected love at first sight. But he hadn't been able to find a reason to keep going out with those women, and so he'd remained alone.

But not lonely. At least, he hadn't felt lonely until today.

Fourteen hours in Emma Foster's company, and now he was questioning everything he thought he knew about his emotional state. How had that happened? And more importantly, what was he going to do about it?

Nothing. The answer came to him almost immediately. He wasn't going to do anything. At least not right now. Emma was searching for her missing baby—the very last thing she needed or wanted was to have a conversation about how she'd triggered this bout of navel-gazing. She had her own problems to deal with. She didn't need to hear about his sad romantic past, or his experiences with Fisher and how he still missed the little guy.

The best approach was for him to treat this as an anomaly. Maybe he and Emma could talk after they found her baby, but until then, he didn't want to spend a lot of energy thinking about what was missing from his life. He'd spent the last year ignoring everything that wasn't work-related, and it had suited him just fine. Emma might have him rethinking his single status, but that didn't mean he needed to do a full-scale reevaluation of his choices.

A shooting star streaked across the sky, a blazing arc of light that bisected the darkness for a brief, thrilling second. Matt's breath caught in his throat, a sense of wonder rising in his chest at the sight. He briefly considered pulling Emma out of the tent—there were bound to be more soon—but decided against it.

Another mountain lion cry split the air. He could tell the animal wasn't close enough to worry about, but the eerie sound made the hairs on the back of his neck bristle. It was easy to think of the park as another pretty spot when he was taking tourists on a guided nature walk, but hearing the roar of a bear or the vocalization of a big cat drove home the fact that the area was mostly untamed wilderness.

That was as it should be, but his body wasn't interested in the logic of ecological preservation. It was dark, he was sitting on a rock alone, and there were predators about. His primitive lizard brain was knocking hard on the door of his consciousness, insisting they head for the illusory safety of the tent.

He chuckled softly, shaking his head at his foolishness. "If the guys could see me now," he muttered. He and his fellow soldiers had faced all manner of threats, of both the human and animal varieties, while in the desert. He'd handled it all with aplomb, except for that one time he'd nearly shot his foot off after being startled by a camel spider. The guys had razzed him pretty hard about it, but in his defense, those things were wickedly scary. Matt considered himself a nature lover, but that was one creature he didn't appreciate at all.

The bushes nearby rustled softly as some nocturnal animal began to forage for a meal. Time for him to go and leave the critters to their business.

Emma was quiet as he slipped inside the tent. He couldn't tell if she was asleep yet, but at least she'd stopped crying. Hopefully she would be able to get some rest tonight—he could only imagine how exhausted she was after the last few days of panic and worry.

Matt curled up on his side, his back to her. It felt rude somehow, even though she was facing the tent and had no way of seeing him. Their positions were a good reminder that no matter how connected he might feel to her, they were still relative strangers. Hopefully they would get to know each other better, but for now, he needed to remember that holding her while she'd cried didn't make him special to her. It was tempting to read too much into the moment, but she'd been due for a breakdown and he'd been the closest warm body. Nothing more, nothing less.

The reality check helped clear his mind, and he shifted a bit to dislodge a pebble digging into his hip. Then he closed his eyes, summoned the discipline he'd learned as a soldier, and fell into a dreamless sleep.

They'd survived the night. Barely.

Joseph poked his head out of the tent and blinked

at the dawning sun. He rubbed his gritty eyes and yawned, wishing he could sleep but knowing it was impossible now that it was light.

Christina didn't seem to have that problem. He glanced over at his niece, lying boneless on the sleeping bag, her rosebud lips slightly parted as she breathed steadily. She hadn't slept more than ninety minutes at a stretch, and each time she'd woken up it had taken forever to get her to go back to sleep. She was out now, but for how long?

Joseph's body cried out for rest, and the thought of enduring two more days of this torture was enough to make him reconsider his plan. Maybe he should give Christina back and find another way to get the money. Perhaps Emma would be so grateful to have her daughter again she'd pay him anyway?

The baby stirred and let out a soft whimper. Joseph held his breath, silently praying she didn't wake. He wanted ten minutes to himself before starting the grind all over again. Was that too much to ask?

Exhaustion clawed at him. He'd been tired before—he'd lost his share of sleep while in the navy. But this was different. Caring for this baby had left him feeling totally depleted on all levels—physical, mental and emotional. How did such a tiny creature have so many damn needs?

Heck, at this point he might be better off taking his chances with Karnov and his thugs. A broken leg was starting to sound a lot better than another day of dirty diapers and temper tantrums.

Speaking of diapers... He grabbed his pack and

checked his supply. His heart sank as he realized he didn't have enough supplies to last more than a few hours. He'd thought one pack of diapers and a few pouches of food would be enough, but he'd quickly learned better. Christina needed to be changed every time he turned around, and she ate constantly. He was going to have to restock or they wouldn't make it to the deadline.

He cursed quietly in the morning air. The only way to get more supplies was to go into town. People would see him and the baby. Had news of the kidnapping reached Alpine yet? It was a medium-sized town hours away from El Paso, but a missing child tended to be a big news story. And in this day and age, their pictures were probably all over social media. Would anyone recognize him or the baby?

It was a chance he was going to have to take. But maybe it would be safer if he went into one of the smaller towns—they tended to be more insular, less connected to the wider world. As a stranger he would stick out, but if the locals didn't have any other reasons to suspect him he might be able to get away with a quick trip.

His mind made up, Joseph began the process of breaking camp. He was a pro at it by this point, since he made sure to move them to a new site every day. Even though he tried to avoid other hikers and campers, it was best not to get too comfortable in one spot.

Christina woke up as he worked. He changed her diaper and gave her one of the remaining pouches of baby food. When she was done, he strapped her onto his chest and began the trek back to his car. He'd hidden it in a patch of scrub not far away, wanting to stay close in case he had to make a quick getaway.

An hour later, he carried Christina into a small grocery store in Terlingua. He waved absently at the cashier's welcome and made a beeline for the baby aisle, scanning the shelves for what he needed.

It wasn't a great selection—certainly nothing like the variety he'd found in El Paso. But the essentials were there, and that would have to be enough. He grabbed a pack of diapers and wipes, and after a quick glance at Christina, threw a second pack into the cart. She probably wouldn't go through that many diapers, but better safe than sorry. He didn't want to have to make this trip again.

After filling the cart with baby food pouches, he wheeled over to the beverage aisle. Might as well restock on water and sports drinks while he was here. Two men looked over as he approached. They both sported beards and tans, and one wore a hat that said Guide. Likely tour guides in the park, Joseph figured. Several tour companies were based out of the small towns on the edges of the park, with the guides often living in the area year-round.

The men nodded at him. "Cute kid," said the one with the hat.

"Thanks," Joseph replied. He turned to study the shelf, acutely aware of the fact that neither he nor Christina had bathed in days. He sniffed at her head, trying to be casual about it. No doubt about it—they both smelled. One more reason to get out of here quickly.

He grabbed a few bottles, trying to ignore the men murmuring a few feet away. From the corner of his eye, he saw them consulting a ragged piece of paper. The guy without the hat noticed him looking over and quickly folded the paper, stuffing it back into his pocket.

Huh. That's odd.

But Joseph didn't have time to dwell on the men's behavior. Christina chose that moment to emit a loud fart, and the accompanying stench left no doubt as to the state of her diaper.

"Oh, man," he muttered. He wheeled the cart toward the back of the store and rolled open one of the diaper packs. Grabbing her and the wipes, Joseph stepped into the restroom.

He had just laid her down on the changing table when the door opened and the two men from the beverage aisle walked in. The hair stood up on the back of Joseph's neck as they flanked him and planted their feet.

"Can I help you?" He tried to keep his voice calm, but he was shaking inside. Why were they here? What did they want?

"What's your name?" asked the guy in the hat.

Joseph kept his eyes on Christina and his hand on her belly to keep her from rolling off the table. "Why do you want to know?"

"Just answer the question, please," said Hatless.

Joseph's mind raced as he changed the baby's diaper. "Chris," he lied.

"Uh-huh," said Hat. It was clear he didn't believe it. But what was he going to do about it?

"And the baby?" said Hatless. "What's her name?"

"Chr—uh, Emma," Joseph said. He could have bitten his own tongue off for the mistake, but it was too late now.

He decided to go on the offensive. He picked up Christina and held her, then turned to face the men. "What's this about? Why all the interest in my baby?"

The two men exchanged a glance. "The thing is, mister, we don't think she's yours."

A chill skittered down Joseph's back, and it was all he could do to keep from running out of the room.

He tried to laugh off the accusation, but all that came out was a strangled sound. "That's ridiculous."

"Is it?" asked Hatless. He pulled out a piece of paper, and Joseph recognized it as the one the men had been studying in the beverage aisle.

It was a "missing" flyer, sporting a few pictures of Christina and a couple of him. His stomach twisted as he scanned the page, his mind racing as he tried to come up with a plausible way to dismiss the proof in his hands.

He decided to bluff. "You think this is me?" He scoffed as he passed the page back. "Please. I look nothing like this guy."

"I disagree," said Hat. "I'd say you look exactly like him. And that's definitely the baby."

"Whatever," Joseph said dismissively. "All babies look alike at this age. Or don't you know that?"

The men blinked, as if they hadn't considered that

point. Joseph tightened his grip on Christina and took a step forward.

"I can see why you guys were concerned, but there's no need. Now, if you'll excuse me."

He made it another step before Hat stepped in front of him. "Not so fast."

Joseph narrowed his eyes at the man. "What the hell do you think you're doing?"

"I can't let you leave here. Not with the baby."

He sucked in a breath, hoping his fear didn't show on his face. "I'm telling you, everything is fine. Now let me by."

"Not until we get this straightened out," said Hatless. "The police are on their way now and should be here any minute."

A cold sweat broke out over Joseph's body, and he felt the blood drain from his head. He couldn't let the police find him—the prisons were full of men willing to do Karnov's bidding in exchange for his approval. Out here, he at least had a chance. In prison, he'd be a sitting duck.

He swallowed, debating. He might be able to make a break for it, but not while holding the baby. She would only slow him down. But she was his bargaining chip. Could he afford to give her up?

He heard Hatless shift behind him and knew his moment was up. If he let the men get their hands on him, he was done for.

There was only one thing he could do. "Here." He thrust Christina forward against Hat's chest, then let go so the man was forced to catch her. Ignoring Hat's startled cry, Joseph pushed past him and ran for the exit.

Footsteps pounded after him, but Joseph didn't risk looking back. He practically dived into the driver's seat of his car, slamming the lock on the door behind him. As he cranked the engine, he saw Hatless closing in on him fast.

Joseph stood on the gas pedal and tore out of the parking lot, passing a black-and-white that had just pulled in, lights flashing and sirens blaring.

He turned onto the main road, the truck bed fishtailing a bit thanks to his speed. His hands were slick on the wheel and his breathing labored as he kept glancing in the rearview mirror, expecting to see the red gleam of sirens in pursuit. But the view was blessedly clear.

His heart rate began to slow, and he eased off the gas—no sense drawing attention to himself now. If he played his cards right, he could get out of town before the cops even knew to look for him.

But where should he go? Not back to the park—there was no reason to stay in Big Bend now. His apartment was in El Paso, but the police were likely watching it.

"Traitorous bitch," he mumbled, anger rising in his chest as he recalled the flyer. Why had Emma done such a thing? He'd made it clear he was keeping Christina safe, and that she'd get her daughter back soon. Why hadn't she believed him? He didn't blame her for calling the police before she knew he had the baby, but once he'd explained the situation, she should have trusted him. Instead, she'd created flyers that made him look like a baby-stealing monster, someone who was dangerous and not to be trusted. Her betrayal stung, and given the fact that she'd already lied to him about the money, Joseph was rapidly losing any affection he'd ever had for her.

How in the hell had those flyers made it down here anyway? Terlingua was hours away from El Paso. Were the police actually searching in this area, or had Emma come down here on a hunch?

He cursed softly. It seemed he wasn't as slick as he'd thought if his sister had thought to look for him here. Had she remembered their childhood camping trips as well, or had she just gotten lucky?

Doesn't matter, he thought as he drove past the city limits sign. Even if she was here, she still hadn't found him. And now that she was getting her baby back, she wouldn't continue to look for him. He had a small window of opportunity to find a new place to hide, and he was going to take advantage of it.

And as for the money? He'd figure that out, too. Emma might not want to help him, but he wasn't going to let her get away with what she'd done. She thought it was acceptable to treat him like a hardened criminal? He was going to show her just how sinister he could be.

Chapter 5

Emma sat in the dirt in front of the tent, holding the peanut butter sandwich in her lap. She knew she needed to eat so she and Matt could pack up and head out, but her limbs felt heavy, and her mind wandered.

It was getting harder to hold out hope. Yesterday's discovery of the empty yogurt pouch had made her think they were getting closer to finding Christina, but as the hours had passed, her initial enthusiasm had waned. She'd spent most of last night staring at the roof of the tent, her brain helpfully supplying all the reasons why the pouch had nothing to do with her daughter. Now, in the light of a fresh morning, Emma had to admit it seemed to be nothing more than a coincidence.

Her daily call to Detective Randall hadn't helped her mood, either. He wanted her to come back to El Paso, even though they didn't have any new leads there. The lack of progress on the case was troubling, but what bothered her most was the way he'd spoken to her— very carefully, his tone especially gentle. She got the feeling he was trying to prepare her for the news that the search had gone cold. With no positive developments and no new clues, it was only a matter of time before the investigation shifted focus, the hunt for her daughter giving way to the search for her tiny body.

For one black moment, Emma pondered which would be worse: never finding her daughter, or knowing for certain she was dead? Being able to bury her would provide some small measure of closure, but Emma decided she'd rather not know. At least if Christina remained missing she could hold out hope that her baby was alive, somewhere out there. The thought of a world without her daughter in it was simply too terrible to even consider.

"It won't come to that," she whispered under her breath. "I won't let it."

As if she had any control over the situation. But somehow saying the words made her feel a little better, like her voice had imbued them with the weight of truth.

She rubbed her eyes with the heels of her hands, digging deep for energy. The physical fatigue didn't bother her—as a nurse and a mother, she was used to that. It was the emotional intensity of the situation that she found so draining. She couldn't relax, couldn't for one minute forget about her baby being gone. Her adrenaline was high nonstop, and it was taking its toll on her body and mind. There was a breakdown coming, but she didn't know how much time she had left until her body simply stopped functioning. Hopefully they would find Christina before Emma hit the wall.

She slid sunglasses on, adjusting them carefully on the bridge of her nose. It didn't hurt as much as yesterday, but the tissue was definitely sore. Still, as she'd told Matt at the time, it could have been worse.

The corner of her mouth curved in a small smile as she recalled his reaction to her injury. He'd been so apologetic, so worried. It had been cute, really, the way such a big, strong man had seemed to shrink before her eyes when he realized he'd accidentally hurt her. His reaction had been sweet and, to be honest, a bit unexpected. Matt seemed so serious and regimented that his show of emotion had surprised her. Once more, Emma wished she'd met him under different circumstances so she could justify her desire to get to know him better. Maybe, when this was all over—

She cut off the thought before it had a chance to take root in her mind. When this was all over, she was taking her baby girl and going home, back to El Paso and to her job. Matt lived near the park—his life, his work, was here, several hours away from her home. While the thought of getting close to him was appealing, it could never be a reality. She was busy enough, between her shifts at the hospital and taking care of Christina. Making sure her brother was brought to justice for what he'd done was likely going to take time, as well. There simply wasn't room in her schedule for a relationship, particularly one of the long-distance variety. So while she found Matt intriguing, he was going to have to remain a mystery.

That settled, she took a bite of sandwich and turned her thoughts to the day ahead. Matt rounded the bend of the trail, looking disgustingly well-rested even though he hadn't crawled inside the tent until quite late. She reached up to brush a strand of hair behind her ear, wondering if she looked as bad as she felt.

He smiled as he walked forward to meet her. "Hi," he said simply. "Doing okay this morning?"

Just like that, his greeting chased away the worst of her bad mood, and Emma felt herself smiling back. "I've been better, but I've been worse, too."

He nodded, his clear blue eyes zeroing in on her nose. "Still hurting?" he said, nodding toward the feature in question.

"A little." She resisted the urge to touch it self-consciously, knowing that would only make it ache more. "But I'll survive."

"Of that, I have no doubt." He knelt and grabbed a radio from his bag. "I'm going to check in with the team, find out if anyone has seen or found anything that might be connected to your brother."

A glimmer of hope broke through the dark clouds of her thoughts. Emma had forgotten they weren't the only ones in the park looking for Christina. It was possible one of the other rangers had gotten lucky, or would do so today.

"Do you think anyone has news?"

Matt hesitated a second, then shook his head. "I probably would have heard about it already if someone had seen or heard anything of interest. But it won't hurt for me to double-check, and to remind everyone to keep their eyes and ears open."

Emma nodded, trying not to feel disappointed. "Can I fix you a sandwich?" She actually wished they had coffee this morning—she'd welcome caffeine in any form right about now.

"I'm good, thanks." Matt rested his hand on her shoulder. "Be right back," he said, squeezing gently.

Emma looked down, busying herself with the bread and peanut butter so she wouldn't stare at him while he contacted the ranger station. Even though Matt didn't think his fellow rangers had noticed anything amiss in the park, she had to believe it was only a matter of time until someone saw something.

He returned a few minutes later, and she could tell by the look on his face there was nothing to report. *He really is kind*, she thought as she watched him struggle to find a way to let her down gently. Even from the beginning, when he'd clearly thought she had a screw loose, he'd treated her with respect and been nice to her. It was a point in his favor, one more thing she appreciated but didn't know how or even if she should tell him.

"It's okay," she said, sparing him the effort. "As long as they keep looking."

He looked mildly relieved by her reaction. "They will," he said. "They're a good group of people. They're worried about Christina, too."

"Are you ready to start looking again?"

"Just as soon as we break camp," he replied. "Do

you want to keep going forward, or try a different direction?"

Emma shook her head. "No, let's stay on this trail. If they really were here before, they might not have moved far."

"Let's hope," Matt said. Working quietly, they packed up their gear. Emma strapped her bag on her back and forced her aching legs to start moving.

They hadn't gone far when she felt a buzz in her pocket. Emma pulled out her phone and saw from the display that Detective Randall was calling. A chill skittered over her, followed immediately by a wave of heat that made her feel dizzy.

Matt glanced over and placed his hand on her arm to brace her. "You okay?"

She nodded, her finger fumbling for the screen so she could accept the call. "Hello?" *Please, let her be alive.* She put the phone on speaker, so Matt could hear what the detective had to say.

"Emma, where are you?"

"I'm in Big Bend." *What? What is it?* She wanted to scream the words, but managed to stay calm.

Before she could say anything else, Detective Randall spoke again. "Good. I need you to get to the Big Bend Regional Medical Center."

"What? Why?" She glanced at Matt, who frowned and shook his head slightly.

Randall's next words made her heart stop.

"They've found Christina."

* * *

"Can you go any faster?" Emma's voice was tight, her expression pinched as she sat next to him, her body drawn taut as a bowstring.

He knew she was eager to get to the hospital. Even though Detective Randall had assured Emma that Christina was fine, he could tell she wouldn't believe it until she saw the little one for herself.

"I'm doing my best," he said, swerving around another slow-moving car. It was difficult to stay focused on driving when he had so many unanswered questions swirling through his mind. Who had found the baby? Where was Emma's brother? How had the two of them been separated? Detective Randall had been maddeningly short on details, which only added to Matt's curiosity. And he was just an outsider looking in on the situation; he could only imagine how Emma must feel at this moment.

The Big Bend Regional Medical Center was located in Alpine, a good-sized town not far from the park. Matt and many of the other park rangers lived in Alpine, so he was familiar with the terrain. He exited the freeway as soon as possible and took a few side streets to avoid the worst of the traffic. It still took longer than he would have liked, but soon enough he pulled into the parking lot of the main hospital.

Emma had her hand on the door handle as he rolled to a stop outside the emergency room entrance. She leaped from the truck without even a backward glance. "I'll meet you inside," he called after her, but she was already halfway inside the place, and he wasn't sure she'd heard him. It was clear the rest of the world had ceased to exist for her—it was all about her daughter now.

Not that he blamed her. It was only natural she'd be anxious to see her baby again.

He parked quickly and jogged inside in time to see Emma walk through a door that led to the back area of the ER, presumably where the patients were seen. Reaching out, he snagged the door before it closed and caught up to Emma in a few strides.

The nurse leading her turned and gave him a questioning look, but before he could explain his presence, Emma glanced back and saw him. Relief flashed across her face. Without a word, she reached out and grabbed his hand, gripping it tightly.

Her silent expression of trust was surprising, and so was the lump that formed in his throat. Since when did he get emotional about holding hands with a woman? But there was nothing normal about this situation, and he knew it.

"Is my baby okay?"

The other woman shot Emma a sympathetic glance. "The doctor will speak with you soon. I should wait for him, but..." she trailed off. When she spoke again, her voice was softer. "She's fine, Mama. No need to worry."

Emma let out a soft sob of relief. "Thank you," she whispered.

Matt smiled as he walked quickly to keep up with Emma. The woman led them through several corridors, finally stopping outside a nondescript door. She rapped on the surface, and a muffled voice from within sounded. "Yes?"

The nurse pushed the door open. Matt kept a firm grip on Emma's hand to keep her from running over the woman to get inside. The nurse stepped to the side and Emma shot into the room, dragging Matt along. He caught a glimpse of two uniformed police officers and a tiny dark-haired figure sitting inside a hospital crib before Emma's body blocked his view.

"Christina!" She practically sobbed the baby's name as she reached out to hold her child.

The baby turned to the door and her face lit up when she saw her mother. "Ma, ma, ma!" she babbled happily, reaching out with chubby arms. Emma scooped up her baby and held her tightly, her nose pressed into the folds of the little one's neck. She inhaled deeply, and Matt watched as the worry lines vanished from Emma's face.

The two police officers exchanged a glance. "That's all the proof I need," one said drily.

"Works for me," said the other.

Emma didn't react. It was clear she wasn't aware anyone else was in the room with her. She simply held her baby, swaying from side to side and whispering in the infant's ear. Christina's little hand rested on her mother's shoulder, her fingers alternately clutching and releasing the fabric of Emma's shirt. Matt could hear the baby coo softly, the sound mostly absorbed by Emma's body.

It was a touching reunion. From the corner of his eye, Matt saw the nurse wipe away a tear. He was feeling a little misty himself at the sight—she looked totally at peace and blissfully happy now that she had her baby in her arms again. The transformation was stunning; he'd thought Emma was pretty before, but now she was beautiful.

"Ma'am?" One of the officers stepped forward, seeking Emma's attention. She didn't respond, making Matt wonder if she'd even heard the man.

He tried again. "Miss?"

When she still didn't react, Matt reached over and touched her shoulder. She jerked, her eyes flying open in surprise. She glanced up at him questioningly.

"The police need to talk to you," he said gently. He hated to interrupt this moment between mother and baby, but the officers weren't going to wait forever.

"Oh," she said blankly. "Of course."

The nurse slipped out of the room as one of the men gestured for Emma to take a chair. The other officer regarded Matt curiously.

"Who're you?"

Emma looked up. "He's a park ranger. He's been helping me search Big Bend for Christina." Her arms tightened protectively around her daughter as she said the baby's name. Matt got the impression she wouldn't be letting go of the infant anytime soon.

"Do you want him to stay?"

Matt felt a spike of unease at the question. While there was no reason for him to remain now that Emma and Christina had been reunited, he wasn't quite ready to say goodbye to the pair just yet. Of course, it wasn't exactly his decision...

"I do," she said simply. "He's my friend."

Her declaration warmed his heart, triggering an unexpected surge of emotions that gave him a lump in his throat. For reasons he couldn't name, Emma's words meant a lot to him.

"All right," the officer said. "There are a few things we need to take care of before we can release the baby into your custody. First of all, do you have ID on you?"

"Um, yes. I should." Emma glanced at her bag, which had fallen to the ground in her rush to hold Christina. Matt bent down to pick it up, and she flashed him a grateful smile as he passed it to her.

She fished out her wallet and passed it to Matt. "My driver's license is inside." She turned to the officers. "Will that work? I have her birth certificate in a safe-deposit box back home."

"The license will do for now," said the man. Matt easily found it and passed it over. To his surprise, underneath her license was a candid snapshot.

It was Emma, standing next to a man who was sitting on a tree stump. She had her hands resting on his shoulders and he was leaning into her, his head resting against her stomach. *This must be Chris*, he realized. The picture had the look of an engagement photo shoot, with both of them sporting the wide, bright smiles of people in love.

Emma looked happy and relaxed, a far cry from how he'd seen her the past couple of days. He knew he should close her wallet and stop staring at the picture, but he couldn't look away. The image was strangely compelling, and Matt found himself focusing on Emma's face and the beauty of her smile.

He glanced at Christina, then back at the photo, this time examining Chris. *She looks like her daddy.*

He felt a pang in his chest as Fisher's face flashed in his mind's eye. The boy hadn't resembled him at all, and it was no wonder since Matt wasn't his father. Would he ever have a child of his own? Or had he tossed aside his one shot at a family? Yes, Jennifer had lied to him, but perhaps with counseling they could have worked things through...

"Here." Matt was pulled out of his thoughts by the officer holding out Emma's ID. "You can put this away now."

He slid the license back into place, hiding the photo once more. Did Emma stare at this picture often, or had she forgotten it was even there?

"Where did you find her?" she asked, glancing from one officer to the other. "And where is my—" She hesitated, grimacing. "Where is Joseph?"

"Two men saw your brother and the baby in a grocery store in Terlingua. They work as guides in Big Bend, and they recognized the pair from a flyer they had picked up."

Emma turned to glance at Matt, her eyes shining with gratitude. A tingling rush went through him at the realization his actions had led to this moment.

"Your brother went to the bathroom to change the baby," the man continued. "They called the police and followed him inside to confront him. He panicked, thrust Christina at them and took off running."

"Did they find him?" Her tone made it clear she wasn't asking out of concern for his safety. Matt hoped that for his sake, Joseph never saw his sister again.

"No, ma'am. We're still looking, of course."

"He's long gone," she said dismissively. "He always did have a flair for self-preservation. There's no way he stuck around here now that he no longer has Christina."

"You're probably right," said one of the officers. "We've put out a statewide bulletin, so hopefully someone will recognize him."

Emma nuzzled Christina's hair, shrugging slightly. Matt got the impression that now that she had her baby back, she didn't care what happened to her brother.

"We'll leave you for now," said one of the men. "But don't go yet. There are still some things we need to take care of before we can officially release your baby to you."

"I understand," Emma said. "As long as you let me hold her, I'll stay here forever."

The two men smiled and nodded, then turned and left the room. Once they were alone, Emma let out a huge sigh.

Matt remained quiet for a moment, unsure of what to say. Did Emma want him to stay with her, or would she prefer some privacy with her daughter? He shifted from one foot to the other, not wanting to interrupt the moment, but not wanting to linger if she wished to be alone with Christina.

Give her some time, he decided. Both she and the baby had been through a hell of an ordeal. It was only natural she'd want a few minutes to herself to process everything that had happened.

He started toward the door, but as he moved he noticed Emma's shoulders drop. She seemed to fold in on herself, and then he heard the unmistakable sound of a sniffle.

She was crying.

The sound just about broke his heart. Before he could think better of it, he moved to her chair and placed his hand on her shoulder. "Emma," he said softly.

She didn't respond, but she placed one of her hands over his, accepting his touch.

Matt racked his brain, trying to come up with the right words. There had to be something he could say to comfort her, to let her know she wasn't alone right now.

Her shoulder shuddered under his hand as she cried. He knelt next to her and gathered her into his arms as best he could. She leaned against him, still holding her little one tightly.

"I didn't think I'd ever see her again," she said. Her voice was a broken whisper, a jagged sound that cut through the defensive walls he'd built around his heart. "I tried to stay positive," she continued. "But as the days wore on, I began to lose hope."

"You don't need to think about that now," he said softly. "She's back with you, and everything is fine."

"Yeah." She exhaled, her breath a little shaky. "But for how long?"

Matt stroked her arm with one hand. "What do you mean?"

"My brother," she said flatly. "He's still out there. And he still needs money."

"You think he'll bother you again? After coming so close to being caught here? I thought you said he was good at self-preservation."

"He is," Emma replied. "But he's also got an impulsive side. He's already demonstrated he's capable of anything. I can't imagine what he'll do once he's truly desperate."

There was real fear in her voice, the kind that wouldn't be assuaged by pretty words. Matt wished there were something he could do to reassure her that she and her baby were safe; despite her worries, he didn't think Joseph would be so stupid as to bother them again. But Emma seemed convinced she had a reason to be concerned, and who was he to tell her otherwise?

"The police will help you," he said, but even as the words left his mouth, he wasn't sure they were true. Unless Emma could demonstrate a real danger to herself or her baby, the authorities would probably not be much help. Her fear that Joseph might try something else likely wouldn't be enough to qualify for assistance. Unless they wanted to use her as bait to draw her brother out again… He clenched his jaw at the possibility, hoping the police wouldn't be so cavalier about her safety.

Matt hated the thought of Emma alone in her apartment, cowering under the covers and jumping at every sudden noise. But what could he do? His life was here—he couldn't very well uproot everything and go to El Paso to guard her against a threat that might never materialize. And even if he could leave, she likely wouldn't want him there. Helping Emma search for her daughter had created an artificial sense of intimacy between them—it wasn't as if they really knew each other.

Besides, he told himself. She was a strong woman. Her actions had made that clear enough. If she thought her brother was going to try to hurt her again, she was more than capable of taking steps to protect herself and her daughter. She didn't need him swooping in like some knight-errant when she could handle things on her own.

He knew it was true, but he still felt a bit uneasy at the thought of Emma facing Joseph alone. He'd kidnapped her daughter, yes, but he hadn't been violent about it. If he came back, would he escalate his behavior and physically hurt Emma or Christina?

The idea made his stomach turn, and his arms tightened involuntarily around Emma. Even as he held her close, the rational part of his brain was questioning his actions. *She's not mine*, he told himself. So why did he feel the need to protect her as if she were?

The baby began to fuss. He released his hold on them, and Emma shifted her into a different position. "We're not ignoring you, sweetie," she crooned. "Mommy's still here."

Matt got his first good look at Christina as she beamed up at her mother. She was an adorable baby— dark curls, bright blue eyes and chubby pink cheeks. She babbled happily, flashing a few white teeth as she spoke. Now that he'd seen Chris's photo, he could tell she looked more like her father than Emma. But she had parts of Emma, in the curve of her smile and the shape of her eyes.

Watching the two of them and the obvious love they shared made Matt's heart feel too big for his chest. That was the kind of bond he wanted—one of absolute trust and total devotion. It was something he'd thought he'd had with Jennifer, but now he knew better. He wanted to wake up next to someone, knowing they had his back no matter what the day brought. He wanted to hold his child close, to revel in the small joys of discovery as they explored the world. To have his baby gaze up at him, totally secure in the knowledge that his father loved him beyond reason.

Maybe it was too much to ask. Maybe no one ever got the total package. Emma had her baby, but she'd lost her partner. Plenty of his friends had unhappy marriages or troubled kids. Perhaps that was just the way of it—he needed to pick one thing and accept that he couldn't have it all.

Christina reached out, grabbing for the brim of his hat. Matt removed it and placed it on her head, laughing as it slid down to cover her face. He waited a beat, then plucked it off. "Peekaboo," he said playfully.

The baby giggled, the sound one of pure joy. She reached up again, so he put the hat back on her head, repeating the game. Playing with her lightened his heart, and he soon cast aside his heavy thoughts and focused on the moment, enjoying the sound of her laughter.

After several minutes, Matt became aware of Emma's eyes on him. He turned to find her watching him, a faint smile playing at the corners of her mouth. There was a strange look in her eyes, one he couldn't read. What was she thinking? Did she not want him to play with her daughter? He could understand if she was leery of Christina being around a man so soon after Joseph had taken her. But surely she knew he wasn't a threat to either of them?

He got to his feet and took a step back, establishing some distance between them. "Well," he said, stalling as he searched for something to say. "I think I'll duck out for a minute and get something to drink. Can I bring you anything?"

"Some water would be nice," Emma replied. She didn't sound upset, but her gaze was still assessing as she watched him. He got the feeling he was being evaluated in some way, and he was curious to know if he'd passed this unspoken test.

"Water it is," he said. He plucked his hat from Christina's head and sat it firmly on his head. "I'll be back soon."

"We'll be here," Emma said. She pressed a kiss to the baby's forehead as he turned to go. He took one last look before heading out the door, enjoying the sight of this woman and her child far too much.

Not yours, he reminded himself as he headed down the hallway in search of a vending machine. He tried to hold on hard to that thought, but a sense of longing was building in his chest. No, Emma and her daughter weren't his family. But perhaps, maybe, one day they might be?

Matt considered himself more of a realist than an optimist. But in this case, hope was starting to take over.

He was setting himself up for a huge fall. He recognized it, knew he should take steps to protect himself. It was the right thing to do.

The problem was, his heart didn't seem to care.

Joseph swallowed hard and entered the truck stop diner, pulling his hat down low as he glanced around. He was here for a meeting—his last chance at saving himself from Karnov's thugs. One of his friends had told him about a man who paid handsomely for kids— the guy apparently worked for some fancy adoption lawyer, procuring children to be placed with wealthy couples desperate for a family. "He pays extra for babies," Jimmy had said.

So after losing Christina in Terlingua yesterday, Joseph had made a call. The man he'd spoken to had said he'd be wearing a green shirt and black cowboy hat; sure enough, someone matching that description sat in a booth near the restrooms. Joseph headed that way, dodging the busy waitress as she made her circuit of tables.

He slid into the booth with a nervous smile. "I'm Joseph."

The man studied him, his dark eyes devoid of any hint of friendliness or welcome. "You a cop?"

The question made Joseph's heart pound. "No. Are you?"

The man's lips twitched with what might have been

a smile. "No." He looked past Joseph's shoulder and nodded once. A second later, two large men appeared at the table. "Let's go."

Adrenaline pumped through Joseph's system, making his limbs tremble and his palms sweat. "Go where?" This was not what he had anticipated. He was supposed to meet this person and talk business. He'd made no mention of going somewhere else when they'd spoken on the phone.

He glanced at the two heavies looming over him, hoping to see some hint of humanity. But their faces were blank, almost bored. He looked at the man sitting across from him, who was smiling now, plainly enjoying Joseph's discomfort. "We're gonna take a walk."

Oh, God. That didn't sound good. But what choice did he have? It was clear if he didn't go willingly the enforcers would simply drag him out of the booth.

Joseph swallowed hard and slid across the fake leather seat. The men moved back a step as he stood.

The man in the green shirt rose, as well. "After you," he said mockingly.

Joseph's stomach churned as he walked back toward the door. Maybe this wasn't such a good idea after all. But he still needed the money, and Emma had betrayed him...

The two men flanked him as they stepped into the parking lot. Green Shirt took the lead, heading for one of the semitrucks parked in a far corner of the lot.

Away from people, Joseph thought, panic building in his chest. *Are they going to shoot me out here and dump my body?*

His throat grew more constricted with every step until he was gasping for air. Finally, they reached the cab of the truck. Green Shirt climbed up and opened the door, speaking softly to someone inside. He nodded, then jumped back down.

"Search him," he said to the goons.

With no warning, the two large men put their hands on Joseph. They were surprisingly gentle as they frisked him for weapons.

"Take off your shirt," one ordered.

Confused, Joseph did as he was asked. He got the impression refusal was not an option.

One of the men removed a small black device from his pocket. He flipped a switch and held it close to Joseph's body, running it up and down the length of his legs.

"He's clean," the man said.

Green Shirt nodded. "Put your shirt back on. Then give me your cell phone."

When he had complied, the man gestured to the cab of the semi. "Up you go."

Joseph climbed the steep steps, fumbling to open the door and maintain his balance at the same time. The last thing he wanted was to fall, especially in front of these guys. They reminded him of a pack of wolves he'd seen on a nature special, circling round their prey, waiting for it to stumble. He knew now he was in over his head, but he still wanted to make it out alive.

He half climbed, half fell into the passenger seat of the truck, pulling the door closed behind him.

"So," came a voice from the back, "you have some business for me."

Joseph turned to find that the back half of the cab was one large mattress covered in what looked like white satin sheets. A huge man reclined in a nest of pillows, his navy silk pajamas shiny in the ambient light. On one side of him sat a plate of cheese and crackers, on the other a small dog of indeterminate breed.

Both dog and man eyed him suspiciously. The dog licked its lips nervously. Apparently, this was some kind of signal. The man plucked a piece of cheese off the plate and held it in front of the dog's nose. The sleek little body trembled as the animal snatched the treat from its master's hand.

Joseph's first impulse was to laugh. How had such a fat man climbed those steps and wedged himself back here? Had the two goons outside pushed and pulled to hoist his girth into the truck? Or had he come in through the trailer? Maybe there was a special door in the back so he didn't have to squeeze himself through such a tiny opening...

His imagination took off, threatening to override his common sense. But one look at the man's eyes made Joseph's blood go cold. In that moment, he understood. He wasn't looking at a man. This was a monster.

Joseph swallowed hard, trying to find his voice. "I heard you're looking for babies."

The man inclined his head. "I might be. Do you have one?"

"Yes." He reached into his pocket and pulled out a

picture. "She's about ten months old." He extended the photo, his arm shaking a bit.

The man didn't take the photo, but he leaned forward to study it. "Cute," he said.

The word didn't sound good coming from him. In fact, it sounded downright scary. Joseph was really starting to have second thoughts now, but it was too late to change his mind.

"How much?"

Joseph named his price. The man leaned back and stared at him, his expression totally blank, giving no hint as to what he might be thinking.

The silence stretched on. Joseph began to wonder if he'd somehow offended the man. Was there something else he was supposed to say, some expected sign or action that came next? He'd never dealt with people like this before and didn't know the procedure.

Finally, the man lifted one eyebrow. "That's pretty steep, considering this is our first time doing business together." He named another figure, one that was much less but would still cover the gambling debt. Joseph was too frightened to do anything but accept.

"Very good. Let my associate know the address, and we will take it from here."

It was clear he was being dismissed, but Joseph still had questions.

"How will I get paid?"

"My associate will explain everything. If things work out, we can do business again. If not…" He trailed off, his meaning quite clear. A chill skittered down Joseph's spine as he silently hoped he never saw this man again.

Was he jumping out of the frying pan and into the fire? He'd thought Karnov was bad, but this man seemed no better.

"Uh, okay," he stammered. "Thank you." He didn't know if that was the right thing to say, but he didn't want to offend, and he figured it was better to err on the side of caution.

"We'll see," replied the man.

Joseph opened the door and practically fell out. He straightened, brushing his hand down the front of his shirt as he fought to regain his composure. The two enforcers merely stared at him. Green Shirt smirked.

"You have information for me?"

"I—uh, yeah," Joseph stammered. "I mean to say, yes. I do." He rattled off Emma's address in El Paso. "Do you need me to write it down?"

Green Shirt shook his head. "Nope." He tapped his temple with his forefinger. "Got it."

"And my money?"

"After," the man said. It was on the tip of Joseph's tongue to insist on getting half now, but he thought better of it. He doubted Green Shirt would respond well to such a demand, and he knew the man in the truck wouldn't appreciate it.

Joseph nodded and swallowed. "So, um, what happens now?"

Green Shirt grinned at him. "Now you leave. Run back to your hole, little rabbit. I'll be in touch."

Joseph didn't have to be told twice. He started for the relative safety of the truck stop diner, moving at a fast clip. He didn't want them to think he was running away, but he also didn't want to stick around any longer than necessary. The spot between his shoulder blades tingled as he walked, but he didn't dare turn around to see if they were watching him.

He slid into the booth in the back, his hands shaking a bit.

"What'll it be?" asked the waitress.

"Just coffee." He didn't think he could stomach any food right now.

She nodded, returning a moment later with a chipped mug. Joseph wrapped his hands around it, his attention focused on the parking lot. He didn't want to leave until he knew those men were gone. He wasn't stupid—he realized they knew his address, probably knew everything about his life already. But the thought they might follow him home tied his stomach in knots.

After a few moments, he heard the low rumble of a truck engine turning over. He scooted closer to the window, trying to catch a better glimpse of the back corner of the parking lot.

The semi crawled out of its spot, making a wide turn onto the main aisle of the stop. It glided past the windows of the diner on its way out of the parking lot. Green Shirt was behind the wheel, the two enforcers next to him. As Joseph watched, Green Shirt turned and gave him a mocking salute.

If he were a braver man, Joseph would have returned the gesture. Instead, he looked away, huddling into his coffee cup as he tried to pretend he hadn't been watching the truck drive away. From the corner of his eye, he saw the other man laugh.

Joseph held his breath until the truck pulled out of the lot and headed for the freeway. *This was a mistake*, he thought. He knew it was wrong to sell his own niece, but he'd justified it in his mind by assuming she'd be given to a family who would love her. After meeting these men, he realized how wrong he'd been.

But what could he do? He'd survived his first encounter with the buyer, but something told him he wouldn't survive a second. And now that they had Emma's address, he couldn't exactly go back on the deal. They'd likely just kill him and take the baby anyway.

Still, there had to be something he could do. He didn't want to die, but he also didn't want his niece sold into a nightmare. Maybe there was a way he could save her without the men knowing he'd double-crossed them. Unlike Karnov, he suspected these men didn't give warnings. And he doubted they would kill him quickly.

As if on cue, his phone buzzed in his pocket. He pulled it out and frowned at the display, not recognizing the number.

"Hello?"

"Two days."

The hairs on the back of Joseph's neck stood on end as his heart began to pound. "Excuse me?"

"You have two days. Then we're coming for blood."

"How did you get my number?" This was a new phone, one he'd never used before. The only person he'd called was that friend, Jimmy.

At least, he'd *thought* Jimmy was his friend... It seemed he'd sold him out to Karnov.

The man on the other end of the line laughed softly, the sound menacing. "You're not as smart as you think you are. Two days," he repeated.

"I-I'm getting the money," he stammered. "Tell Karnov I'm good for it."

The man laughed. "I've heard that one before."

"It's the truth."

"For your sake, I hope so." The man disconnected without another word.

Joseph returned the phone to his pocket, taking a deep breath to calm his racing heart. He tugged at the collar of his shirt, feeling an invisible noose tighten around his neck. *I'm sorry, Christina. So sorry.*

But what other choice did he have? It was a matter of self-preservation; his back was against the wall, and Joseph wasn't about to simply surrender. He was going to stay alive, and once his debt to Karnov was paid, he'd figure out a way to get the baby back. It would all be okay—he would come up with a plan that would take care of everything.

Somehow.

Chapter 6

Emma lay curled on her side, watching the rise and fall of Christina's chest as the baby slept beside her. She normally didn't bring her baby into bed with her, but she still couldn't bear to be apart from her for very long. This was the second night they'd been home, and the memories of finding an empty crib were still too fresh for Emma's liking. Hopefully she'd soon find the courage to put Christina back into her own room, but she was probably going to have to replace the crib and rearrange the furniture in the nursery to erase any similarity to that horrible night.

She rolled onto her back with a small sigh as her mind sifted through her other memories—calling the police, talking to Detective Randall. And the lonely drive down to Big Bend, the miles blurring as she struggled to see through her tears.

Thank God for Matt, she thought. If it weren't for him, she might have given up. And if it weren't for the flyers he'd made, Christina wouldn't have been recognized. Her baby would still be missing, in the care of her deranged uncle.

She shuddered at the thought, cutting off her imagination before it could go down that road. The what-ifs and maybes weren't important. All that mattered was that her daughter was with her again, safe and warm and loved.

While Emma had been eager to return to El Paso and put this nightmare behind her, a part of her had been reluctant to leave Matt. Although their time together had been brief, she'd grown used to being around him and had begun to rely on his emotional support. He'd been so wonderful in the hospital, taking care of many of the details so she could simply hold Christina and reassure herself that her baby was fine. He'd been supportive without being intrusive, as if he'd sensed her need to focus on her daughter to the exclusion of everything else. It was exactly what she had needed, and she wished she could have spent more time thanking him for all his help.

Their goodbye had been brief but heartfelt. He'd helped her load Christina into the car, dropping a sweet kiss on her baby's forehead before shutting the door. Then he'd turned to her, his blue eyes bright.

"I don't know how to thank you," Emma had said, tears springing to her eyes once more.

"You don't have to," Matt had replied, his voice gruff.

She had smiled then, touched by his response. She had wanted to say more, but Christina had begun to fuss, unhappy with her stationary position.

"Sounds like it's time for you to go," Matt had said.

"I guess so." Seized by impulse, Emma had reached for him, bringing his face down as she rose to her tiptoes. She'd pressed a brief kiss to his mouth before releasing him, then climbed in the car before Matt could do or say anything. She'd driven away then, her mouth still tingling from the feel of his lips and the brush of his stubble.

She placed her fingers to her lips now, smiling a little at the memory. Matt was the first man she'd kissed since Chris, if you could really count what she'd done as a kiss. She normally wasn't so impulsive, but the knowledge she wouldn't be seeing him again had made her bold. And what a shame it was that he was out of her life. Now that she could really think about it, he was exactly the kind of man she wanted to have around— kind, dependable, supportive, helpful. Not to mention good with kids, specifically Christina. Her daughter had really taken to him, giggling with joy when he'd played peekaboo with her. The sight of such a large, strong man paying attention to her baby had hit her hard, drawing her to him all the more.

Did he have any idea? Likely not. She'd watched his face when he'd played with Christina. There had been no hint of calculation or artifice, no indication he was doing it simply to score points. He'd been genuinely interested in her baby, and his smile at her responses had been real. Matt seemed to truly like children, and Emma had to wonder why it was he didn't have a wife and babies at home.

Maybe he just hasn't found the right person yet. He'd flinched when she'd asked if he had kids of his own; was that because he didn't think he'd be able to have a family? Maybe he'd grown tired of looking for Ms. Right and thought he'd be alone forever. For a few minutes, Emma allowed herself to indulge in the fantasy that *she* was the one he'd been waiting for. Since she didn't know him all that well, it was easy to imagine that he was the ideal man—always attentive and sweet, never having a bad day. And never leaving dirty socks on the floor or the toilet seat up. It was fun to picture that life, the both of them blissfully happy and in love, Matt bonding with Christina as if she were his own child. A house in a nice neighborhood, with the requisite dog and cat as pets. She'd have room for a small garden; he'd have a shed where he could tinker around on weekends. He'd teach Christina how to ride a bike and throw a ball. It would be the perfect suburban life, the American dream live and in color.

Christina stirred in her sleep, settling with a small sigh. Emma smiled at her little girl, so beautiful and perfect. "One day," she whispered. "One day I'll be able to give you that." No one could replace Chris, but Emma wanted her baby to have a father. Someone who loved her and would protect her, someone who would laugh with her and hold her when she cried. Emma's own father had been wonderful, so she knew how important it was for a little girl to have a daddy in her life. Part of her had hoped that Joseph could be a positive male influence, but those dreams were dashed.

Just thinking about her brother made anger bubble up in Emma's chest. Joseph had better pray Emma never found him. Emma wasn't normally a violent person, but if she got her hands on him, he wasn't going to walk away from the encounter.

Her phone buzzed on the bedside table. She rolled over and grabbed it, frowning at the unfamiliar number. Then she saw the text message, and her blood ran cold.

Get out now.

Her first thought was it was a wrong number. That was the only logical explanation. She returned the phone to her bedside table and tried to relax again, but the ominous message lingered in her mind.

I'll check the apartment. Once she convinced herself that things were normal, she'd be able to go to sleep. She slid out of bed, moving slowly so she didn't wake the baby. Then she began her circuit of the place, double-checking the windows and making sure the curtains were drawn tight. She'd already had the building supervisor change her door locks—now she was the only one with a key.

She was in the nursery when she heard the first sound, a furtive scratching that made the hairs on the back of her neck stand on end. It sounded like it was coming from the living room, so she crept back down the hall, straining to hear the noise again.

More scratching, coupled with a few soft taps. It was coming from the door. The knob jiggled slightly, and Emma realized someone was trying to pick the lock.

Oh, God, she thought, her breath catching in her throat. *OhGodohGodohGod…*

She raced back into her bedroom, closing the door behind her and locking it. Then she shoved her feet into a pair of tennis shoes and grabbed the baby wrap draped across the chair. The warning hadn't been a wrong number—it had been meant for her. Someone was coming for her, and she was about to run out of time.

She shoved her phone in her pocket. She'd call the police later, after she and Christina were safe. Whoever was trying to break in would be in the apartment in a matter of seconds, and there wasn't time to wait for the authorities to arrive. She had to get out now, while she still had a chance.

She held her breath as she picked up the baby, hoping her daughter wouldn't wake up and start crying. Fortunately, Christina snuggled quietly against Emma's chest as Emma put her in the baby wrap. *Please stay asleep*, she pleaded silently.

They were inside the apartment now, whoever they were. She heard the sound of footsteps as they headed down the hall toward the nursery. Horror filled her as Emma realized they weren't after her—they were here for her baby.

Not again, she thought grimly. She didn't know what

Joseph had gotten into this time, but she wasn't going to let him use her daughter as a pawn in his game.

She opened the sliding glass door and stepped onto the balcony. Her apartment was on the second floor— too high to jump safely. But there was a wide ledge that ran around the building. If she could make it over the railing, she could use the ledge to shimmy over to her neighbor's balcony.

The plan sounded great in her mind, but when Emma looked over the railing, the ground looked so very far away, and the ledge seemed impossibly small. Maybe she'd be better off barricading her bedroom door and waiting for the police...

She pulled out her phone and dialed.

"Nine-one-one, what's your emergency?"

"Some men have broken into my apartment," Emma whispered, hoping they couldn't hear her. "I think they're trying to kidnap my daughter." She gave the operator her address. "Please hurry."

"Help is on the way, ma'am. Please stay on the line with me."

A crash sounded from inside the apartment. Whoever was here was no longer worried about keeping quiet. She had to leave—she had no other choice.

"I can't—I have to hang up now."

"Ma'am—"

Emma ended the call, cutting off the operator mid-protest. She stuck the phone back in her pocket, praying the police were close by.

Emma gripped the railing tightly, took a deep breath and swung a leg over. Her foot landed on the ledge. She brought her other leg over, letting out a sigh of relief when both feet were on the ledge.

But now came the tricky part. With Christina strapped to her chest, Emma wouldn't be able to hug the side of the building as she inched along. She was going to have to put her back to the building, which meant she'd have to turn around now.

Her heart pounded hard as she prepared to flip herself around. *Don't look down, don't look down*, she coached herself. If she caught a glimpse of the ground she wouldn't be able to move, and she couldn't stay here. She was a sitting duck right now.

"It's too late to turn back," she muttered. Gathering her courage, she took one hand off the railing and pivoted on one foot until her back was to the building. Gripping the railing blindly with both hands, she began to shuffle along the ledge until she came to the spot where the balcony met the edge of the building. Her stomach cramped, but she couldn't stop now.

Leaving the relative safety of the balcony, she slid along until her back was against the brick of the building. After a few steps, she was at the corner.

It was dark here, the shadows thick. She was tempted to stay here and wait for help, but she heard a crash and figured her bedroom door had just been kicked in. Sure enough, a few seconds later she heard angry voices, the sound growing louder as two men stepped onto her balcony.

"She can't have gone far," said one.

"But how did she even know to leave in the first place?" asked another.

"My guess?" said the first voice. "Her brother."

"You think he warned her?"

Emma held her breath, a million thoughts running through her mind. Was Joseph the source of the mystery text? Had he really tried to protect her from these thugs? And who were they?

Before she could process that possibility, Christina stirred and let out a faint cry.

The two men stopped talking. "Did you hear that?"

Emma placed one hand on the infant's back, patting frantically. *No, not now. Not now, baby girl…*

Christina snuffled and began to wiggle in earnest. Emma recognized her behavior and knew her daughter was on the verge of waking up. And if history was any indication, she wasn't going to be quiet about it.

The men remained silent as Emma inched farther away from her place. She stepped softly but tried to move quickly, headed for her neighbor's balcony. The building was arranged in a staggered fashion, with each unit's balcony set back from the one next to it to afford some measure of privacy to the occupants. If she could make it to Josie's, she could hide there until the men left.

If she could make it that far…

"We can't stay here all night," said one of the men.

"I'm not telling the boss," said the other.

They continued to grumble as their voices faded. Emma began to relax—maybe they would leave and she could return to her apartment and call the police.

Christina apparently had other ideas. Her baby chose that moment to open her mouth and release an ear-splitting wail, her cry echoing in the otherwise still night.

Emma cursed softly. There was no way the two men had missed that sound.

"She's still close," one of them said.

Thinking quickly, Emma tried to bluff. "Why so unhappy, little one?" She spoke softly, so that they might think she was in another unit. "Do you want to go inside and see Daddy?" She shoved her knuckle in Christina's mouth to head off any further cries. The baby let out a small squawk, but soon set to work gumming Emma's finger.

"That's just the neighbors," said the second man. Emma nearly sobbed with relief—her ploy had worked!

"I'm not so sure," said the other one. He sounded doubtful, and Emma realized this was a pivotal moment; if Christina remained quiet, he might be persuaded to go. But if the baby made another sound, he was going to stick around and search until he found them.

Please, baby. Christina was starting to grow impatient with her position. She began to huff and grunt, gearing up for another loud cry.

Panic filled Emma as she realized she couldn't keep her finger in her daughter's mouth and continue inching along toward Josie's balcony—she needed both hands on the wall to maintain her balance on the ledge. She was going to have to make a choice; stay on the ledge and keep Christina relatively quiet, or let her yell and head toward the safety of her neighbor's place.

In the end, Christina made the choice for her. The baby let out another cry, this one louder than the first.

"That's not the neighbors," said the skeptical one. "She's out here, and she's close." He stepped to the edge of the railing, leaning over to look down. Emma inched farther away, her eyes locked on his form as he walked to the left side of her balcony and looked around. Apparently not seeing anything, he made his way to the right side, which was the path she'd used for her escape.

She froze, hardly daring to move as he bent over and checked the ground. Then he lifted his head and began to scan the side of the building, leaning out so he could see the neighboring balconies.

"All the lights are off next door," he reported. "There's no one awake to make that noise."

"Then where is it coming from?" asked his partner.

The man continued to peer into the darkness. The light from her bedroom illuminated his face, revealing a wicked scar along the curve of his jaw as his dark eyes moved from one spot to the next. Then he stopped, his mouth curving in an evil smile.

"Right there," he said, satisfaction filling his voice. "It's coming from right there."

Emma's heart stopped as she realized he'd seen her. He threw one leg over the balcony railing, clearly intent on following her. But before he could throw the other leg over, a car with flashing lights turned into the parking lot.

"Cops," said his partner. "We need to leave."

"No," said the determined one. "Not without her."

He made to climb over, but the first man put a hand on his shoulder.

"We'll get her later," he said. "You know what will happen if we get picked up."

The man hesitated, clearly torn. Then he swung his leg over the railing to stand on the balcony once more.

"You got lucky this time," he called out. "It won't happen again." Then he turned and both men disappeared into her apartment.

Emma leaned against the building, the chill from the brick seeping through the thin fabric of her T-shirt. A shudder ran through her body, making her limbs tremble.

Dozens of questions jockeyed for position in her mind, each more disturbing than the one before. Who were those men? Why had they targeted her? They clearly wanted Christina, but why? Who was behind this...this...the word "attack" sprang to mind, but they hadn't come here to beat her or rob her. Would they have taken her with them, or did they only want her baby?

One thing was certain—the man was right. She had gotten lucky tonight. Thanks to the mysterious text, she'd been given a few seconds' warning. They weren't giving up, though; he'd all but promised they'd be back. But she wasn't going to sit around and wait for their return. Now that she knew they were coming for her, she wouldn't be caught unawares again.

A swell of determination washed over her, stiffening her spine and giving her flagging courage a boost. She had more questions than answers at this point, but it didn't matter. The danger was clear, and so were her next steps.

She was going to protect her baby girl and keep her safe.

Or die trying.

Matt jerked awake, his hand reaching for the army-issued rifle he no longer kept by his side. *Incoming!* The buzzing sound persisted, and he was half out of bed before his sleep-addled brain suddenly remembered he wasn't a soldier anymore, but a park ranger.

Rattlesnake, was his next thought. Just the word was enough to send a burst of adrenaline through his system. He froze, heart pounding, knowing that any movement would antagonize the snake. Rattlers weren't known for their patience, and he didn't want to get bitten.

He opened his eyes, saw the ceiling fan hanging over him and frowned. He was in his bed, his apartment. How had a snake—

The last of the sleep fog cleared his mind and he realized the buzzing wasn't an incoming round or a rattlesnake. It was his phone, vibrating against the wood of his bedside table.

Feeling foolish, he reached for the phone without bothering to glance at the display before answering.

"Matt?" It was a woman calling, her voice distraught.

"Emma?" he said hesitantly. He shook his head, rubbing his free hand down his face. It couldn't be her—he just had her on the brain after her parting kiss.

It had been the nicest surprise, the sudden and un-expected feel of her lips on his. If he hadn't been so overcome with shock, he'd have taken her in his arms and kissed her properly. But the moment had flown by, and before he could get his arms to respond to his brain's commands, she'd slipped into the car and driven out of his life.

He'd kicked himself repeatedly over the missed op-portunity, but hadn't thought he was so far gone as to hallucinate the sound of Emma's voice. Clearly, she'd affected him more than he knew...

"Wait, who is this?" he asked. Not many people had his number, and this definitely wasn't his mother on the other end of the line.

"It's Emma," she said. She continued before he had a chance to respond. "I need your help."

Matt bolted out of bed, his eyes scanning the floor for his pants. "What can I do?"

"There's a truck stop just past the junction of I-10 and Highway 90. Can you meet me there?"

Matt paused in the act of stepping into his pants. "Uh, sure. It'll take me a while to get there, though. That's a couple hours away, at least."

"I know." She sounded tense, and he imagined her biting her bottom lip. "I'll wait."

"Is everything okay?" It was a stupid question—of course something was wrong. She wouldn't be call-ing otherwise.

"No," she said. "But it will be."

He heard the thread of determination in her voice and had to smile. Emma had a spine of steel. She was capable of taking on the world, and it was both humbling and flattering to know that such a confident woman was asking him for help.

"I'll be there as soon as I can," he promised. "Stay safe, and call me if anything changes."

"I will."

Matt hung up and hurried to dress, a sense of urgency nipping at his heels. "I'm on my way," he muttered as he climbed behind the wheel of his truck.

But would he get there in time?

The cops stayed in Emma's apartment for what seemed like forever. Joseph thought his bladder might burst, but he didn't dare leave his car. He was parked in the shadows of the lot, and he'd watched as the traffickers had first broken into Emma's place and then emerged several minutes later, empty-handed and cursing.

She hadn't left after his text, but apparently it had been warning enough to keep her safe. The fact that Christina was still with her mother made him feel marginally better, though he knew it would be a long time before he could look at himself in the mirror again. His deal with the devil plagued him—there had to be a way to make things right.

The door to the apartment building opened, spilling out four uniformed cops. They headed for their cruisers, the streetlights winking off their badges as they walked.

Joseph felt his eyebrows rise. That's it? They were leaving, just like that? Emma's apartment had just been invaded by human traffickers seeking to kidnap her baby, and the cops were going to leave the two of them alone?

Indignation filled his chest, making him sweat. Didn't they realize the men were going to come back? Guys like that didn't just give up and walk away. How could the police leave a woman and her baby alone and unprotected, knowing they were targets?

He was halfway out of his seat before he remembered Emma would be more likely to shoot him than accept his help. And really, if he was a smart man, he'd be getting out of town while he still could. At this point, he still had one day before Karnov's men would start looking for him, and the traffickers didn't know he'd double-crossed them. Yet. This was the time to make his escape; he could be long gone before anyone even knew to check.

But his sister's safety weighed on him. It was his fault she was in danger. If he hadn't tried to punish Emma for denying him money and then putting out those missing person posters, none of this would have happened.

"Actually," he muttered, "it's because of that damn horse." He'd put it all on Lucky Penny, only to have the horse come up lame on the final turn. If the jockey had done his job, the horse would have won as projected. Joseph was supposed to be swimming in money right now, but thanks to a cruel twist of fate he was sitting in his car in the dark, trying to remember if there was an empty water bottle in the back seat.

The building door opened again, and this time a

woman walked out. All thoughts of his bladder fled as Joseph realized it was Emma, toting Christina in her car seat. She made a beeline for her vehicle, her head swiveling from side to side as she scanned the parking lot. Joseph sat up straight, holding his breath as he watched her move.

She didn't waste any time. In a matter of seconds, Emma had put Christina in the back seat and climbed behind the wheel of her car. She pulled out of the parking spot with barely a backward glance.

Joseph watched her drive away, feeling torn. Should he follow to make sure she got to her destination safely? Or should he run? He might not get another chance to escape the powerful men waiting in the wings for their pound of flesh. But could he really leave Emma and Christina alone, knowing the danger they were in?

No, he decided. At least not yet. He grabbed the empty bottle from the back seat, cranked the ignition and stepped on the gas, following his sister into the night.

Chapter 7

Matt yanked open the door to the truck stop diner, ignoring the squeal of protest from the hinges as he walked inside. He scanned the tables anxiously, the twangy music filling his ears grating on his nerves as he walked among the tables.

Movement caught his eye, and he turned to see Emma, waving at him from a booth in the back. The tension drained from his body as he approached the table; she was safe.

Without thinking, he walked over to the booth and leaned down, planting a kiss on her mouth. He cupped her face with his hands as he savored the feel of her soft, warm lips against his. This wasn't the brief kiss she'd given him before leaving; he took his time, sinking into the moment and letting her feel all his worry for her and his relief at seeing her again.

Emma reached for him, her hands fisting in his shirt as if to anchor him in place. Little did she know, he had no intention of going anywhere.

After a few seconds, Matt reluctantly came up for air. The sight of Emma's face hit him in the gut. She was so damn beautiful, even under the harsh lights of the truck stop diner. Her pale skin was flushed, her lips parted slightly and a little swollen. But it was the look in her eyes that really did him in—sleepy-soft with a hint of surprise.

Matt cleared his throat, feeling a small degree of shock over his actions. He hadn't planned on kissing her. But when he'd walked in and seen her safe, he'd been so overcome with the need to touch her he hadn't questioned it. And now he was going to have to spend the next few hours trying to forget the feeling of her lips against his.

He slid onto the bench across from her, craning his neck to see into the car seat sitting next to her. "Is the baby okay?"

Emma shook her head as if to cast off a fog, then gave him a look of such warmth that his stomach did a little flip-flop. "She's fine," she replied. "Still sleeping."

"What happened?"

Emma began to talk, pausing only when a beleaguered-looking waitress appeared to ask if they wanted anything. Matt ordered a cup of coffee, more to stave off any protests about loitering than because he actually wanted it. The woman returned a moment later, sliding the steaming cup across the chipped laminate table with a little huff.

Matt gripped the cup, his blood going cold as Emma recounted her story of the two men breaking into her apartment and her desperate escape on the ledge of the building.

"You could have fallen to your death," he said quietly, a little surprised that his voice didn't shake. Even hours after the event, with her sitting safe and whole across from him, fear gripped his heart.

"I know," she said grimly. "But I didn't see another choice. I wasn't going to let them take my baby girl."

"I wish I had been there." He wasn't quite sure what he could have done—two against one wasn't exactly fair odds, especially if the men were armed—but he could have held them off while Emma and Christina escaped.

"It's okay." Emma reached across the table and wrapped her hand around one of his wrists. "You're here now, and that's all that matters."

"I don't know what you have planned, but I want you and Christina to stay with me until this is all over. We can hunker down at my apartment, or go hide in some rinky-dink no-tell motel off the beaten path, it doesn't matter to me. But I don't want you and the baby to be alone again." There was no telling where the would-be abductors were now, but Matt figured they'd be back. Emma and her daughter wouldn't be safe until the police arrested those men. Matt knew Emma was a proud, capable woman, but he wasn't going to let her face that kind of danger on her own.

Not again.

"I was hoping you'd say that," she said, smiling a little. "I don't know what the best choice is right now, but I can't tell you how relieved I am to know I don't have to make a decision by myself."

Her look of gratitude made him feel ten feet tall, and he fought the urge to puff out his chest.

"I just wish I knew who those men were and why they came after us," she continued.

Matt frowned. "My guess? They're traffickers. Someone probably tipped them off about Christina."

Emma's eyes widened. "You mean someone tried to sell my baby?"

Not someone, Matt thought. *One specific person.* But he didn't want to rub her nose in the fact that her brother was probably the one behind the kidnapping attempt.

Fortunately, he didn't have to. Emma's expression turned thunderous. "That rat bastard," she muttered darkly.

Matt merely nodded once to show he agreed with her. "He probably got cold feet and sent you the text telling you to leave."

"Yeah, and a lot of good it did me," she said. "If Joseph had really meant to help, he'd have given me more than thirty seconds of warning."

She had a point. Whoever had sent the message hadn't given her enough time to make an escape before the men arrived. So why send the text at all?

"Maybe he didn't know the men were so close?" Matt suggested.

Emma snorted. "No, he probably just felt guilty and was trying to absolve himself by warning me. If the men abducted Christina after I got his message, he figured it would be my fault because I hadn't taken the anonymous text seriously."

"Is that really how your brother thinks?"

"Yes." She rolled her eyes. "Everything is always someone else's fault. He's never responsible for anything that happens, unless it's something good. Then he can't wait to take all the credit."

"Sounds like a fun guy," Matt commented. "I know you're angry with him, but we can't waste our time on him. We need to figure out our next move."

"If those men really are traffickers, this is more serious than I thought." Emma glanced at the sleeping face of her baby, her features softening a bit. "I've read a few news articles about people like that. They don't give up easily."

"That's true," he confirmed. "I think the first thing we should do is find someplace safe to sleep for a few hours. We'll take my truck. The people looking for you won't know what I drive, so they won't be searching for it. Once we get on the road, why don't you call the El Paso police and tell them our suspicions? They might not take us seriously, but there might be someone there who knows about the traffickers operating in the city."

"I told the officers who came to my apartment everything that had happened. I also left a message for

Detective Randall," she said. "I'm waiting to hear back from him."

Matt nodded. "That's good. Maybe he can arrange to have you and Christina placed under protection until the threat is handled."

A shadow crossed Emma's face. "That's probably for the best." She looked down at her hands, which she had clasped on the table. "I was hoping things would go back to normal now that Christina has been found." She met his eyes, her lips pursed as if she'd tasted something sour. "So much for that."

It was Matt's turn to reach for her, to wrap his hand around hers. "It'll be okay," he said. "This is just a detour. We'll handle it, and soon you'll be settling in to your old routine again."

She smiled shyly. "You said 'we.' Do you mean it?"

The look on her face made him suck in a breath. All at once, he realized what his words meant to her. He'd spoken without thinking, but as he watched relief and hope flicker in her eyes, he understood he'd extended a lifeline. Emma was a single mother, used to doing everything by herself. She had to be exhausted and probably a little lonely. He'd only meant to offer her some encouragement, but could he give her something more?

Yes. The voice in his head was quiet but insistent. *The answer is yes.*

Matt nodded, swallowing hard. "I did say that. And I do mean it."

The weight of his promise settled over his shoulders, but he didn't feel trapped or bogged down. Rather, it felt like he had slipped into an old shirt, one he hadn't worn in quite a while. Since leaving Jennifer and her baby, he'd retreated into himself, shrinking a bit to hide his heart from the world. But now he was starting to stretch again, to unfurl his soul and reclaim his true size. It was a heady sensation, one that made him feel like he could take on the world if it meant keeping Emma and her daughter safe.

Her eyes were shiny as she looked at him. "Thank you," she whispered. She glanced away, discreetly wiping her cheeks. "I need to use the restroom before we go. Do you mind watching Christina?"

"Not at all." He stood and took Emma's place next to the baby. Christina was still asleep, one hand curled into a tiny fist next to her chin.

Matt watched her for a few breaths, a wave of tenderness spreading through him as her breath hitched a little. She was so small, so full of potential. Did she have any idea what was going on?

Of course not. How could she? Hell, he was an adult and he still had a ton of questions. Still, his heart did a funny little flip as he watched the baby's peaceful slumber.

Watch out, his head warned. He'd felt this tingle before, when he'd seen Jennifer standing there with a baby in her arms. If he wasn't careful, he'd fall in love with little Christina and her mother, and get his heart broken all over again for his efforts.

Christina shifted in her sleep, and he felt some of his resistance crumble away. He could protect Emma and her daughter and still guard his heart. There had to be a way, even if he couldn't see it right now. He'd figure it out as they went along. Somehow.

"I don't know what's going to happen, little one," he whispered. "But I will do everything in my power to keep you safe. You and your mother."

Joseph sank low behind the wheel of his car, his eyes darting left and right as he continuously scanned the parking lot of the truck stop. Of all the places for Emma to go, she'd brought him right back into the lion's den.

His stomach had dropped to his shoes when she'd exited the freeway and turned in here. It was the same place he'd met with the traffickers only a couple of days ago. Fortunately, he didn't see the boss's semi parked anywhere, and it didn't look like Green Shirt was in the diner. But how long could his luck last?

A flash of movement inside the diner caught his eye, and he watched as Emma rose from the table and headed to the bathroom, leaving Christina in the care of the blond man who'd walked in about ten minutes ago. Joseph narrowed his eyes as he studied the guy. His face was turned away from the windows, his head bent as he looked at the car seat. Who was this stranger? And why had his sister called him?

Emma seemed to trust him, that much was obvious. She wouldn't have left him alone with Christina otherwise. He had a no-nonsense vibe that made Joseph wonder if he was a cop. But no, a police officer wouldn't be meeting her at a truck stop diner. He'd have come to her apartment, or had her come to the police station. Not a cop, then…

Joseph studied the man's back as he leaned down. He had broad shoulders, and even from this distance Joseph could tell the man had a fair bit of muscle on him. Maybe a private investigator? Then he straightened, and Joseph saw a bit of color peeking out from under the edge of his sleeve. A tattoo.

Soldier. The word flashed in his mind, the pieces falling into place as he continued to study the man. Short hair? Check. Good posture? Check. Alert, wary gaze, scanning the place for potential threats? Check and check. Yep, this guy was a soldier, or had been at one point.

The realization made him feel a little bit better. Whoever he was, he could likely protect Emma and Christina from danger.

At least he hoped so.

Joseph heard the rumble of a truck engine and turned to see a semi pull into the lot. It drove past his car, headed for the back corner. He couldn't see the driver, but a sense of horror filled him as he watched the truck glide into a parking spot.

Oh, no. Oh, please no.

He blinked, hoping the stress of the last few days was causing him to see things. But no. It was the same semitruck he'd climbed into not that long ago, pulling into the same spot along the far edge of the lot.

The traffickers were back.

He swiveled his head to look into the diner. If Emma and the baby left right now, they might be able to get away before the traffickers noticed them. Christina was in her carrier, so her face wouldn't be that visible.

His heart thumped hard against his chest as he watched the blond man take the baby out of her car seat. He put her up to his shoulder, patting her back gently.

Joseph glanced in the direction of the bathrooms, cursing when he saw the doors remained closed. Where was his sister? What was taking her so long?

His stomach lurched as he looked at the semitruck once more. It was parked now, and as he watched, the driver flipped off the lights. They were getting ready to go inside...

Joseph couldn't let them see Emma and the baby. She'd already escaped them once—she might not be so lucky a second time.

Acting on instinct, he climbed out of the car and headed for the diner. If he could give his sister a bit of a head start, she and the blond guy might have a fighting chance.

He darted across the parking lot, forcing himself to walk so he didn't draw the eyes of the traffickers. It probably would have been safer for him to text her again, but there was no guarantee she'd see the message in time. Besides, he was committed now. He twitched with the sensation of being watched, though in truth, no one bothered to glance at him. For one brief second he allowed himself to hope that the boss had a different set of guys with him today, but Joseph knew he was unlikely to be so lucky. He had to get in, warn Emma and get out before they found him. Otherwise, he was in for a world of hurt.

"Come on," he muttered, stepping into the warm, greasy air of the diner. "In and out. It's that simple."

And that complicated.

* * *

Emma finished washing her hands, then bent and splashed water on her face. The cold was a shock to her system, helping her reset her thoughts and get her mind back on track.

"What are you doing?" she asked her reflection. But the answer was clear.

She was attracted to Matt. And if she wasn't careful, she was going to fall for him.

But come on, who could blame her? He'd come when she'd called in the middle of the night, without hesitation. And when he'd walked into the diner, his first question had been about her daughter. That alone was enough to make her want to jump over the table and kiss him.

Again.

She shivered a little at the memory of his greeting. There was something so deliciously sensual in the way this big, strong man had walked in and kissed her without saying a word. An electric shock had raced through her body as he'd held her, his soft, careful touch an enticing contrast to the muscles of his chest and arms. For the first time since Chris, Emma had felt wanted. It was something she could get used to.

But not now.

She shook her head, casting aside her selfish desires. Right now, she had to focus on her baby.

Having Matt here was a huge relief, and not just because she was attracted to him. Even though she knew Christina was still in danger, being with Matt made her feel like everything would turn out okay. Matt's presence by her side took away some of her stress and fear. She wasn't alone anymore; she didn't have to face the bad guys without help.

But she had to be careful, or she'd mistake his offer of help for something more. Matt was a good man—she knew that already. But that didn't necessarily mean he had feelings for her. Yes, his kiss had made her toes curl, but that didn't mean he wanted a real relationship. He might only be interested in a short-term fling once this was all over. It was a truth she had to keep in the front of her mind, or she would start to read too much into his actions and wind up with her heart broken.

"He's just being nice," she muttered. As a former soldier, he likely had an overdeveloped sense of responsibility. A tinge of worry crept along the edges of her thoughts. Was she taking advantage of him?

She dismissed the possibility almost immediately. Matt was a grown man. He'd answered her call because he wanted to. She hadn't held a gun to his head and forced him to meet her here, nor had she blackmailed him into helping her. Everything he was doing was of his own volition.

Emma glanced at her watch as she dried her hands. It was almost five in the morning. Hopefully they could find a hotel before the sun was fully up; it had been a long night, and she was quickly losing what little energy she had left.

She stepped out of the bathroom and started back for the table. Her heart warmed as she caught a glimpse of Matt holding Christina. His head was turned to the side, and Emma could see his lips move as he spoke to her daughter. He seemed like such a natural with kids, and once again Emma wondered why he didn't have any of his own.

Just as she took another step, she noticed a man walking up the aisle of the diner, headed toward Matt and Christina. A jolt of fear went through her, but then she recognized him. It was Joseph.

She relaxed instinctively at the sight of him, and in the next heartbeat stiffened as rage filled her body. A white-hot anger flooded her system, propelling her forward as the rest of the world faded into insignificance.

Emma moved past Matt and Christina, barely registering the worried look on Matt's face as she made a beeline for her brother. For his part, Joseph didn't try to run. He actually looked a little relieved to see her, but she couldn't say the same for him. All the familial affection she'd once had for her brother was gone, replaced by a gnawing sense of disappointment and a potent anger, the likes of which she'd never felt before.

"What the hell do you think you're doing?" She practically spat the words at him, her jaw muscles so tight she could barely speak. Just the sight of him was enough to override her self-control, and she lifted her hand, the need to slap him overwhelming.

Joseph caught her wrist before she could strike. "Emma, I'm so sorry," he began, but she cut him off.

"No. You don't get to say that to me."

"Emma, what's going on?" Matt's deep voice floated over her shoulder. "Are you okay?"

"Get her away from here," she said, not daring to look back. She was never going to take her eyes off her snake of a brother again, so long as he was near her child.

"Emma—" Matt started.

Joseph spoke at the same time. "You have to get out of here," he said urgently. "Right now."

Emma cocked her head to the side. "Sure," she said, the word dripping with sarcasm. "I believe you."

"You're Joseph," Matt said quietly. Suddenly, he was standing next to Emma, trying to pass the baby over. Emma reflexively took her daughter and immediately realized her mistake. Now that Matt had his hands free, he looked like he was going to take a piece out of Joseph.

She appreciated the thought, but this wasn't the place to start a fistfight. She didn't really care if Joseph got hurt, but she didn't want Matt to get into any trouble with the police. Nor did she want him to get injured—Joseph wasn't afraid to fight dirty, especially when his back was against a wall.

To her surprise, Joseph barely glanced at Matt's towering figure. "Emma, please listen to me. I know you don't trust me, but you have got to get out of here now."

Something about his tone broke through her anger. "Why?" she asked warily.

"Those men that broke into your apartment tonight," Joseph said. "They work for a human trafficker."

"How did you—?" Emma shook her head, not bothering to finish the question. Joseph's knowledge of the attempted kidnapping merely confirmed his involvement. Emma didn't think it was possible to be any more disappointed in her brother, but her heart sank a bit further.

Joseph glanced over his shoulder. "Please," he said urgently. "They're here now—their semitruck just pulled into the lot. This is where the boss meets people."

"You mean, where he met you?" Matt cut in. His voice was lethally quiet, tripping a primal fear response in Emma that made her shiver.

"Yes." Joseph didn't bother to mince words. "Emma, you have to take Christina and get out of here before they see you."

He sounded like he was telling the truth, but Emma no longer trusted her brother. Was he lying to manipulate her into doing something that would put her in even more danger? Or was he truly trying to help?

She looked up at Matt, trying to read his expression. He was staring at Joseph with open suspicion, his jaw clenched tightly and a deep furrow between his eyebrows.

Joseph glanced over his shoulder again. When he turned back, his face was pale and Emma noticed a line of perspiration on his forehead. "Emma, it has to be now. They're coming inside." She heard the note of panic in his voice, saw his feet start to shuffle toward the exit. She still couldn't tell if he was lying to her, but one thing she did know for certain—her brother was frightened.

"Emma." Matt's voice was steady, his hand warm on her arm. "Let's go."

She glanced up to see his eyes fixed on the door

to the diner. She followed his gaze and noticed three men climbing out of the cab of a truck. Moving in unison, they began walking across the parking lot toward the entrance. They didn't look familiar, but something about the way they moved triggered a rash of goose bumps on her arms.

"Okay," she agreed. She turned to grab Christina's car seat and saw Joseph dart into the men's bathroom. *Trying to save his own hide,* she thought bitterly.

Matt reached past her, taking the bulky carrier from her grasp. "Out the side," he said quietly.

Emma wasn't quite sure where the exit was located, but Matt gently pushed her along until she saw the door in front of her. Clutching Christina against her chest, she pushed on the horizontal bar, glancing back at the diner entrance to see where the men were now.

It was a mistake. The trio had made it inside. One of the men met her eyes, recognition dawning on his face as he focused on her. It was the one from the balcony, his scar even more obvious in the fluorescent lights of the diner. He let out a yelp and grabbed his buddy's arm.

Matt cursed behind her, propelling her through the doorway and into the chilly air. "They've seen us."

"It's my fault," she babbled as he steered her toward his truck. "I looked back."

Matt didn't reply. He unlocked the truck and tossed in the carrier, then boosted Emma into the passenger seat. Just before he closed the door, she spotted her brother running across the parking lot.

"Joseph!" she yelled out. He flinched but didn't respond. "Why did you do this to me?"

The door to the diner burst open, spilling out the three men. They zeroed in on her and began to run for the truck. Emma slammed her door just as Matt jumped behind the wheel. He cranked the engine as she fumbled to put Christina into the car seat.

Matt stomped on the gas and the truck shot forward. As Matt headed for the exit, Emma caught sight of Joseph. He was running toward the men, waving his arms with his mouth open wide.

"Oh my God," she said, staring in disbelief as her brother turned and started to run again. "He's trying to distract them."

"About time he did something to help you," Matt said sourly, not bothering to turn his head. He tore out of the parking lot onto the access road of the freeway, the engine roaring as he dodged cars.

Emma turned around in the seat, trying to keep Joseph in her sight. Despite her anger and disappointment, he was still her brother and she didn't want him dead. But the other vehicles at the truck stop obscured her view, and as Matt sped onto the freeway, the parking lot soon shrank in the distance.

"Is she okay?"

Emma turned around, realizing for the first time that Christina was crying. In all the excitement, she hadn't registered the sound over the pounding of blood in her ears.

"Yes," she said, feeling guilty at having ignored

her daughter. She bent over the car seat, shushing her and stroking her forehead until her baby fell asleep once more.

Matt gripped the steering wheel tightly, his eyes darting from the road to the rearview mirror. Emma buckled herself in, craning her neck to see behind them. "Do you think they're following us?" Her heart pounded at the thought; they were miles from any major town, with long stretches of lonely road ahead. What would they do if those men caught up to them?

"I'm not sure," Matt said. "But they know what my truck looks like now."

Emma didn't respond. What could she say? It wasn't clear if the men only had the semitruck, or if they had other vehicles parked at the truck stop they could use to give chase.

"Should I call the police?"

Matt considered the question, then nodded. "Can't hurt. But I'm not stopping, and I don't know how helpful they'll be. We don't have any proof of wrongdoing—just three guys who chased us out of the diner."

"Still, maybe they can stop the truck or detain the men for questioning. Give us a bit more time to get away."

"Go ahead." Emma made the call, explaining the situation to a skeptical-sounding 911 operator.

"I got a partial plate," Matt said. He rattled off the digits, which Emma repeated into the phone.

"I'll dispatch some units, but it might take a while for them to arrive," the officer on the other end said.

Emma thanked him and hung up, feeling like her call had been futile.

"Should have told him there was a fight going on," Matt said. "That would have lit a fire under them."

"You're probably right," she said. Matt began to slow down, steering for the next exit. "What's going on?"

He took the off-ramp, gliding to a stop at the light on the corner. "I'm going to double back."

Emma's anxiety spiked, sending her heart into her throat. "You're *what*?" she squeaked.

Christina whimpered in her sleep. Emma stroked her baby's cheek, lowering her voice. "Why are you turning around?"

"Because," Matt answered calmly, "they saw us hop on the freeway going in this direction. If they're following us, they expect us to be headed east. By doubling back, we can lose them without them ever knowing it."

"Oh." She had to admit, it was the smart thing to do. But the knots in her stomach grew tighter as they drew nearer to the truck stop.

They drove by it without incident. The parking lot was clear, with no sign of Joseph or the three men.

"Their semitruck is gone," Matt commented, keeping his voice low.

Emma curled her fingers into the fabric of her shirt and focused on taking deep breaths. "Did we pass them after turning around?"

"I'm not sure," Matt said. "I saw a few trucks that resembled theirs, but I wasn't able to get a good enough look to know for certain."

"I guess we just have to keep our fingers crossed

then," she said. Hopefully the traffickers were driving east, away from them.

And her brother? Emma wasn't sure what to hope for where Joseph was concerned. She didn't want him dead, but she also never wanted to see him again. It was strange, feeling so detached from her brother. They'd been close growing up, but now that seemed like a lifetime ago. Joseph's actions felt like a double betrayal, his roles as brother and uncle damaged beyond repair. She didn't know where he was now, but a small part of her worried.

She sensed Matt gradually relax as the miles stacked up. He still checked the rearview mirror, but his knuckles were no longer white as he held the wheel. "What do we do now?" Emma asked quietly. The sun was rising behind them, causing the truck to cast a long shadow on the road ahead.

"We find a place to rest," Matt said. He glanced over, offering her a small smile. "I don't know about you, but all that excitement has me tired."

Emma chuckled softly. "Tired is a bit of an understatement." She was exhausted. The night had lasted a lifetime, and it still didn't feel like it was over. She needed to sleep, to let her brain and body rest so she could process everything that had happened.

Matt took one hand off the wheel, stretching his arm across Christina's car seat with his palm up. Emma slid her hand into his, drawing strength from his touch. She wasn't alone, at least not right now. As she stared at their clasped hands hovering over her sleeping daughter, a sense of peace bubbled up inside her chest, crowding out the sour residue of panic.

She didn't know what was going to happen. But they would face the danger together.

Chapter 8

"You tried to double-cross me."

Joseph swallowed hard, the metallic tang of blood thick on his tongue. "No, no, I—"

His words were cut off by another slap, causing his head to snap back and tears to fill his eyes. He blinked to clear them, trying to focus on the man in front of him.

The boss sat in a large chair in the trailer of the semitruck, swaying slightly as the vehicle moved. Joseph was on his knees, hands bound behind his back. His body vibrated with the rumble of the engine and the small bumps in the road. He wasn't sure where they were going, but he knew they were on a freeway.

Emma's face flashed through his mind. Had she gotten away? He thought so—he'd seen the truck peel out of the parking lot, headed for the freeway. But after the three men had caught him, he'd overheard the boss making some calls, instructing his men to give chase. If Emma was looking for the semi, she might miss the men who were actually trying to follow them.

"Do you know what I do to people who betray me?"

The boss's words brought Joseph's attention back around to his current situation. Things were not looking good; he was flanked by the two large bodyguards, and based on the state of the floor, this trailer was no stranger to bloodshed. He was in a rolling torture chamber, and it was only a matter of time until the boss started working on him.

He bit his lip, deciding silence was the wisest course of action. Apparently, he was wrong.

Another slap. "Answer me."

Joseph looked into the man's dead eyes, ignoring the cold sensation creeping up his spine. "I didn't lie to you," he said. "It's not my fault your men were unsuccessful."

"Is that right?" The boss gestured to one of the men. The goon searched Joseph's pockets, digging out his burner cell phone.

The boss held up the phone. "You're telling me if I look at your messages, I won't find a warning to your sister?"

Joseph didn't flinch. "No."

It was the truth; he'd already tossed that burner phone and moved on to the next, anticipating this very possibility. The phone he'd used to text Emma was now in pieces, scattered along the side of the road.

If the boss was surprised, he didn't show it. "We'll see." He stared at the screen, thumb scrolling as his free hand stroked the small dog in his lap.

The animal looked even more nervous than Joseph remembered. His small body trembled as a pink tongue darted out, swiping across his shiny black nose.

The boss tossed the phone to the ground. "You're smarter than I thought," he said. "But I know you tried to double-cross me. That little stunt back at the truck stop proves it."

Joseph looked away, not bothering to deny it. "You haven't paid me," he pointed out. "You're not short any money. We can both walk away and pretend this never happened."

The man laughed, his ponderous belly undulating. "That's not how this works. I might have been willing to do that, had you not undermined my men. But now this is personal."

"It doesn't have to be," Joseph tried. "I didn't mean to offend you—"

"Oh, yes, you did." The man leaned forward as much as his girth would allow. "And I can't have word getting out that you disrespected me and were allowed to go unpunished."

Joseph latched on to the final word. "Unpunished" made it sound like the man wasn't planning on killing him. Torture, yes. But Joseph could withstand pain.

"What are you going to do to me?" It was a loaded question, one he probably shouldn't have asked. But better to know his future than to be left wondering.

"You'll find out soon enough," the boss said with a

smirk. "But in the meantime, we're going to find your sister. You still owe me a baby."

"Emma's gone. I don't know where she went."

"That's fine. You're still going to help me get her back."

"I don't see how." The boss sounded very certain, but Joseph didn't find his confidence reassuring.

"I'm going to use you as bait."

The idea of it made Joseph laugh. "I hate to disappoint you, but Emma is not going to care if you threaten me. She hates me after what I did to her."

"You're probably right," the man agreed. "Which is why I'm not going to threaten you to draw her out."

Joseph's stomach dropped as his imagination kicked into overdrive. "You're not?"

The boss shook his head. "No. What would be the point? The bond between siblings is nothing compared to the love between a mother and daughter."

It took a second for his words to sink in. Joseph's body went numb as he realized what the man was saying.

"No," he whispered. "Please, leave her out of this." His mother was a good woman; she deserved better than to be used as a pawn in this monster's game.

The man laughed again. "I wanted to. But you leave me no choice." He shrugged. "I gather from your reaction you haven't told your mother about me?" He didn't wait for Joseph's response. "No matter." He stroked the dog in his lap, his lips twisted in a cruel smile. "You'll be introducing us soon enough."

* * *

It wasn't a bad hotel, for a small town.

Matt eyed the building as he parked the truck. The stucco finish looked fairly new, with no major cracks or stains of disrepair. There were a few flowers planted here and there, adding spots of color to the parking lot. He glanced around, taking note of the other cars; lots of slightly older midrange models that looked like solid family vehicles. Nothing too flashy or unusual. His truck looked right at home here.

"This looks like a nice place," Emma said, echoing his thoughts.

He nodded. "It'll do. Stay in the truck with Christina. I'm going to go get us a room."

"We can't go with you?"

Matt shook his head. "I don't want them to see you. Traffickers often use hotels as stops along their route. It's possible they have connections to people working here, and I don't want the staff to know you're with me. If the traffickers come sniffing around, the front desk won't be able to tell them you and Christina are here."

Emma's eyes widened. "Good point. I hadn't thought about that."

Matt smiled wryly. "You shouldn't have to worry about it. No one should." He hopped out of the truck and strode into the lobby.

"Good morning, sir." A young man stood behind the front desk, his black hair shiny under the lights. "How may I help you?"

"I'd like a room for the night." They'd start with one night. Hopefully Detective Randall would call Emma soon. The sooner she and Christina were placed into protective custody, the better. Matt would do all he could to keep them safe, but he was only one man against a group of ruthless traffickers. It was only a matter of time before the criminals found Emma and the baby again.

"Very good. Would you like a king-size bed or two queens?"

Matt hesitated, wondering how to reply. Since he was ostensibly a single man traveling alone, the king-size bed was the logical choice. But he didn't want Emma to think he had made any assumptions about sleeping arrangements, or to feel like he was trying to pressure her into something she wasn't ready for.

"Two queens," he said. "I can spread my stuff out on the extra bed."

The man smiled. "Most of our guests do that," he said, typing on a keyboard as he spoke.

"Glad I'm not the only one," Matt replied, trying to sound casual. He handed over his credit card and driver's license to complete the process.

After a moment, the man handed him a card in a small envelope. "All right, I've got you in room 536. The elevators are down the hall behind me, and we have a complimentary continental breakfast every morning. Please let us know if you need anything during your stay."

"Great, thanks," Matt said. "I need to move my truck around back. Can I get in the building from that direction?" He didn't want to parade Emma and the baby through the lobby—hopefully there was a way to sneak them in the back door.

"Yes, sir. There is a door leading to the parking lot on the other side of the building. You'll just need to use your key card to unlock it."

"Wonderful." The knot of tension in Matt's belly eased a bit. He'd get Emma and Christina up to the room, then head out to grab some food and supplies. He'd feel a lot better knowing they were safe behind a locked door, and he wouldn't draw too much attention if he was out and about on his own.

He walked to his truck, offering Emma what he hoped was a reassuring smile as he opened the door. "We're all set," he said. "We can go in through the back door, so they won't see you."

She climbed down, and he reached over to grab the car seat. Christina blinked up at him, her blue eyes bright. She gave him a big grin, two pearly teeth peeking out behind her lower lip. Matt's heart seemed to swell as it soaked up the sweet sight of this little one. It tickled him to know that she was happy to see him, and he was struck by a pang of longing for a family of his own. He smiled back at the baby, which made her kick her legs and coo up at him.

"She really likes you," Emma said quietly. Matt glanced over to find her watching him, a hint of sadness in her eyes.

"Feeling's mutual," he said gruffly. If he wasn't careful, he'd fall in love with this baby. He cleared his throat, casting aside his inconvenient emotions. "Let's get you both inside." He pulled the shade of the car seat lower to hide Christina's face from immediate view. "Don't look up as we walk in," he advised.

Emma slid him a glance. "Why?"

"Security cameras," he said. "I don't want them to get a good view of your face." Maybe he was being paranoid, but he didn't want to make it easy for Emma to be identified.

"Good point," she replied. She immediately looked down, watching her feet as they walked. "I hadn't thought about that."

The elevator was empty as they rode up, as was the hallway to their room. Emma took the carrier as he unlocked the door and ushered them inside.

She let out a deep breath as the door snicked shut behind them. "Finally," she breathed. Her shoulders slumped slightly as she unbuckled Christina and pulled her free from the confines of the car seat. "I feel like I can relax and catch my breath."

Christina seemed to echo her mother's sentiment, babbling happily as Emma set her on one of the beds and began changing her diaper.

It was a simple, domestic task, the kind of thing mothers all over the world performed millions of times a day. But Matt could see the love Emma had for her daughter in the way she smiled down at her, talking softly as she worked. Her hands were gentle but quick and when she was finished, she lingered a moment, leaning over Christina to rub her nose against the baby's cheek. "Eskimo kisses," she said, the words coming out in a singsong refrain that Christina seemed to enjoy.

The bond between the two of them was unmistakably strong, and it was a joy to watch how mother and baby responded to each other. Matt felt privileged to be part of this ordinary, yet special, moment.

Emma glanced behind her, saw him watching them and smiled. "Come sit with us," she invited.

"Maybe later," he said. In truth, he wanted nothing more than to join them, to feel like he was part of their world. But he had to be careful. He couldn't let his desires for a family overshadow the truth. Emma and her daughter were vulnerable. She'd called him for help and protection, not because she wanted him in her life on a personal level. So even though Emma and Christina seemed like the answer to his hopes and dreams, he couldn't let himself get sucked into a fantasy.

"I thought I'd go get some supplies," he said, ignoring the flash of disappointment on Emma's face.

"That's a good idea," she said, sounding oddly reluctant. "That was my last diaper."

"Why don't you write a quick list for me? I'll get diapers and some food for all of us."

"That sounds great," she said. "I was so flustered when I packed that I didn't include enough diapers or food for Christina. Instead, I wound up grabbing a lot of things we don't need." She made a face as she held up a toy truck. "I'm not sure why I brought this. I think it was on the table and I just swept everything into a bag before running."

"Understandable." In truth, he was impressed she'd thought to pack at all. He knew she'd been terrified in the aftermath of the attempted kidnapping. The fact that she'd had the presence of mind to grab a few essentials before taking off spoke volumes about her courage.

Matt grabbed the complimentary notepad and pen from the bedside table and passed them to her. "Jot down what you need. I know she likes that yogurt in the pouch—what else can I get for her?"

Emma gave him a crooked smile and shook her head.

"What?" He could tell she wanted to say something, but as he recognized the glint of gratitude in her eyes, he wasn't sure he wanted to hear it.

"It's just amazing to me how tuned in you are to my baby," she said. "You played with her in the hospital. You didn't hesitate to hold her in the diner. And you remember her favorite yogurt based on a wrapper I showed you briefly a few days ago."

Matt ducked his head, feeling his cheeks warm. "It's no big deal," he said.

"It is to me," Emma replied. "Most men aren't terribly interested in a baby, especially one that's not their own. But you've been so amazing with Christina. It means a lot to me."

"It's the least I can do," he said. How could he explain it to her? He wasn't ready to tell Emma he was developing feelings for her—to say the words out loud would make it real, and that was something he couldn't embrace at the moment. But he could admit to himself that Emma was becoming important to him. And because Christina was important to her, he paid extra attention.

But in the shadows of his heart, he knew it was more than that. He was attentive to Christina not just because she was Emma's daughter, but because she was special in her own right. In the short time he'd known her, he'd seen glimpses of the little one's personality. She was a sweetie, and she was quickly burrowing into his heart. He was doing his best to maintain some distance, but her wide grins and soft coos made it difficult to stay impartial.

"If you say so," Emma said quietly. Her tone made it clear she didn't agree with him, but she didn't press the issue.

As she bent her head to write a list, Matt felt a tinge of frustration. "I'm not a hero," he said gruffly. His attraction to Emma went beyond an affinity for her personality. He wanted to take her to bed, to lose himself in her arms and take pleasure from her body. Based on the way she'd responded to his kiss in the diner, she wanted him, too. But he'd seen the way she looked at him sometimes, her eyes starry and emotional. If and when they took the next step, he wanted her in his bed because she was interested in *him*, not because she felt indebted to him for the way he'd helped her, or because he'd been nice to her baby.

Emma's eyebrows drew together in confusion. "Okay…"

Matt held up a hand, cutting off any further reply. "I'm going to hit the head. I'll take that list when you're done."

He walked away before she could respond and entered the small bathroom, shutting the door behind him. Bracing his hands on the counter, he took a deep breath.

What are you doing? His brain began to rattle off a list of all the reasons why he shouldn't acknowledge his growing attraction to Emma. She was alone and in trouble, which made for the worst timing in the world. She was a single mother who'd built a life for herself and her daughter; did he really have a right to insert himself into their relationship and upset that applecart? And furthermore, she lived in El Paso and he lived in Alpine. Long-distance relationships were a recipe for disaster, as he'd learned the hard way. Maybe he wasn't really attracted to her at all—perhaps he was simply interested because she'd awakened his protective instincts. Once this business with the traffickers was sorted, they'd both go back to their normal, boring lives, and the pull he felt for her would lessen.

But even as he formed the thought, his heart scoffed at the idea. Circumstances might have brought Emma into his life, but his feelings for her went beyond a knight-in-shining-armor complex. He found her fascinating and wanted to know everything about her. The intensity of his interest surprised him; Emma was different. There was something about her that spoke to him. Without his noticing, she'd sneaked past his defenses and touched his heart.

Could she say the same for him? She liked him—that much was clear. But were her feelings simply in response to his help? It was possible. Perhaps she was still getting over the death of Christina's father, and her heart wasn't ready for someone new. Or maybe she saw him as a potential dad for her daughter—a puzzle piece she could insert to complete her family. Matt wasn't opposed to parenting another man's child, but he refused to let someone use him like that again.

Jennifer's face flashed in his mind, filling his mouth with a bitter taste. *Not all women are like that*, said the logical voice in his head. He knew it was true. Emma's apparent interest didn't mean she was plotting to trap him the way Jennifer had. But he couldn't shake the worry that she was trying to draw him closer, and not just because of his winning personality.

So don't let her. He could maintain his distance until he was certain of her feelings. He didn't have to let his curiosity rule his actions, even though she was the first woman to intrigue him in what felt like forever. He'd spent the last few years running on a kind of emotional autopilot. He could maintain that status a little bit longer.

Right?

Chapter 9

The room felt bigger without him there.

Normally, Emma would have appreciated the sense of extra space. But now it made her nervous.

She'd gotten used to Matt's presence, his quiet strength. Even though they'd only been together for the last few hours, the stress of the situation made it feel like time had been stretched. Minutes became hours, hours pulled into what felt like days. It gave their time together a sort of intimacy she'd only experienced once before, with Chris.

It was strange, this closeness between them. Did Matt feel the same way, or was she projecting her emotions onto him? He was a difficult man to read sometimes—perhaps she was simply filling in the blanks with what she wanted to be there, as opposed to what he actually thought.

His behavior a few minutes ago was exactly the kind of thing that made her wonder. She'd felt him watching her and Christina, and when she'd turned to face him, she'd seen such powerful longing in his eyes it had nearly stolen her breath. It had been one of those rare, unguarded moments when his emotions had been plain to see. But then she'd asked him to join her and the baby, and the wall had shot up between them again.

Matt struck her as a man who deeply wanted a connection, a family. But for whatever reason, he was letting fear stand in his way. Emma was frustrated by his behavior; if he would let his guard down—just a little—maybe they could get to know each other better. Heaven knew she was tired of being alone. But she wasn't going to force herself onto him.

Christina's laugh drew Emma's attention back to her baby. She was another element in the equation that Emma couldn't overlook. As attracted as Emma was to Matt, she had to be careful. He'd been great with Christina so far, but he might not want to get involved in her daughter's life. Emma couldn't afford to fall for a man who didn't want to be a father to her child.

It was a lot to ask; she recognized that. It would take a special man to step into her life and take on the responsibility of being a dad to Christina. Not many guys were ready for that kind of commitment. It was one thing to raise your own child. Quite another to take over for someone else.

But she was getting ahead of herself. It was possible she and Matt could explore this attraction between them one step at a time. They didn't have to start in the deep end of the relationship pool; even though she already felt close to him, it was important they actually took time to get to know each other.

Provided he was interested.

Emma sighed and turned her attention back to her baby. She hadn't been this twisted up over a man since the early days of her relationship with Chris. She'd forgotten how mentally exhausting it was to try to read someone else's mind, wondering how they felt and what they thought. She had to stop letting her curiosity distract her from the situation at hand. Once she and Christina were really safe, then she could try to untangle her feelings concerning Matt.

Her phone buzzed, pulling her out of her head. She recognized the number on the display as Detective Randall's. A rush of relief shot through her, leaving her limbs tingling. He was calling to arrange protection for her and Christina, she just knew it.

"Hello?"

"Emma, it's Doug Randall. I got your message. Are you and the baby okay?"

She sighed, some of the tension draining from her body. "We're safe for the moment."

"That's good," he replied. "I spoke to the officers who responded to your call last night." There was an odd note in his voice, and Emma's relief began to morph into apprehension.

"And?"

"And I'm not sure what more we can do for you." He had the decency to sound sheepish, but it didn't stop Emma's temper from bubbling over.

"How can you say that?" Emma snapped. Christina made a distressed sound and looked up, her small features scrunched in worry. Emma forced a smile for her daughter and modulated her tone. "The men were clearly looking for Christina. When they saw me, they said they'd be back for us both. What more do you want?"

"I believe you," he said, sounding tired. "But we simply don't have the resources to put you in protective custody at this time. We've stepped up patrols by your apartment, but no one matching the suspect descriptions has been seen in the area."

"So that's it?" she said, not bothering to hide her disappointment. "You're just going to leave me and my baby to fend for ourselves?"

"It's possible this was a one-off thing. Maybe you misheard what they said, and thought they were targeting Chris—" he said, but she cut him off.

"No. I'm not confused." She told him about the encounter with Joseph at the truck stop diner, and the way the traffickers had chased after them. "They're not going to stop," she said finally.

His sigh rattled over the line. "This changes things a bit."

"Oh?" She didn't dare hope for a safe house, but perhaps her revelation would move her case up on the list.

"There are some new players on the trafficking scene," Randall said. "Rumors are swirling the head honcho uses a mobile office to avoid detection. If that's who your brother contacted, we and the FBI would be very interested in hearing how he did it and finding out who these guys are."

Emma heard the door open behind her and turned to find Matt entering the room, his arms laden with bags. She nodded at him, then pressed the button to activate the speakerphone function. "So now you're interested in helping me?"

Randall paused. "I always wanted to help you," he replied. "But I have finite resources and limited time. I have to make choices about what to focus on, and as much as I'd like to, I can't save everyone." He was quiet a second, then added, "Believe me, I've tried." He let out a short, harsh laugh, and in that instant she saw beyond the bureaucratic lines he'd spouted to the man underneath.

His words had the ring of truth, but Emma still wasn't satisfied. It wasn't right that people who needed help couldn't find assistance thanks to budget cuts. How many criminals walked free because the police couldn't do their jobs?

"So what happens now?" she asked.

"I'm going to reach out to some people who know more about traffickers in this region. I'll call you once I know more. In the meantime, where are you?"

She glanced at Matt, who shrugged. "We're in a little town off Interstate 10. I'm not even sure of the name. We stopped at a hotel to get some rest."

"We?"

She glanced at Matt again, looking for reassurance. "Matt is with me."

"That's good," Randall said, relief evident in his tone. "I'm glad you're not alone. Did anyone follow you?"

Matt shook his head. "I don't think so," she said. "They tried, but by the time they got the semitruck going again, we were gone."

"All right," said Randall. "Stay there if you can. If you notice anything suspicious, call the local police and then me. I'll be in touch as soon as I have anything on my end."

"All right," she said. She hung up, feeling a bit more settled than before. She still wasn't happy about the lack of police protection, but at least Detective Randall seemed to take the situation seriously and was trying to help.

"Why isn't he putting you in protective custody?" Apparently, Matt felt the same way.

Emma put the phone on the bed, realizing her mistake when Christina immediately lunged for it. She plucked it from her daughter's grasp and offered her favorite toy car as a substitute to stave off tears. "Apparently, there aren't enough resources, and we aren't high enough of a priority."

Matt frowned, his lips pressing together in a thin line. "What a load of horsesh—" He stopped just in time, his eyes darting to Christina. He cleared his throat, his cheeks turning pink. "That's unacceptable," he amended.

Emma smiled despite her frustration. "I agree," she

said. "With both sentiments. But I can't exactly force him to do what I want."

"Too bad," Matt muttered. He began to unload the bags, pulling out baby food pouches, diaper packs and wipes. He arranged the supplies neatly on the desk, then passed her another bag. "Here are some clothes I picked up for you both. I hope I got the right sizes."

She peeked inside, touched that he'd been so thorough. He'd gotten two outfits for Christina, and for her he'd selected black yoga pants and a couple of T-shirts. "This is perfect," she said gratefully. She reached the bottom of the bag and found a package of ladies' underwear. Her cheeks flushed, though she had no cause to be embarrassed. Still, the thought of Matt selecting her panties made her duck her head. Chris had been the last man to see her unmentionables.

Her imagination kicked into overdrive, picturing Matt standing in front of the display. Had he put a lot of thought into his selection, or merely grabbed the first package he saw, wanting to get it over with? Was he at all curious to know how she'd look in these panties?

And speaking of underwear, what was his status in that department? She sneaked a glance in his direction, watching as he pulled his own clothes from another bag. A couple of pairs of boxer shorts landed on the pile, answering her question.

He looked up, caught her watching him. He lifted one brow in interrogation, then lowered it as awareness passed between them. The corner of his mouth curved up, his blue eyes growing warm. He glanced down, then back up to her face. Emma realized she was clutching the package of underwear to her chest and dropped it like a burning coal. Matt grinned.

"I hope those will work," he said. "You didn't strike me as a thong person."

"You're right about that," she replied. He was having entirely too much fun teasing her—it was time she got some of her own back. "But I usually don't go for the briefs, either."

"Oh?"

She shook her head, leaning forward a bit as if she were about to impart a close secret. "I'm a bikini-cut kind of girl."

Matt's smile faded as his eyes took on a faraway look. He swallowed hard. "Yeah, I can see that." His voice was a bit husky, and it was Emma's turn to grin.

"I'm sure you can," she said sweetly. She folded everything into a neat pile. It felt good to flirt with Matt, even if only for a moment. A nice reminder of what normal felt like, or could feel like, if she found someone worth flirting with. Maybe when this was all over, they could take things up a notch...

Matt cleared his throat. "Would you like to take a shower?" He held up another bag, heavy with what she assumed were toiletries. "I can play with Christina while you take some time for yourself."

His offer made her knees wobble. A hot shower sounded like heaven. It would feel so nice to wash the fear-sweat stink from her skin, to put on fresh clothes. "You really don't mind?" she said, already edging toward the bathroom.

"Not at all." He passed her the bag and sat on the bed

next to Christina. "We'll be fine. There's lots to play with out here." He reached for a little ball and rolled it toward Christina, who smiled up at him.

Emma stepped into the bathroom, closing the door softly behind her. Even though Christina liked Matt, it wasn't uncommon for her to fuss when Emma had to leave her. Fortunately, Matt's distraction seemed to have worked, as it remained blessedly quiet in the room.

It didn't take long for the water to heat up. Emma stripped down and stepped under the spray, stifling a groan as the heat worked on her aching muscles. The stress of the last few days weighed heavily on her, from the hikes in the park to the near-constant tension she'd been feeling since last night. She was sore all over, exhausted in both body and mind. But knowing her daughter was safe gave her a small sense of peace. As long as Christina was okay, Emma could bear any number of difficulties.

Her mother's ears picked up a quiet cry from the room. Apparently Matt's luck had run out. She hurried to rinse off and turned off the shower, grabbing a towel as she stepped out.

It was quiet in the room again, but she knew from experience it might not last long. Emma dried off and dressed quickly, then opened the door and stopped short.

Matt was standing with his back to her, swaying from side to side as he held Christina. He spoke to her in a low, soft voice, his words slightly muffled but still audible from Emma's spot in the bathroom doorway.

"Did I tell you about the little boy I once knew?" he said. "You remind me of him. Fisher."

Emma knew she shouldn't eavesdrop, but Matt's words kept her rooted in place. Who was Fisher? And what had happened to him?

"You're a little older than he was," Matt continued. "But you're just as sweet. His eyes were brown, though, not blue like yours."

Emma's heart began to melt as she listened. It was clear Matt cared for Fisher, whoever he was. No wonder he was so good with Christina—he had experience with babies.

"I think you two probably would have liked each other," he said. "He loved it when I would rock him like this."

Christina cooed happily. "I know," Matt said "They didn't teach me this in the army. I had to figure it out on my own. But Fisher helped me, and now you're getting the benefits."

The baby continued to babble. "I do miss him," Matt said, continuing his one-sided conversation. "A lot."

Emma's heart broke for Matt. Had Fisher been his son? She wanted to know what had happened to the child, but she didn't want to cause him more pain by asking. It was clear the child wasn't part of his life now. No wonder he seemed so distant at times; if Emma had lost Christina for good, she wouldn't be able to function, much less be around another baby.

Matt continued to talk to Christina, but Emma had heard enough. She felt like the worst kind of snoop, as if she'd cheated this information out of Matt. He certainly hadn't meant for her to learn about Fisher. She needed to stop this before he inadvertently revealed more of his secrets.

She quietly closed the bathroom door, then made a show of opening it loudly. "Christina," she sang out as she walked into the room. "Mommy's back."

Matt turned to face her, his cheeks a little pink. "I had to pick her up," he said. "She started getting unhappy."

"That's okay," Emma said, reaching up to catch her daughter, who was leaning toward her. "Looks like you had things under control."

"For a moment, anyway," Matt replied. He ran a hand through his hair, watching Christina as Emma snuggled her close. The longing was back in his eyes, and now Emma knew why.

"Do you want to grab a shower?" she offered.

He shook himself a bit, and she could tell he'd been lost in thought. "That sounds great," he said. "Thanks."

She watched him walk away, more curious than ever. It seemed she wasn't the only one who knew the pain of loss. At least she could comfort herself with the knowledge that part of Chris lived on in her daughter. If Matt's son had died, he was left with nothing but memories.

She wanted to know his story, to learn more about his life. Maybe she could convince him to share it with her. He might not want to talk about it, but then again, there was a chance he wanted to open up about his past. His memories were probably in the front of his mind, thanks to being around Christina. Talking sometimes helped. Perhaps he was ready.

It was worth a try.

Matt stepped out of the bathroom, running the towel over his head to dry his hair. The shower had felt good and helped reset his mind. Holding Christina had been a powerful reminder of Fisher, and he missed the little guy now more than ever. For the millionth time, he wished things had turned out differently. But despite his attachment to the boy, he knew he'd made the right choice. He never would have been able to make a life with Jennifer after her lies. It just seemed karmically unfair that her deceit had cost him everything.

Emma glanced up, finger to her lips. He followed her gaze to the bed and saw Christina's sleeping form stretched out on the mattress. He nodded and made his way over to the other bed. She held up the remote and at his nod, switched on the television and turned the volume down. Matt arranged the pillows against the headboard and leaned back. Emma climbed up next to him, settling into the spot at his side. She flipped through the channels, settling on reruns of a recent sitcom.

"Okay?" she whispered.

"Works for me," he said softly.

They sat there in companionable silence, enjoying the show. It was such a normal, domestic activity, the kind of thing couples all over the world did every day. But to Matt, the moment was special. It was a treat to sit next to Emma, to spend time with her, even though they weren't talking.

He faced the television, but his senses were tuned to her. Focusing on the soft cadence of her breathing, he felt the vibration of the headboard when her shoulders shook with suppressed laughter at a particularly funny moment. She smelled clean from the shower, and he imagined her skin was soft and warm.

"How long will she sleep?"

"Usually a couple of hours," Emma said. "But all bets are off since she didn't sleep well last night."

"You should nap, too," he suggested.

"Maybe I will," she replied. "What about you?"

Is that an invitation? What he wouldn't give to snuggle up next to Emma and sleep. Or not. He was tired, but there were other, more enjoyable ways to pass the time. But he'd promised himself he would keep his distance and sleeping with Emma, even in the most literal sense of the word, was not going to help him in that regard.

"I'm going to keep an eye out. I'll rest later."

"Are you sure?"

He nodded. She smiled at him, wriggling down until her head was resting on one of the pillows. "Thanks," she whispered. She scooted away from him, turning on her side to present him with her back. A moment later, her breathing took on a deep, even rhythm, and he knew she was out.

Matt turned back to the TV, determined to focus on the show and not the woman lying next to him. But his eyes kept straying, glancing over to watch her as she slumbered.

Don't be a creep, he told himself. Emma trusted

him to look after her and her daughter, not act like a stalker. It was difficult to ignore her, though; she was the first woman he'd shared a bed with in a long time.

Even if it was only in a platonic sense.

Matt crossed his arms and closed his eyes, determined to keep his thoughts on the right track. It shouldn't be that hard to pretend that she wasn't there— she was quiet and still, practically a part of the bedspread. Still, his awareness of her didn't fade. With a mental sigh, he turned his thoughts to something more mundane: listing the species of birds found in Big Bend.

Great blue heron… Red-tailed hawk… American kestrel…

Matt woke with his nose buried in Emma's hair and his arm around her torso.

What the—?

His first instinct was to pull back, but he checked the impulse. Emma's body was relaxed and warm against him, her back snug against his chest, her legs bent and molded to his. He felt the even rise and fall of her chest and knew she was still asleep. Why, then, had he woken up?

He heard the soft sounds of Christina's breathing behind him as she continued napping. The room was otherwise quiet, with the still, peaceful air that accompanied slumber. It was a nice change after the tension of their drive to the hotel. He'd tried to put on a brave face for Emma's sake, but in truth, he'd been worried the traffickers would find them. As the hours had passed with no sign of the men, his worry had faded, as well. Now, as he lay in bed with Emma in his arms, he could almost pretend the threat was gone.

How long had he been asleep? He couldn't see the clock on the bedside table; didn't care enough to move, either. He certainly hadn't meant to fall asleep, especially after telling Emma he'd stay awake to watch over her and her daughter.

Nice job, he thought sarcastically. He'd grown soft since leaving the army. A few years ago, he would have never fallen asleep while on guard. If his buddies could see him now, he'd never hear the end of it.

Emma stirred in her sleep. Matt froze, his mind racing. Was she waking up? He needed to move before she did—otherwise, she might get the wrong idea. The last thing he wanted was for her to think he was trying to cop a feel while she was unconscious.

He carefully lifted his arm, then began to inch backward, putting space between their bodies. The loss of contact made him cold, sending an involuntary shiver down his spine.

Just as he made it over to the other side of the bed, Emma rolled to face him. Her brown eyes were open, her gaze alert. She was awake then, had been for a while it seemed. Why hadn't she moved away? His thoughts raced, trying to puzzle out the implications of her actions, or lack thereof. She studied him for a few seconds, and he got the impression she was doing some sort of mental calculation.

"Where are you going?" she whispered.

Matt could feel his cheeks burning. "Nowhere," he said softly. "I just didn't want to bother you."

"You weren't." She scooted across the bed until they were only a few inches apart. This close, he could see the subtle flecks of gold in her brown eyes.

"What are you doing?" His heart began to pound at her proximity. Waking up to find himself accidentally holding her was one thing; having her seek him out was another.

"Snuggling," she said. "I'm cold."

"Let me get you a blanket." He had to move away from her or he was going to do something they might both regret.

Disappointment flashed in her eyes as he drew the bedspread across her body. "Sorry," she said. "I shouldn't have done that."

Matt shook his head. "It's okay. Body heat is the best way to get warm." He knew he should get up and leave the bed, but he didn't want to break this connection between them. Right now, with the soft glow of the television washing over them and the gentle sound of the baby's breathing in the bed next to them, he felt content. If he closed his eyes, he could pretend he was on vacation with his family. It was a special kind of torture, but he savored it nonetheless.

"Do you think Detective Randall will call soon?" Her voice was barely above a whisper, but they were so close he heard her clearly.

"I hope so," he replied softly. The sooner the police stepped in to keep Christina and Emma safe, the sooner he could return to his normal life.

Except frozen TV dinners and weekends spent doing laundry didn't hold much appeal.

"I wonder…" She trailed off, looked away.

"What?"

"I wonder if they caught up to Joseph." She met his eyes, her expression apologetic. "I can't forgive him for what he did to me, but he's still my brother."

"I know," he said. "You don't have to explain it to me." Against his better judgment, he ran his hand along the outside of her arm. "Family is family. Love doesn't switch off, even though you might want it to."

She closed her eyes briefly. "That's exactly it. I'm so angry with him, but I don't want him dead."

"He's probably fine," Matt said.

"You think so?" He saw the hope in her eyes and nodded.

"I do." He wasn't saying that just to make her happy. Weasels like her brother tended to land on their feet, though he didn't want to explain it in quite those terms. "He's got street smarts," he said instead.

"I suppose." She sounded a little subdued, so he tried to change the subject.

"So tell me," he said, smiling at her, "what does a nurse do for fun?"

She snorted and rolled her eyes. "This nurse doesn't do anything exciting. Between work and Christina, I don't have the time or energy for fun."

Sympathy welled in his chest. He hadn't meant to make her feel bad about her life. He'd simply wanted to know more about her. "Sorry," he said, feeling mildly embarrassed. "I should have known. Of course you work all the time, in one way or another."

Sadness flickered across her face. "Pretty much. I

used to have friends, but once I had Christina, I didn't have time to go out anymore. They understood at first, but eventually they stopped asking me."

"Doesn't sound like they were very good friends," he observed. Matt felt a surge of anger on her behalf, unable to understand how these anonymous individuals could leave Emma when she needed them most.

"It's not their fault," she said. "They were all married, or about to be, with no kids. After Chris died, they didn't really know how to talk to me. I think they were afraid of saying or doing something to upset me. And then when I had the baby, they really couldn't relate to me anymore. At that point, I was so overwhelmed I didn't know how to connect with them either."

"They're still jackasses," he said.

She laughed softly. "Thanks. I think. But I've kind of gotten used to being alone."

Matt looked away, unable to meet her eyes. He could relate to her solitude all too easily. He'd fallen into a routine of work-errands-sleep, which didn't leave much room for a social life. It was funny, though; until meeting Emma, the lack of company hadn't bothered him much. Now? He felt an acute sense of loneliness and a longing for connection.

"I know what you mean," he said softly. "I'm not exactly a party animal either."

She was quiet a moment. When she spoke again, her voice was barely more than a whisper. "I have a confession to make."

He looked up, surprised at the sheen of vulnerability

in her eyes. Without thinking, he reached out to touch her shoulder. "What is it?"

Emma swallowed, and he got the impression she was gathering up her courage. "I like you. And not just because you're helping me. You're the first person I've wanted to learn more about in a long time."

Her words sent an electric tingle through his limbs. A bubbly sense of anticipation filled his stomach, as if he'd just downed a bottle of champagne. He leaned a bit closer, unable to keep the smile from his face. "I feel the same way about you," he said.

"You do?" She inched toward him, her lips curving up.

"Yeah. I've been trying to talk myself out of it, but it hasn't worked."

"Why would you want to do that?" Her tone was teasing, but he could tell she was curious.

"It didn't seem right, given the circumstances. I figured my feelings are the last thing you need to deal with now."

She hummed thoughtfully. "Maybe you're right," she said. She settled her palm on his chest, just above his heart. Her hand was warm through the fabric of his shirt, her touch soft but impossible to ignore. "Or maybe you're exactly the kind of distraction I need."

Reading the question in her eyes, he didn't stop to think, leaning forward and closing the distance between them. She met him halfway, her lips soft and yielding against his own.

The contact sent an arc of sensation down his spine. Emma grabbed his shirt with both hands, her short nails digging into his flesh as she pulled them together. Their bodies met, chest to curves, her knees to his thighs. Heat raced through Matt's system, making his skin feel tight and overly sensitive. Every brush of Emma's lips, every graze of her fingertip or pass of her hand, registered in high definition, his brain hyperaware of her movements and responses.

The kiss quickly took on a desperate edge as Emma yanked on the hem of his shirt and his hands tangled in her hair. More, he needed more of everything—her lips, her breath, her skin. Her scent filled his nose, soapy and clean from the shower. She tasted like tooth-paste and sleep, a combination that was at once both familiar and exotic. What was it about this woman that turned even the most ordinary things into something so heady and sensual? How did she have such a po-tent effect on him?

She touched his stomach, setting off a spark of static electricity that had them both jumping apart. "Sorry," she whispered breathlessly.

"It's okay." He leaned back down to recapture her mouth, but paused before his lips met hers. Maybe this wasn't such a good idea... As much as he wanted her, it might be better to keep his distance until the traf-fickers were no longer a threat. It was all too easy to succumb to temptation in the face of danger. He didn't want Emma to regret anything that happened between them once cooler heads prevailed and they faced the very real issues that might sink a relationship before it even got off the ground.

"What's wrong?" Her brown eyes shone with a mix of arousal and concern. "Are you okay?"

"Yeah," he said, reaching up to cup her cheek with his hand. "I just think we might want to slow down a little. I don't want you to feel pressured, and I can't make you any promises…"

"I know," she said shortly. She kissed him quickly, then drew back. "Unless you want to stop? I'm not going to chase you if you're not ready."

"It's not that," he replied. He searched for the words to explain his thoughts, trying to ignore the increasing demands of his libido. His body was trying to wrestle away control of the situation, and as Emma continued to rub circles on his chest with her fingertip, he was rapidly losing the ability to think rationally.

"Matt." The sound of her voice cut through his mental fog. He focused on her face, saw the glint of determination in her eyes. "I know what I'm doing. I know what this is, and what this isn't. I'm tired of being lonely. For once, I want to put myself first."

He nodded, relief filling his system as her words sank in. She understood what he'd so badly tried to communicate. The pressure lifted at her acknowledgment that they were on the same page, relationship-wise.

"What about Christina?"

Emma glanced to the other bed. "She's out. I don't think she'll wake up anytime soon, as long as we're quiet. And even if she does, she won't understand what's going on."

"That's true." Her reassurances made him feel better about his desires. He gave himself permission to turn his brain off and reached for her, surrendering to sensation as she eagerly returned his embrace. "Then let's keep each other company," he whispered, dipping his head to kiss her once more.

Chapter 10

Is this really happening?

The question kept rattling around in Emma's brain, even as Matt's hands traveled over her body. It was hard to believe she was here in his arms, sharing this bed. She'd thought about this moment, imagined what he would feel like, how he would respond to her. But she'd never truly hoped her fantasies would become a reality. Matt was so quiet and reserved, she'd almost convinced herself her attraction to him was one-sided. But as his lips blazed a trail down her neck, she had to acknowledge this wasn't all in her head.

Nerves fluttered to life in her stomach as he slowly peeled the hem of her shirt up. Gone were the flat tummy and smooth skin of her youth. Pregnancy had left her with a softness to her belly, the curves decorated with the shiny tracks of stretch marks. Her souvenirs, as she liked to think of them. Reminders of a time in her life that was both heaven and hell, as she'd simultaneously celebrated the miracle of the life growing within her and tried to piece together the heart broken by Chris's death. She'd gotten used to the changes in her body to the point she no longer really noticed them. But what would Matt think?

His blue eyes glowed with warmth as he ran his gaze over her exposed flesh. "Beautiful," he murmured, lowering his head to kiss her belly. His fingertip traced the lines across her stomach, his touch featherlight.

"You think so?" She laughed nervously, trying not to let her insecurities ruin the moment. It was hard, though—Matt was the first man to see her like this since she'd given birth. It was enough to make her feel almost virginal again.

He raised his head and met her gaze. "I do," he said seriously. "You're a beautiful, sexy woman. And not in spite of your being a mother. Because of it."

Tears sprang to her eyes, blurring his face. "Thank you," she said.

"Be proud of your scars," he said. "I know I am."

"You have scars?"

"Oh yeah." He sat up quickly, tugging his shirt over his head to reveal his broad chest. Then he lay back down, hiking his hips off the bed so he could shimmy out of his pants.

Emma's heart began to pound at the sight of him sprawled on the bed next to her. He was all muscle and tanned skin, anointed with the perfect dusting of golden hair. In the low light of the hotel room, he looked like a Greek god come to life.

"Check this out." He drew her attention to a starburst on his right shoulder. "Got hung up on some barbed wire during army basic training."

"Ouch." She frowned, imagining how much that had hurt.

"And this one." He tapped his left thigh, which bore a thick stripe just above his knee. "Fell out of a tree when I was a kid. Landed on a bush. One of the branches tore through me."

"Your poor mother," she murmured.

His mouth turned up in a quick grin, giving her a glimpse of the rambunctious boy he must have been. "She wasn't too pleased with me that day," he admitted.

"What about this one?" She reached out to trace an irregular patch on the side of his stomach, just to the left of his belly button.

His cheeks flushed. "Oh, that. I, uh…" He trailed off, quietly cleared his throat. "I may have burned myself while making macaroni and cheese once."

Emma smothered a laugh. "Oh my. Cooking can be dangerous."

"You have no idea," he said seriously. "The water just jumped out of the pot and got me."

"You poor thing."

"It wasn't one of my finer moments, I'll admit. But I persevered."

"Such courage."

He lifted a brow. "I feel like you're making light of my struggles."

"I would never," she said, with mock seriousness.

"It's not easy being a single man with no desire to cook," he said with a sniff. "The options are pretty limited. And kitchen mishaps like the attack of the boiling water don't make me want to roll up my sleeves and try again."

"I can imagine your struggles," Emma said, trying to maintain a straight face. The idea of this big, tough former soldier balking in the kitchen tickled her funny bone. Apparently he was only human, after all.

He covered the old burn with his hand, his smile fading. "Your scars are prettier," he said softly.

"You think so?"

He nodded, reaching for her again. "In this light, the marks look like veins of silver running across your belly."

She glanced down, trying to see the lines through his eyes. They did seem to shine a bit compared to the surrounding skin, but she wasn't sure they were quite as pretty as he thought. Still, it was a nice idea, and she appreciated the poetry of the sentiment.

"I'll take your word for it," she said.

"Good," he replied, pulling her close once again. "Because it's true."

His breath was hot on her neck, his lips insistent as he nibbled and kissed his way along her collarbone. Slowly, carefully, he pulled her shirt up, exposing more of her skin with every gentle tug. He didn't rush, didn't try to hurry the process. Instead, he took his time, caressing and tasting each exposed stretch until she melted bonelessly into the mattress.

Need built inside her even as her bones turned to jelly. She ran her hands over Matt's body, enjoying the feel of his muscles flexing and relaxing as he moved.

They explored each other with hands and lips and tongues, learning secret places and hidden spots. Her nerves disappeared as she surrendered to the pleasure of touching and being touched, of kissing and being kissed. Of loving, and being loved.

He rolled onto his back. She threw one leg over his hips, then rose up on her knees to straddle him. But just as she was about to lower herself, his hands gripped her hips, keeping her suspended.

"Wait," he said. The word sounded pained, and she looked up to find his expression anguished.

"What's wrong?" Concern flooded her system—was he hurt? Had he changed his mind?

"I don't have a condom."

"Oh." Relief washed over her, making her smile. "It's okay. I have an IUD."

"So you're protected against pregnancy? Because my last health check came up clean."

"As did mine," she said.

A playful glint entered his eyes as he stared up at her. "I'm happy to continue if you are," she said, grinning as anticipation chased away the last of her worries.

"I thought you'd never ask." Matt grabbed her legs and flipped her onto her back. Emma had to bite her lip to stifle a shriek of surprise at her sudden change of position. Her head was still spinning as Matt covered her body with his own, and as they joined together, she felt her heart take flight.

* * *

Emma wasn't sure how long they lay together, legs tangled and skin cooling. Her mind was pleasantly blank, but as the air conditioner hummed to life, her brain began to engage again. She had meant to talk to Matt about what she'd overheard earlier. Instead, she'd let her emotions rule her actions and jumped into bed with him.

Matt trailed his fingers along her arm. "You're thinking."

She turned her head to face him. "How did you know that?" She hadn't said anything, hadn't even made a sound.

"You tensed up. Not much, but enough." He rolled onto his side, planting his elbow in the mattress and propping his head with his hand. "Everything okay?"

Emma stared up at him, marveling at his perception. "Yes."

He studied her face for a few seconds. "Do you regret what we did?" He sounded a little shy, but he held her gaze.

"No." She reached out to touch his cheek, needing him to believe her. She may have acted impulsively, but she wasn't sorry about it. Being with Matt had made her feel alive again. It was an experience she knew she'd always treasure. "I'm not unhappy about that."

"Okay," he said simply. "But I can tell something is on your mind. You can talk to me, if you want."

It was the perfect opening. So why did she find it so hard to start talking?

"Well…the thing is…" Embarrassment filled her,

making her cheeks go warm. She'd never had to confess eavesdropping before. It was such a childish activity she almost didn't want to admit it.

But she owed it to Matt to be honest with him. So she took a deep breath and plunged in.

"I overheard you talking to Christina earlier. I came out of the bathroom while you were telling her about Fisher, but you didn't hear the door open. I feel bad about listening in, but my curiosity got the better of me."

Matt's expression went blank, and she sensed him start to withdraw. Under normal circumstances, she would let him retreat to the safety of his emotional fortress. But she still carried the scent of him on her skin and felt the ghost of his touch. They had shared their bodies with each other; it was time for him to share some of his heart.

"Please," she said softly. "I don't want to cause you pain by bringing up hard memories. But I want to know about Fisher."

Matt let out a heavy sigh and rolled onto his back, staring up at the ceiling. He was quiet for so long, Emma feared he wasn't going to say anything. But then he began to speak, his voice so low she had to strain to hear.

"When I was in the army, I was engaged. Her name was Jennifer. We had met through mutual friends, dated through most of college. I was in ROTC, and she knew I'd be on active duty following graduation. Everything was great, for a while. We got engaged shortly before my first deployment. I wanted to have a quick wedding so she'd be my beneficiary in case something happened, but she insisted on waiting until I got back. Said she wanted a huge wedding with all the bells and whistles." He smiled ruefully. "That probably should have been my first clue, but I was too blind to see."

Emma scooted closer to Matt but was careful not to touch him. She sensed he was lost in his memories, and she didn't want to interfere.

"As my deployment wore on, she kept telling me she had a surprise for me when I got back. I figured she'd found a house, or maybe gotten a new job. She wouldn't tell me what it was, just kept saying I'd be so happy." He snorted. "I nearly had a heart attack when I stepped off the plane and saw her standing there with a baby in her arms."

"Oh my," Emma murmured. "That is quite a surprise." Was that the little boy he'd mentioned earlier when talking to Christina?

Matt nodded. "She swore up and down he was mine. The math worked out, but he just didn't feel like my baby. I can't explain it—I just knew deep down he wasn't my child."

A small stone of worry formed in Emma's stomach. "What happened?"

"We lived together for a while. I got pretty attached to Fisher, but I couldn't shake the feeling he didn't belong to me. After several months, I took a paternity test and it confirmed what I already knew."

"What did Jennifer do?"

"She broke down and confessed. She'd been cheating on me for a while and I hadn't known. When she turned up pregnant, she was scared because she didn't know who the father was. She broke it off with the other guy and decided to recommit to me. But once the truth was out, I told her we were done."

A cold chill swept over Emma, making her shiver. "You left them?"

"It was kind of the other way around. She took up with Fisher's father again. Last I heard, they're married and living in the suburbs."

"That's good," she said. She knew from experience how hard it was to be a single mother.

Matt blew out a breath. "Fisher was a sweet little guy. I still miss him, but I just couldn't stay. He never really felt like mine, you know?"

"Sure," she replied automatically. Her thoughts whirled as she processed this new information. Matt hadn't wanted to raise another man's child. Why had she ever thought he'd want to be a part of Christina's life?

Embarrassment filled her as she recalled her earlier fantasies of a future with Matt. He'd seemed like a good potential partner for her, and the way he'd played and interacted with Christina had made her think he might be willing to step in as a father for her. But after hearing his story about Fisher, she knew that would never happen.

I'm such a fool. She'd let her loneliness and desire for connection overrule her head. Of course Matt had been sweet to Christina—her daughter was adorable and good-natured. Most people enjoyed being around her. But just because he'd played with her a few times didn't mean he wanted to stay involved in her life. She should have known better than to assume otherwise.

Emma rolled off the bed and began to pull her clothes free from the tangle of sheets. Her chest felt tight and her eyes burned, but she refused to show any emotion.

Matt sat up, watching her curiously. "You okay?"

She nodded. "Yep. I was starting to get cold." She didn't look at him, didn't trust herself not to burst into tears. It wasn't Matt's fault she was disappointed. He'd never volunteered to star in her fantasies of love and a family. Could she really blame him for not wanting to take on such weighty responsibilities, especially after his experience with Jennifer?

"Are you sure?" Matt asked. "Because I feel like I've upset you somehow."

Emma fumbled with the clasp of her bra. Damn him for being so perceptive! The sooner she got her clothes on, the better. Being naked around him made her feel even more vulnerable.

He climbed out of bed and reached for his boxer shorts. She turned around, tugging her shirt down before stepping into her pants. Once she was dressed, she took a deep breath to center herself.

Matt's story had upset her, yes. But she didn't want him to know it. If he knew how she'd been building him up in her mind, the way she'd hoped they might have something together...at best he would pity her. At worst, he would leave. And she still needed him to help her keep Christina safe.

She turned to face him again, pasting a smile on

her face. "You haven't upset me," she said. "I really was getting cold. And I wanted to get dressed in case Detective Randall calls and we need to leave quickly."

"I hope he'll have good news," Matt said, zipping up his jeans. He walked over to the table and reached into one of the remaining bags he'd brought in earlier. He pulled out a loaf of bread, a jar of peanut butter and a small bottle of honey. "In the meantime, can I make you a sandwich? I've worked up a bit of an appetite." He winked at her, and despite her churning stomach, she smiled.

"That sounds nice." She walked over to the second bed to check on Christina. Her daughter had rolled onto her stomach, her arms and legs tucked underneath her and her little bum slightly raised. It was her favorite sleeping position, and Emma was glad to see her baby was resting so comfortably.

She sat on the edge of the bed, trying to process this new information about Matt. She knew she had no right to be upset with him, and yet her mother's heart was bothered by the fact that he had walked away from Fisher. No, the boy hadn't been his. But Matt had lived with him for several months. Why couldn't he have gotten over his reservations about the child's paternity and let his love for the baby take over? Couldn't he have found a way to forgive Jennifer, if only for Fisher's sake? Did Matt really think that a genetic connection was what made a family?

He walked over and passed her a sandwich on a paper plate. "Thanks," she said reflexively.

The mattress dipped as he sat next to her. "Sure

thing." They ate in silence for a moment, Emma's mind cycling through dozens of questions she wanted to ask. But she didn't know where to start, or even how to phrase most of them. Should she even bother to try to understand why Matt had made the choices he had, or was it better to just let her feelings dic on the vine?

She felt Matt's eyes on her and turned to meet his gaze. "I'm not sure of what I did," he said softly. "But I want to make it right."

Tears sprang to her eyes, and she blinked hard to dispel them. He was a good man. Even though she didn't understand some of his choices, she wanted to give him the benefit of the doubt. She just needed to recalibrate her dreams to reflect reality. And really, it was better to face the music now rather than later, after her feelings for him had been given a chance to grow.

"You didn't do anything," she said. But before she could say more, her phone buzzed on the nightstand.

Emma lunged for it, one eye on her sleeping baby. Christina sighed but didn't otherwise stir. Moving quickly, Emma took the phone into the bathroom and partially closed the door.

She glanced at the display but didn't recognize the number. "Hello?" Hopefully it was Detective Randall, calling with an update…

"Emma, don't hang up."

Joseph's voice made her tense. Her grip on the phone tightened to the point of pain. "What do you want?" Part of her was relieved to hear his voice—he was still alive! But her anger and frustration quickly took over.

"I need your help."

She snorted. "You need my help? Oh, that's rich."

"It's not for me." He spoke quickly, almost pleading. "It's for Mom."

Emma paused, silently debating. Was he telling the truth? Or was he simply trying to manipulate her by invoking their mother?

It took a split second for her to decide. Joseph may well be lying to her again, but she wasn't willing to risk the possibility her mom really needed her. She'd hear him out, and if his story didn't add up, she'd cut him off without a second thought.

"What's going on?" She didn't bother to hide her skepticism. He needed to know he was skating on thin ice.

"It's the traffickers. They've got her."

Emma's heart dropped to her toes. "What?" Numbness stole over her body as Joseph's words sank in. The thought of those men anywhere near their mother made her blood run cold. She'd seen the ruthlessness in their eyes, their total lack of compassion. Their mom was a gentle, kind woman who deserved no part of that.

"They have her," Joseph repeated. He sounded a little impatient, which sparked Emma's temper.

"And where are you?" she snapped. "Off spying from a safe distance? Did you do anything to stop them from taking Mom, or were you too busy trying to save your own ass?"

Matt poked his head into the room, and she realized her voice had carried. She waved him inside and put the call on speakerphone. Might as well let him listen, so she wouldn't have to repeat everything later.

Laughter drifted over the line. She heard a muffled voice speak, and it sounded like he said, "She is feisty." Emma frowned. It sounded like her brother wasn't alone.

"I'm here with her," Joseph said. "I can't believe you think I'd just watch them take Mom." He sounded hurt, but Emma didn't care.

"Don't let them hurt her," she warned.

"I'm doing my best," he said. "But I can't stop them. I'm outnumbered."

"I don't care," she said ruthlessly. "If they touch one hair on her head, it's on you."

"Emma—"

"Shut up. Just tell me what they want." She wasn't stupid. Joseph wouldn't be calling if the traffickers didn't want something. And it didn't take a genius to figure out what.

Another voice came on the line, calm and composed. "You're a smart woman, Emma. You know what we're after."

They still wanted Christina. It stood to reason they'd taken her mother to use as a bargaining chip, probably because they'd correctly assumed she wouldn't lift a finger to save her brother after what he'd done.

"You think I'll give you my daughter in exchange for my mother?" It broke her heart to ask the question, especially because she already knew the answer. She loved her mother and would do almost anything to help her. But Christina was her heart and soul. Emma would give her life to keep her baby safe. There was no way she could willingly put her daughter into harm's way, even if that meant throwing her own mother to the wolves.

"I think you should consider it," the man said. "Because if you don't cooperate, we're going to kill her by inches. Maria will feel pain like you've never imagined. And we will make it last."

"Why are you doing this? Why can't you just leave my family alone?"

The man chuckled. "Your brother insulted the boss. Can't have that. Now it's personal."

She heard a meaty thud followed by a feminine cry. Joseph's voice rang out in protest, but he was met by laughter.

Emma's stomach turned at the sounds. "Stop it!" she cried.

The laughter stopped, but the painful gasps continued. "Let me talk to her," she insisted. She didn't want anyone to suffer abuse, but she wasn't ready to believe they had her mother just yet. Joseph was a consummate liar, and she doubted the men he was with were honest.

There were fumbling sounds as the phone was passed around, then a thin, pained voice came on the line. "Emma?"

Emma's legs gave out at the sound of her mother's voice. Matt caught her before she hit the floor, pulling her against his broad chest as he took on her weight. He guided her over to the bathtub, gently lowered her to sit on the edge.

"Mom?" Her voice cracked on the word, and her

chest tightened to the point she couldn't breathe. "Are you there?"

"I'm here. But don't listen to them, baby. You forget about me—keep Christina safe." Her mom let out a yell which was quickly stifled by the sound of another blow. Emma's shoulders shook as she sobbed silently, her face pressed into the hollow of Matt's shoulder.

"I'll find you, Mom," she said loudly. She wasn't sure if her mother could hear her, but she wanted her to know she wasn't giving up. "I won't let them hurt you."

Another pained gasp, this time accompanied by a yelp from Joseph. Apparently the men were starting in on her brother, too.

"Better hurry," taunted the man who'd spoken to her earlier. "Your mother seems healthy for her age, but she won't last forever."

"Where are you?"

"All in good time," he said. "I'm not going to tell you yet. I'll call you in twenty-four hours, with a location and a time. Stay by your phone."

Emma drew in a shuddering breath, knowing she couldn't argue. "Please don't hurt her," she whispered.

"We'll see," said the faceless tormentor. "And Emma, one more thing."

"What?"

"No police. If you even think about contacting the authorities, the next time we speak you'll be listening to the sound of your mother's execution. Is that clear?"

"Yes." She nodded though he couldn't see her. The harsh buzz of the dial tone echoed off the tile, making her jump. She hung up and buried her head in her hands, the phone dropping with a clatter against the floor.

I can't do this. The thought circled around her brain on infinite loop as images assaulted her from all sides. Her mom, kissing her goodbye as she headed off to the bus. Her smile of pride the day Emma graduated from nursing school. Her tears at Chris's funeral. The look of total joy in her eyes as she held Christina for the first time.

Most of Emma's important memories involved her mother. She'd been there for all of life's major ups and downs, and Emma couldn't imagine moving forward without her.

But every cell in her body rejected even the idea of putting Christina in danger. She simply couldn't do it, no matter what the stakes.

Still, as Emma stared at the bathroom tiles, tears blurring her vision, she knew she couldn't sit back and let those men torture her mother. She wasn't willing to sacrifice her daughter, but she wouldn't write off her mother, either.

Gradually, she became aware of Matt's hand stroking down her spine. He held her against his chest, his voice low in her ear as he murmured something over and over again.

Emma focused on his voice, tuning in to what he was saying.

"It's going to be okay."

His words hit her like a jolt, a powerful reminder that she wasn't alone. His support was nice, but she wasn't sure she shared his confidence. "What am I going to do?" she whispered.

"We," he corrected immediately. "And I don't know. But we will figure it out together."

Chapter 11

She looked haunted—that was the only way to describe it.

Matt watched Emma as she pasted on a smile while she played with her daughter, but he saw the blankness in her eyes and knew she wasn't really there. Her thoughts were with her mother, her imagination likely running wild at the thought of what the traffickers were doing to the poor woman.

He wanted to comfort her, but nothing he could do or say would help. Truth be told, he was still processing the news, as well. They hadn't had much time to talk after the call from the traffickers. Emma's voice had woken Christina, and she'd left the bathroom to tend to her daughter.

They sat playing on the bed now, Christina cooing

happily while her mother pretended to be okay. Once again, Matt marveled at Emma's strength and composure in the face of such terrible circumstances. It was clear she was used to doing everything on her own, but Matt wasn't about to let her handle this alone.

He wasn't sure when it had happened, but somewhere along the way, Emma had begun to matter to him on a personal level. His feelings for her went beyond admiration and respect, and his attraction wasn't merely for her body. He wanted to truly be a part of her life, to take care of her the way only a lover could. And as for Christina? The baby already had him wrapped around one of her fat little fingers. If he let his mind wander, he could easily picture helping her learn to walk, teaching her to drive in an empty parking lot and walking her down the aisle at her wedding.

But would Emma want the same? Perhaps she didn't want to find a father for Christina. Maybe she was worried another man would try to erase Chris from their lives. Matt could tell her he wasn't interested in replacing Chris, but would she believe him?

And really, did it even matter now? His feelings were all stirred up after making love to Emma, but the timing couldn't possibly be worse. Besides, his thoughts weren't important at the moment—all that mattered was finding a way to save Emma's mom while keeping her and Christina safe. He couldn't come up with a plan while distracted by his own worries, so it was time to clear his head and push his issues to the side.

"What do you want to do?" Maybe she was already working on a plan—he didn't want to assume anything.

Her eyes flickered to his before returning to Christina. The look of defeat on her face hit him like a punch to the gut. It wasn't like her to lose hope. "What can I do?" She shook her head. "I won't give them my baby. I've basically signed my mother's death warrant."

"No, you haven't." He hated her feelings of guilt, the fact that she thought she was somehow responsible for the actions of those men. He felt a renewed surge of anger toward her brother. Once again, Emma was paying the price for Joseph's carelessness.

She looked at him, her eyes full of desolation. "Do you think they'd really know if I called Detective Randall? I want to tell him, but what if they have cops on their payroll? I don't want them punishing my mother because I disobeyed them."

"I'm not sure," Matt admitted. "I think we can assume they probably do have police connections, but it's impossible to know how far they extend. Randall seems like one of the good guys, but I've been wrong before."

"I don't know if I can risk it," she said.

"We might have to," he replied. "I have the beginnings of a plan, but it's going to take a few more people to pull it off."

"What are you thinking?" There was a note of interest in her voice, which he took as a good sign. He needed to get her thinking about offense, not defense. The only way they could regain control of the situation was if they started calling the shots again. It was tricky, but he had some ideas of how to make that happen.

"I've got some buddies from the army I can call. I think they'll help us take these guys down."

"How?" she asked. "Even if they do agree to help us, we don't know where the traffickers want to meet, or when. I doubt they're going to give us enough warning to get any kind of backup in place."

"That's true," Matt said. "Which is why we're not going to let them tell us where to go. We're going to dictate to them, not the other way around."

She stared at him in disbelief for a moment, then huffed out a laugh. "I admire your confidence, but I don't see how that will work. They have all the leverage. Why would they possibly agree to cooperate with our demands?"

"Because you're the one with the power." At her blank look, he reached over and picked up Christina, tucking her against his chest. "They want your baby. That's what this whole thing is about. They're not willing to give up on stealing Christina because of some stupid slight that damaged the boss's ego. You're the one who holds all the cards, and they're trying to distract you from realizing it by threatening your mother."

Awareness began to dawn on her face, and with it came a glimmer of hope. "Oh," she said, sounding a little surprised. "I hadn't thought of it like that."

Matt stuck his finger against Christina's palm. She reflexively grabbed it, and he waved it a bit, making her smile. "They're hoping you won't. They called you to shock you, put you on the defensive. They want you reacting, not planning. And they know threatening your mother will play on your emotions, keep you from thinking rationally."

"It worked," she muttered.

He nodded. "Of course it did. Most people would be horrified to learn their mom is in danger. They'd do anything to save her."

Emma climbed off the bed and moved to stand in front of him. Christina smiled at her mother, but was happy to remain in Matt's arms. She laid her small head against his chest, and his stomach did a strange flip. This baby had been through so much in the past few days, and yet she seemed to trust him, even though he was a relative stranger. He was happy to know she wasn't afraid of him. In fact, she seemed to like him. Maybe even love him, if babies that young could feel love for someone. He'd certainly fallen head over heels for her, and as she snuggled against him, he silently promised to keep her safe.

"I'm not so sure they'll react well to us flipping the script on them," Emma said. She stroked Christina's hair, but didn't try to take her from him. Matt began to sway gently, and Emma matched his movements. They stood there together, rocking in the age-old dance of parents, the baby cradled between them. Christina's thumb found her mouth; soon her breathing settled into the deep, regular rhythm of sleep.

Moving carefully, Matt laid her on the bed. She stirred, but didn't wake. He watched her for a second, his arms feeling oddly empty. Then he turned to find Emma staring at him, tears in her eyes.

"What's wrong?" He moved to hold her, but she stepped back, shaking her head with a slight smile.

"It's nothing. I'm fine." She waved off his concern and swiped at her eyes. "Just worried about Mom."

"Of course," he replied. "And to answer your earlier question, I don't think they'll be pleased when you take control. But they don't really have a choice. If they're going to be driven by the boss's ego, they can't go against him. They're going to have to cooperate if they want to have any chance of making this guy happy."

"But what if they hurt Mom to get back at me? I don't know if I can have that on my conscience." Emma bit her lip, her worry plain.

Matt drew in a breath. This is where things got complicated. She was going to have to make a decision, but first he wanted her to be aware of all the possible outcomes.

"They might." *No, be honest*, he told himself. "Scratch that—they probably will hurt her." He took her hand and drew her down to sit next to him on the other bed. "Here's the deal, Emma. They are going to kill your mom if they don't get their hands on Christina. In fact, they'll kill her even if they do get your daughter. There is no scenario that ends with them letting her go. Not after what she's seen and heard. If we do nothing—if we simply run and try to disappear—they will murder your mother. We can try to save her, but I can't guarantee we'll be successful."

She was quiet, clearly digesting his words. Matt knew what he wanted to do, but it wasn't up to him. This was Emma's mother, her family. She had to be the one to decide.

"Running would be easier," she said. "But I can't just abandon my mom. I'd rather try to save her than leave her to die." She met his eyes, her gaze determined. "But I'm only willing to do this if you can promise me Christina won't be in any danger."

He glanced at the sleeping baby, his heart softening as he watched her thumb fall from her relaxed mouth. "There are no guarantees in life," he said, swallowing hard. "But I promise you this—they'll have to go through me to get to this little girl."

Emma searched his face, perhaps looking for confirmation he truly meant what he'd said. He met her gaze unflinchingly, letting her see his absolute determination to keep her daughter safe.

Apparently satisfied, Emma nodded. "All right," she said softly. "What do we do now?"

"I'm going to make a few phone calls," he said, already reaching for his cell. "In the meantime, we wait."

The hours ticked by slowly, each moment seeming to last longer than the one before it. Emma's anxiety mounted as the day wore on, her worries for her mother increasing as her imagination ran free. Every time she closed her eyes, she pictured her mother bound and gagged, her face bruised and bloody as a circle of faceless men surrounded her, laughing at her fear and pain.

She tried to keep herself occupied, to keep her mind focused on the mundane. She slipped into the shower while Matt made his calls and Christina slept. The hot water felt good, and the hotel soap washed away the last of Matt's scent from her skin. Her heart ached a little at the memory of their time together. In the moment, she'd opened her heart to him, secretly hoping they might have a future together. But as she'd listened to his story about Fisher, she'd realized Matt would never be able to accept Christina as his child. The recognition had hurt, but she couldn't bring herself to be angry with him. Besides, it was better to find out how he really felt now, before she let herself fall all the way in love with him. Knowing he couldn't accept Christina should make it easier for Emma to give up on her dreams of a relationship with him.

And yet she still found herself yearning for him, hoping he might change his mind. It was hard to reconcile Matt's lack of interest in being a father to another man's child with his actions toward Christina. He said he couldn't do it, and yet he kept playing with her daughter, holding her, rocking her, putting her to sleep. He was a natural, and he seemed so comfortable with her baby. What's more, Matt seemed to genuinely enjoy Christina.

His promise to keep her daughter safe had been heartfelt; Emma had seen the emotion in his eyes, and at this point, she knew him well enough to realize he didn't make empty assurances. The fact that he was still here was a testament to his own feelings. He could have left her and Christina at several points over the last day or so. She wouldn't have blamed him if he'd simply driven them to the nearest police station and washed his hands of them. But he'd stayed. And even now, he was working on a plan to save her mother from the traffickers. Those weren't the actions of a man who was simply trying to do the right thing. The fact that he cared enough about her and Christina to help them so extensively had to mean *something*.

But deep in her heart, she knew it wasn't enough. As much as she liked him, as much as he seemed to care for her...none of it mattered if he couldn't step up and be a father to Christina. Emma wasn't willing to put her own happiness before her daughter's. It would be easy to overlook his reluctance to care for a stranger's baby, especially since he seemed to like Christina. She and Matt could have a relationship and build a life together. But not if it meant Christina felt forever disconnected from Matt. Children were often more perceptive than adults acknowledged. It wouldn't take long for her daughter to realize Matt didn't see her as his own. That he held part of himself back when it came to his relationship with her. And if she and Matt were to have a baby together? Her heart broke at the possibility Matt would show obvious favoritism to his biological child, leaving her daughter out in the cold.

No, she couldn't do that to her baby. Better for Christina to lack a father figure than to have one who was distant and reserved, or worse, one who saw her as a burden and grew to resent her presence over time.

She dressed and returned to the room, rubbing her hair with a towel as she turned her thoughts in a different direction. No sense in spending time worrying about something that was never going to happen. Better to focus her energies on Matt's plan so they could save her mother.

She sat on the bed, waiting for him to finish with his call. Christina still napped, but Emma knew from experience it wouldn't last much longer. Hopefully she would wake up in a good mood...

Matt nodded at her in acknowledgment, his voice a low murmur as he spoke into the phone. Something about his body language told her he wasn't going to be finished anytime soon, so she propped some pillows against the headboard and leaned back to wait. Before she recognized what was happening, her eyes drifted shut and she surrendered to the pull of sleep.

Emma jerked awake, her heart jumping into her throat as she stared at the unfamiliar surroundings. A breath later, it all came flooding back; the diner, the traffickers, the hotel.

Christina.

She rolled over, her eyes searching the other bed for her sleeping daughter. But her baby wasn't there.

Her stomach twisted as she clawed her way free from the bedsheets. "Christina," she croaked, blinking back tears as she scanned the bed, hoping perhaps her daughter had rolled behind a pillow or snuggled under the comforter.

"Easy, Emma."

At the sound of Matt's voice, she whirled around to find him sitting in the corner, her daughter in his lap. "She's okay," he said gently. "I told you, I won't let anything happen to her."

Emma sank down on the bed, relief making her a little light-headed. "How long has she been awake?"

"About forty minutes."

She rubbed her forehead, trying to piece together the timeline. "How long was I asleep?"

"Almost an hour and a half."

"What?" She hadn't meant to sleep that long, hadn't meant to sleep at all, for that matter. How had she not heard her baby wake?

"You were out," he confirmed. He smiled, a twinkle of amusement in his eyes. "Snoring like a band saw."

Emma sniffed, choosing to ignore that particular statement. "Why didn't you wake me up?"

Matt tilted his head to the side. "You needed the rest."

"Yeah, but once Christina woke up—"

"I handled it," he interrupted. "It's not a problem."

Emma frowned slightly, trying to reconcile his actions regarding Fisher with his treatment of Christina. The contradiction was enough to drive her mad, if she let it.

She shook her head, dismissing the questions swirling in her mind. "Thank you," she said instead.

"You're welcome."

Christina reached for her, grinning widely enough to expose her teeth. "Ma, ma, ma, ma," she babbled.

Emma gathered her into her arms and pressed her nose against her daughter's neck, breathing in her sweet baby smell. "Hi, love," she said gently. "Did you have a good nap?"

"Ah-bah," Christina confirmed.

Matt chuckled, his eyes full of warmth as he watched her daughter. "She's got a lot to say."

"Tell me about it," Emma replied. "I look forward to the day I can actually understand her."

"It'll probably be sooner than you think," he said. "I can tell she's a smart one."

His observation pleased her, but Emma was determined not to read too much into it. "That's true," she said. Time to change the subject. "Did you get all your calls made before she woke up?"

"Yes." Emma took a step back as he got to his feet. He stretched his arms above his head with a yawn, the hem of his shirt lifting to expose a stripe of skin. Emma averted her eyes, trying to ignore the heat creeping up the back of her neck, while her fingers tingled from the memory of touching him there.

If he noticed her reaction, he didn't show it. "In fact," he continued, headed for the bathroom, "I have to leave soon to meet some people."

She waited for him to return to the room. "Who are you meeting?"

"Some friends of mine from the army." He walked to the desk in the far corner of the room and slipped his wallet in his back pocket, then reached for his watch. "A few guys I served with retired early and started their own private security company. They're going to help us out."

That sounded promising. Emma's spirits brightened a bit, but she was careful to keep her sense of hope under control. "They're local?"

"Not really. But they're nearby. And they agreed to meet me here. They started driving after we finished talking, so they'll be getting close by now."

"I want to come with you." She took a deep breath, bracing herself for the argument that was sure to come.

Matt paused in the act of fastening his watch. "All right."

Some of the wind left Emma's sails. "That's it?"

He lifted one eyebrow. "Isn't that what you wanted to hear?"

She blinked, a bit taken aback. "Well…yes. But I figured you'd protest."

Matt's lips curved in a knowing half smile. "Would it have done me any good?"

"Probably not," she said sheepishly.

"You're an adult," he said simply. "I'm not going to waste my time trying to tell you what to do, especially where your family is concerned. If it were me, I'd want to meet the people who were going to work to save my mom, too."

She nodded, feeling mildly embarrassed at having doubted him. He'd been nothing but good to her and Christina. It wasn't his fault she'd started to hope for more after this was all over.

Matt stepped into his boots, then walked over and opened his hands. Christina offered him a toothy grin, leaning forward until Emma had no choice but to decant her daughter into Matt's waiting arms. "Go ahead and get ready. I'll change her diaper and give her a snack."

It was such a normal offer, a simple division of labor negotiated by parents all the time. But for Emma, it was a novelty. She was so used to being a single mother she hadn't even thought to ask him for help in that respect.

She headed for the bathroom, pausing at the door to watch Matt gather a fresh diaper before placing Christina on the bed. It felt a little strange to watch someone else care for her baby, but at the same time, seeing Matt and Christina together gave her an unexpected sense of peace during this troubled time.

He glanced up, saw her watching. He flashed a smile and made a shooing motion with his hands. Emma nodded, stepping into the bathroom with a lightness in her heart. Her mother was in danger, her own safety far from guaranteed. But in this moment, the man she'd grown to care for was gently tending to her baby. Her troubles were far from over, but right now, she couldn't bring herself to care.

Chapter 12

The restaurant hostess greeted them with a bright smile. "Good evening. Table for two?" She eyed the car seat Matt carried. "And a high chair?" she amended.

"Actually," Matt said, glancing past her. "I see our party has already arrived." He put his hand on the small of Emma's back and guided her around the hostess stand, steering her toward the booth in the corner where his buddies sat waiting. He jerked his chin up in greeting as they approached, tried to ignore Dave's knowing smirk.

"Gentlemen," Matt said. "Thanks for coming."

He gave Emma a gentle nudge into the booth and pulled over a chair for the car seat. He slid in next to Emma and placed the bulky seat next to him, being careful not to jostle it too much.

"LT," Dave said. "Good to see you."

"LT?" Emma asked questioningly.

"Lieutenant," Matt answered quietly.

"Ma'am," Dave said, nodding politely at her.

"Hello," she replied.

"Emma, this is Dave Lowden and Skip Hardy. They're the ones I told you about earlier. Guys, this is Emma Foster."

"Nice to meet you," said Dave. Skip gave her a nod but didn't speak.

"Who's the little one?" Dave craned his neck to see into the car seat, but Matt had pulled the hood down to keep the bright lights out of Christina's sleeping face.

"That's my daughter, Christina," said Emma.

"Damn, I was kind of hoping you'd settled down and made yourself a family," Dave said. He elbowed Skip with a grin. "Don't you think LT needs a woman's touch in his life? It's unnatural for a man to be single for so long."

Matt gritted his teeth but tried not to look affected. He'd known he was going to have to deal with a certain amount of teasing before they could get down to business. In fact, he'd made a point to warn Emma in the car, so she wouldn't be offended when Dave started mouthing off. And it was always Dave—Skip either couldn't be bothered or had too much sense to join in.

Emma's hand rested lightly on his thigh, a silent, hidden gesture of support. He subtly moved his hand to cover hers, giving it a gentle squeeze of acknowledgment.

Skip eyed Emma and then slid his gaze to Matt. He

tongued his wad of dip to the other side of his lip, then spit discreetly into a bottle that he returned to his lap. "Maybe," he said shortly.

"How is life as a park ranger?" Dave asked, grinning as he took a sip of his beer. "Aren't you tired of campouts and s'mores yet? Why don't you come work with us, make some actual money?"

"You mean babysitting American businessmen working in Juárez?" Matt shot back. "No, thanks."

Dave shrugged off the insult. "It's steady work."

"And the tips are nice," Skip put in.

"And you two are bored out of your skulls," said Matt.

"Now what makes you say that?" Dave asked.

Matt tilted his head to the side. "You about jumped through the phone when I told you I had a situation that needed handling. I figure if you were really happy, you'd have told me to buzz off."

"LT, you wound me." Dave clapped his hand to his chest in dramatic fashion. "I can't believe you think we would leave you in your time of need." He nudged Skip again, who tolerated the intrusion into his personal space with an expression of long-suffering patience. "Are you hearing this?"

"Yep," Skip confirmed.

"So what exactly do you need us for?" Dave continued. He focused on Emma. "Excuse my language, ma'am, but are you some kind of damsel in distress?"

Matt expected Emma to blast Dave for his sexist assumption, but instead she chuckled softly. "Not exactly," she said.

"Bummer," Dave replied. "It's been a long time since I've rescued a pretty lady."

"Try never," Skip said drily.

It was Matt's turn to laugh as Dave took another drink, ignoring Skip's comment.

"You boys about ready to listen?" he asked.

"What's the story?" Dave asked, leaning forward to plant his elbows on the table. All trace of joking was gone from his tone, and his expression was now deadly serious. "You didn't share a lot of the particulars over the phone, so I wasn't sure what to bring."

"Out of curiosity, what did you bring?" Matt asked.

"Everything," Skip said.

Matt lifted one eyebrow. "Really?"

Both men nodded. "I've got an armory in my trunk. Say the word, and we're ready to deploy."

Matt felt a surge of appreciation rise in his chest. This was what he missed the most about the army— the unwavering loyalty and ready willingness to help a fellow soldier, no questions asked. It was frustrating, not knowing if they could trust the police right now. But the fact that Dave and Skip had his back made all the difference in the world.

"Here's the situation." He briefly explained the backstory, filling them in on Emma's run-ins with the traffickers. Both men listened intently, their eyes flickering to Emma's face every so often, as if to gauge her reaction. For her part, she remained quiet, letting him brief the guys without interruption.

"What do we know about these men?" Dave asked.

"Not much," Matt admitted. "There were three men

at the diner, and I counted two more in the cab of the semitruck as we drove by. There might be more in the trailer."

"Armed?" said Skip.

"Definitely. Pistols on the ones who chased us. Probably more substantial weapons in the truck."

"Did you get a plate?"

"Only a partial," Matt said.

Dave made a tsking sound. "You're slipping, LT."

"Don't remind me," Matt replied, feeling a flush crawl up his neck. There was a time he wouldn't have missed a detail like that; civilian life had made him soft.

"Police?" Skip asked.

Emma shook her head. "We called them after the encounter at the truck stop, and I spoke to a detective in El Paso. He said he was going to talk to some people and get back to me, but I haven't heard from him again. I'm scared to call him now, after the threat to my mother."

"You think the traffickers have men on the inside?" Dave asked.

"I think we have to assume that, until we know otherwise," Matt said.

"Smart." Skip made another deposit into his bottle. "So we're on our own."

"I'm afraid so," Matt said. "Is that a deal breaker?"

For the first time, Skip smiled. "More like a deal maker," he said. "I prefer not tripping over cops while we work."

A waitress approached their table, and Skip clammed

up again. Matt and Emma ordered drinks, and she left with a promise to bring Dave another beer.

Matt leaned forward, pitching his voice low even though the surrounding tables were empty. "I know there are no guarantees for this kind of work, but I'd prefer if you gentlemen aimed to maim rather than terminate, if you get my drift."

Emma tensed beside him, drawing in a quick breath as she processed his words. He hated to talk about such matters in front of her, but she needed to know this wasn't going to be a bloodless endeavor. People were going to get hurt, perhaps even killed. And while he wouldn't shed a tear if any traffickers didn't make it out alive, he'd much prefer for them to face the justice system.

"Gotcha," Dave replied. "We'll try to keep the training wheels on."

"What are you going to do?" she asked. She fumbled with the napkin wrapped around a bundle of silverware, her fingers picking at the edges of the paper ring that held it all together.

Dave noticed her actions and slid a glance to Matt, as if to say, *You sure she can handle this?*

Matt nodded confidently. Emma might look fragile to an outsider, but he knew she had a core of steel. She was as tough as any man he'd served with, something Dave and Skip would discover for themselves soon enough.

"I'm not sure yet, ma'am," Dave said. "Once we decide where to set the meet, we can draw up a more concrete plan."

"I already know where we're going to meet them," Matt announced.

Emma's head swiveled to face him. "You do?"

He nodded. "The truck stop diner, Donuts and Diesel."

Her expression was incredulous. "Where they found us before?" She sounded less than impressed with his idea.

"The one and the same."

Dave nodded in agreement, even as Emma asked, "Why do you want to go back there?"

"Makes sense to me," Skip said.

Emma shot him a look. "Well, I'm not getting it. So can someone please explain it to me?"

Matt placed his hand over hers, stilling her nervous fingers. "The traffickers aren't going to like it when you take control and dictate the location of the meet. They'll be even more suspicious if you suggest some remote spot—they'll figure they're being set up. So you're going to request a public place, one they know you're familiar with. They won't anticipate any trouble, because they know you're on the run."

"Okay," she said slowly. "But what about the other people? I don't want anyone to get hurt because they were in the wrong place at the wrong time."

"I don't either," Matt said.

"Which is where we come in," Dave interrupted. "Begging your pardon, ma'am, but we have our own people. Once you tell us where this diner is, we'll put the wheels in motion and take care of things."

"I see." But her tone made it clear she wasn't convinced. "Won't the traffickers realize something is wrong as soon as they walk in? No offense, but if your people all look like you—" she gestured to Dave and Skip's military-issue buzz cuts and muscled arms "—it's going to be pretty obvious things aren't what they seem."

Dave turned to Skip. "She doesn't think we can blend in."

"Nope," said Skip.

"I'm guessing you didn't tell her what we did in the army?" Dave asked.

Matt ran a hand through his hair. "It didn't come up."

Emma looked at the men, then back at Matt. "What am I missing?"

Dave smiled, baring his teeth. "We won't be in the diner. We'll be watching over you from the rooftop, or maybe a nearby building."

Matt could tell by her frown she still wasn't getting it. "They're snipers," he explained. "Masters of disguise."

"Oh." Realization dawned on her face, followed by a shadow of worry. "So I'm going to have to talk to these guys alone?"

"Nope," Skip repeated. "Remember, our people will be there. You'll just look alone."

"I see."

They fell silent as the waitress returned with their drinks. They ordered food, and as the woman walked away, Christina began to stir.

Matt flipped up the shade on her car seat and extracted her from its confines. "Morning, sunshine," he said softly.

Christina blinked and looked around, clearly try-ing to reorient herself. Matt didn't envy her confu-sion—it had to be hard being a baby. Fall asleep in one place, wake up in another with no explanation of how you got there.

She saw her mother and let out a plaintive cry. Matt passed her over, his heart softening as he watched the baby nuzzle into the side of Emma's neck.

"I'm going to go change her," Emma said. Matt rose from the table, putting a hand on her arm to help her scoot free of the booth.

"Need help?"

Emma shot him a startled look. "No, I've got it. Thanks, though." She shouldered her bag and headed for the bathroom, rubbing Christina's back as she walked.

Matt watched them until the door closed behind her. When he turned back to the table, Dave and Skip were eyeing him with undisguised curiosity.

"So, LT," Dave began. "Got anything you want to add to your situation report?"

Matt resisted the urge to shift in his seat, know-ing the men would pick up on the gesture. "What do you mean?"

"Pretty lady," Skip said. "Cute kid."

"That's true," he hedged.

"Does she know?" Dave asked.

"Know what?" Matt had a sinking suspicion Dave was onto him; his next question confirmed it.

"Does she know how you feel about her?"

Matt sighed and reached for his water. "I think so."

"Just think?" Skip's gaze was disturbingly perceptive. Matt normally appreciated that quality in the other man, but found he didn't enjoy being under the microscope himself.

"We haven't really talked about it," Matt replied.

"You should," Dave said.

Matt shook his head. "What is this, some kind of messed up intervention? Since when did you two become guidance counselors?"

Dave shrugged. Skip brought the bottle to his mouth again.

"Life's too short, man," Dave said.

"Yep," agreed Skip.

Matt looked away, focusing on the door to the restroom. "Yeah, well," he muttered. "We haven't exactly had a chance to sit down and talk." Though they *had* taken advantage of the earlier lull in other ways. Heat suffused his body as he recalled the feel of her skin, the scent of her hair. The way she'd moved with him, joining him perfectly. For those endless moments, they'd held each other's hearts. Surely she'd sensed his emotions, realized the depth of his feelings?

"Make time," Dave urged. "You need to take a chance."

Matt slid a glance at the man. "You're sounding awfully new agey. Got anything of your own you want to tell me?"

Dave shut his mouth, but he couldn't control the flush that appeared on the tips of his ears.

Matt grinned. "I see."

"He's in love," Skip confirmed.

"Congratulations," Matt said, meaning it. He was glad his friend had found happiness, even as he pitied the woman who was going to have to put up with him.

Dave smiled, his eyes going soft. "Thanks. Can't believe I actually found someone. For a while there, I figured Skip and I were going to grow old together."

"Me, too," Skip drawled. "That's why I'm paying her."

Dave ignored the jab. "Take it from me. If you think she's the one, don't let her slip through your fingers."

"It's not that simple," Matt began, but Dave cut him off.

"It is. It really is."

Matt sighed quietly, knowing his friend was right. If all went well, Emma would be free from the reach of the traffickers soon. If he really wanted to have a relationship with her, he had to talk to her sooner rather than later.

His brain recognized the fact that he was running out of time, but his heart didn't want to bring up the topic while she was still worried about her mother. She was clearly grateful to him for his help—he needed to make sure she was free from danger before talking to her about the possibility of something more. The last thing he wanted was for her to feel that his assistance was in any way conditional.

"I'll talk to her," he said, taking another sip of water. "Soon," he added, to stave off any further comments from Dave. The man was experiencing the first blush of love, and it was clear he was trying to recruit all his friends to join him in couple land. Matt wanted to be annoyed with him, but in truth, he would love to have a relationship with Emma. To feel that heady rush of excitement over something new, tempered with the comforting knowledge that he had a partner by his side.

"I'm glad to hear it," Dave said. "Now, let's get into the nitty-gritty before Miss Emma comes back."

Matt nodded and leaned forward, grateful for the change of subject. He wasn't sure what it said about him that he'd prefer to talk paramilitary strategy rather than discuss his feelings about Emma. Fortunately, he felt his normal confidence return as they began to iron out the basic details of the upcoming operation.

He might not know how to tell Emma about his feelings, but he was damn sure going to keep her and Christina safe.

Emma finished changing Christina, but she didn't go back to the table right away. She gathered her daughter into her arms and swayed back and forth, enjoying the solid, warm weight of her baby against her chest. With so much going on, it felt good to take a time-out and simply be with her.

Dave and Skip seemed like they knew what they were doing. Both men sported wary eyes and hard smiles. They'd clearly seen combat, and while she wasn't going to pretend to know what that was like, she'd watched enough news stories to recognize it was an experience that changed a man.

Matt apparently trusted the pair—he wouldn't have called them otherwise. But Emma wasn't ready to make that leap quite yet. They were only two men against the traffickers; Dave had promised her they had more people to call, but how long would that take? And would they really be able to plan something that wouldn't tip off the traffickers?

She knew Matt had confidence in his friends' ability to blend in, but did that extend to the other people who worked with them? Her mind kicked into overdrive, easily imagining a scenario where the men realized they were being played and shot her mother without pause.

But more than that, more than her worries over her mom and yes, even Joseph, too, Emma was scared to death of putting Christina in jeopardy. The unpredictability of the situation bothered her most. Matt and his friends were starting from the assumption the traffickers were rational men. She wasn't so sure. What was going to stop them from shooting her on sight and taking her baby? Once they had her in arm's reach, there would be no further need for them to pretend they were there to make an exchange. It would be easy for them to kill her and make off with Christina before Dave or Skip or their friends could act.

And what about Matt? Where would he be while this was going on? She'd feel a lot better if he was by her side. From searching in the desert to the events of the past day, she'd grown used to having him around. She was starting to take his presence for granted, even though she recognized it was a mistake to do so. When all this was over, she and Christina were going back to El Paso. Given her earlier conversation with Matt, he wasn't going to be interested in joining them there.

Emma pressed her cheek against the side of Christina's head, breathing in the scents of shampoo and her soft skin. "I'm sorry, baby," she said quietly. "I know life has been crazy lately. It'll go back to normal soon, I promise."

Though after this scare, she wasn't sure she could leave Christina in day care while she worked. She was going to have a hard time with any separation from her baby, no matter how routine it may have been before.

"We'll figure it out," she promised. There wasn't any other choice; she wouldn't have Matt's help any longer.

A woman entered the restroom and gave her a funny look as she skirted Emma to enter a stall. Emma realized it probably seemed strange that she was standing in the middle of the place, rocking her baby as if she were trying to put her to sleep. "Time to go back," she said softly. Maybe the food had been delivered by now. Hopefully they could eat quickly and leave—being out of the hotel room made her feel exposed and vulnerable, despite knowing she was safe with Matt and his friends. Paranoia nipped at her heels, making her wonder if everyone they saw was somehow connected to the traffickers. That woman, for instance—did she have her phone out in the stall, punching in a text message to her contact?

Emma shook her head, hating the way her nerves were hijacking her brain. But until she knew the traffickers were no longer a threat, she was going to wonder...

She shouldered her bag once more and headed back

to the table. Matt stood to allow her to slide back into the booth. "Want me to get a high chair?"

"Yes, please."

He left, and she glanced over at Dave and Skip. Their food had arrived, but she noticed neither man had started eating. "I hope you weren't waiting for me," she said. "I didn't mean to take so long."

Skip shrugged. Dave said, "It's not a problem, ma'am. We all eat pretty fast, thanks to the army. Didn't want you coming back to find our plates empty."

"Well, thanks, then."

Matt returned with a wooden high chair that looked like it had seen better days. But the safety strap seemed to be in working order, so Emma buckled Christina in and silently vowed to bathe her when they returned to the hotel.

"I'll switch places with you," Matt offered. "That way you can still sit by her."

She stood, allowing him to move past her. Space was tight, and he brushed against her butt as he entered the booth. The contact was innocent enough, but it sent a zing through her legs and made her stomach flutter.

She sank down, hoping the men didn't notice her blush. Her skin felt tight, like it was too small for her body. She focused on mashing up some vegetables for Christina, waiting for her unwanted reaction to pass.

They all ate quietly for a few minutes. "Did you finish making your plans?" she asked. She wasn't sure how long the men needed to come up with a strategy, but since everyone seemed more interested in chew-

ing than talking, she figured maybe they hadn't required much time.

"Pretty much," Dave said. He took a healthy bite
of his burger but offered no additional information.

"And?" Was she going to have to beg them to fill her
in? Her jaw clenched in frustration—whatever they'd
come up with, she was going to have to play a part in
the activities. Why didn't they seem interested in making sure she knew what to expect?

"I'll tell you later," Matt said. "You've got nothing
to worry about."

He sounded so calm, but his words of reassurance
didn't help her nerves. Still, he'd brought her this far.
She was just going to have to trust him a bit longer.

What other choice did she have?

Chapter 13

It was late when they returned to the hotel room. Matt had spent the drive back from the restaurant filling her in on the basic details of the plan to stop the traffickers. He could tell from her body language that Emma wasn't totally on board with the strategy, but she'd put on a brave face. He wondered if there was anything he could do or say to make her feel more comfortable—she had to be nervous, but he wanted her to understand that tomorrow she was going to be safer than she thought.

The plan was for Skip to drive her to the diner. He'd stay in the car, pretending to be Matt, while Emma met with the men. Dave was going to provide cover from the overgrown lot across the road from the truck stop.

Dave and Skip were two of the finest men he'd

served with. They'd stayed in touch after they'd all left the army, and he'd followed their burgeoning private security business with interest. They'd offered him a position several times, but he'd always turned them down. Now, though, after feeling the rush that came with planning an operation, he was starting to wonder if he'd made the right decision.

"You're excited."

Matt turned to face Emma. She was sitting on the bed, snapping Christina into her pajamas. She didn't look unhappy with him; if anything, her expression was one of acceptance, as if she'd come to peace with something.

"I am," he confirmed. "But not in the way you think."

"Oh?"

He ran a hand through his hair, trying to find the words to explain his mood. "My adrenaline is up, that's true. But not because I'm happy about what we're going to do tomorrow. I wish we didn't have to confront these men, that your mother wasn't suffering at their hands."

A shudder passed through her. "Me, too."

"We've got a solid plan, though," he said. "And I'm confident we can save her."

"Are you looking forward to being in the action again? It's probably a lot different from your normal day-to-day activities."

"It is," he said. "And again, it's not something I'm going to celebrate. But I'm not going to shy away from it, either."

She didn't reply, instead busying herself with arranging the pillows on the bed. He recognized her behavior for what it was: an expression of nervous energy.

"We can handle this." He didn't approach the bed, didn't want to crowd her.

Emma looked up, her eyes bright with unshed tears. The sight hit him in the gut, made him want to reach out and fold her into his arms.

"I'm scared," she whispered. "I want to believe you, and I hope Dave and Skip can deliver on their promises. I just can't stop imagining the worst."

"That's only natural," he said. "I trust these guys because I served with them. We have a history together, and I know how they act when everything goes to hell. You don't have that benefit—you just met them. It makes sense you have doubts."

She nodded, appearing a little relieved. "That's exactly it. I'm trying to stay positive, but it's hard not to let my fear take control."

"If it makes you feel any better, I'm afraid, too."

She lifted one eyebrow. "No, actually. That doesn't help me."

He laughed at her dry response and stepped over to the bed, holding his arms out for the baby. "Let me take her. They should be calling soon."

Emma passed the baby over as she swallowed with an audible gulp. "Do you really think they'll agree?"

He shrugged. "What choice do they have? If they truly want Christina, they'll do whatever you ask."

"I hope you're right," she muttered. As if on cue, her phone buzzed.

"Hello?"

"Emma Foster?"

"Yes, it's me."

"So you can follow directions." The man's voice was smug,

Emma ignored his tone, wanting to get down to business. "You said you have my mother. Is that still true?"

"Maybe."

She bit her lip, glancing at him for guidance. Matt nodded encouragingly—he'd warned her they might try something like this to scare her, keep her on the defensive. She took a deep breath and spoke again.

"You're going to have to do better than that," she said. He was proud to hear a note of steel in her voice.

"Oh?"

"If you no longer have my mother, then I have no reason to talk to you."

"Okay, okay," said the man on the other end of the line. "We still have her."

"Prove it," Emma said.

The man cursed, but they heard the sound of shuffling. After a few seconds, a new voice came on the line. "Emma?"

Matt could tell by the look on her face it was her mother. "Mom, I'm coming for you. I'm going to get you out of there." Her tone was emotional, her distress written in the lines of her face. Matt reached out and grabbed her hand, squeezing it gently to remind her she wasn't alone.

"Emma, no. Forget about me. Protect Christina—"

She was suddenly cut off, and the sound of a muffled protest made Matt think she'd been gagged again.

"Happy now?" said the man who'd called.

"Hardly," Emma replied. "But at least I know she's still alive."

"Only if you do what we say," he threatened.

"I want to meet. Tomorrow."

"That's not your call," he said.

Emma ignored him. "I'll be at the truck stop off I-10 and Highway 90 at ten thirty tomorrow morning. If you don't meet me in the diner, I'll assume you no longer want my baby."

"Now wait just a—"

Emma hung up without another word and turned off the phone so they wouldn't have to listen to the traffickers try to call her back. She placed the phone on the nightstand with a sigh.

"You did great," Matt said encouragingly. It was the truth. She'd held up extremely well, under the circumstances. If it had been his mother's safety on the line, he doubted he could have been so composed.

Christina seemed to echo his sentiment. "Ga, ga, ga," she babbled. She patted his cheek with her pudgy hand, giggling as her palm made contact with his stubble. The sound wrapped around his heart, another invisible thread anchoring him to this little girl.

Emma smiled at them. "If you say so," she said. She sounded a little dejected, and sympathy welled up in his chest. He hated that she'd had to hear her mother in pain again, but it was important they knew she was still alive.

"What happens now?" she asked.

"I've got some things to take care of, but you need to get some rest."

She let out a humorless laugh. "I don't think I'll be able to sleep tonight."

"Maybe not, but you need to at least try," he said. "At least lie down and close your eyes for a bit."

"What about Christina?"

Matt shifted his hold on the baby, bouncing her a little to keep her happy. "She and I are good friends now. I'll take care of her until she falls asleep."

Emma studied him for a moment, and he got the impression she was debating whether or not to argue with him. He found himself silently urging her to let him stay with Christina. He wasn't sure how or when it had happened, but somewhere along the way he'd fallen head over heels for this baby. Since their time together was growing short, he wanted to be with her as much as possible.

"Okay," Emma said finally. "If you really don't mind watching her for a bit, I'm going to take a bath. I need to wash that man's voice off my body."

"We'll be here," he replied. He watched as Emma entered the bathroom, wishing there were something he could do to take away her fear and anxiety. But maybe he was helping; hopefully by watching her daughter, he was giving her an opportunity to focus on herself for a change. She just needed to take advantage of it.

"Come on, little one," he said. "We've got a project to work on."

He placed her on the bed, arranging the pillows to

make a soft fence around her. He'd seen her crawl and knew the pillows were no match for her skills, but the point was to make it harder for her to motor off the bed. While she was occupied with a toy, he grabbed the bags sitting nearby on the floor and dumped their contents on the spread.

She played contentedly while he worked, apparently happy to listen to his running commentary as he narrated what he was doing. She seemed to enjoy the sound of his voice, so he kept talking to her after he was done.

"I don't know how to tell you this," he said quietly. "But I've fallen for you and your mother."

Christina babbled a reply. It sounded encouraging, so he continued. "I'm not sure what will happen after all this is over. I just know that I want to stay in your life. If you and your mom will have me, that is."

It was so easy to talk to the baby. She looked up at him with those big blue eyes, seeming wise beyond her years. He poured his heart out to her, confessing all his hopes along with the worries holding him back.

"I want a family so badly," he finished. "And you came into my life. It almost seems like a sign."

Christina sighed as if in agreement.

"That settles it. I'm going to have to say something to your mama." If only he knew where to begin!

The baby yawned and rubbed her eyes, clearly over this conversation. He checked her diaper and laid her down on the bed, then sat next to her, gently stroking her back until she fell asleep.

It was a humbling thing, to help a baby drift off.

They were so innocent, so trusting. It made him feel special to know Christina was comfortable enough around him to settle down quickly.

"We're going to take care of you," he promised softly. "Your mom and I. We won't let anything bad happen to you again."

The bathroom door opened and Emma emerged, her skin pink from the heat of her bath. "Is she out?" she whispered.

He nodded. "Just now."

She walked over to the bed and gazed down at her baby, her heart in her eyes. "Thank you," she said softly.

"It was my pleasure."

She turned to him, her expression shy. "Do you mind if we share the other bed tonight? Just to sleep, not for anything else..." She glanced away, tucking a stray strand of hair behind her ear.

"That's fine," he said. He nodded at Christina, who was lying diagonally across the mattress. "Not much room in this one anyway."

Emma smiled. "True." She turned around to face the other bed. "Which side do you prefer?"

"I don't care," he replied. After sleeping in the desert, he was just happy to have something soft to sleep on. "I've got to take care of a few more things. Go ahead and pick a side."

"Do you need my help?"

He shook his head. "Thanks, but no. You get some rest."

She offered him a half smile. "I'll try."

Matt scooped the keys off the dresser and headed for the door. He drew it closed behind him, his eyes on Emma's slender figure under the sheets. She looked so small, so vulnerable.

But you're not, he told her silently as the door snicked shut. *I'm with you. And I'm not going to let you down.*

She wasn't sure what time he came to bed. It was late, that much she knew. Or rather, very early.

He slipped between the sheets, moving carefully. It was clear he was trying not to wake her, but he needn't have worried about that. She'd been staring at the ceiling all night, counting heartbeats in a vain attempt to lull her brain into a stupor.

Without thinking, she rolled over and reached for him. He jerked when her hands found his body, but he didn't pull away.

She scooted across the mattress until she was lying flush against him, feeling his warmth in a continuous line from her shoulders to her toes.

"Emma?"

She heard the question in his voice, knew what he was asking. "Just hold me, please," she said. She wasn't opposed to sex—it might actually help her fall asleep. But she'd already given him a large piece of her heart the first time they'd made love. She didn't think she could give him another and still survive when he walked away. Christina needed a mother who could take care of her, not a lovesick wreck who spent all day crying.

Matt's arms folded around her, and she rested her head on his chest. The steady thump of his heart echoed in her ear, a reminder that no matter what the future held in store, right now, in this moment, they were together.

It wasn't enough. If she had her way, she'd stop the world so she and Matt could spend more time together. She wanted the opportunity to explore the attraction between them. Her silly heart still held out hope he might change his mind about being a father to Christina. He was so good with her—why couldn't he just let himself love her?

It was on the tip of her tongue to ask, but she swallowed the question. She couldn't make him love her daughter, any more than she could control the tides. She wasn't sure what it said about her, that she'd fallen for a man who didn't want to help her raise her child. No matter, though. He'd be gone soon enough.

But he'd take a piece of her with him.

Emma could already feel it happening. Right next to the Chris-shaped hole in her heart, new cracks were starting to appear. She wasn't sure how extensive the damage would be, but she knew this experience—this man—would leave her forever changed.

Would Christina remember him at all? She was still so little, but growing more aware every day. Maybe Matt would be no more than a warm memory for her, a sensation of strength and safety. But at least the experience was a positive one, hopefully erasing any fear and anxiety left over from her kidnapping.

Matt stroked her back, his touch gentle and reassuring. Emma focused on the repetitive sensation, using it as an anchor to help her ignore her swirling thoughts.

She heard a low hum in his chest, followed by what might have been a whisper. "It's going to be okay."

I hope you're right, she thought, desperately wanting to believe him. She was ready to wake up from this nightmare, once and for all.

Chapter 14

"Emma. It's time."

She stirred, letting out a soft moan. Matt hated to wake her—she hadn't fallen asleep until the wee hours of the morning, and even then, her rest had been fitful.

He placed his hand on her shoulder, gave her a gentle shake. She rolled onto her back, her eyes blinking as she focused on his face.

He offered her a faint smile. "Morning."

She reached up to rub her eyes. "Is it?"

"I'm afraid so."

Emma sat up with a sigh, pulling her legs up to rest her arms on her knees. Her head drooped, and he could tell she was exhausted.

"I'm sorry," he said, sitting on the mattress next to her. "I wanted to let you sleep longer, but you've got to get going. Skip texted me—he's already in the parking lot waiting for you."

Skip was going to drive Emma and the decoy baby Matt had rigged up to the meeting at the diner. If everything went according to plan, the bad guys would be momentarily fooled by the fake baby, allowing Skip and Dave time to incapacitate them and free Emma's mother. They'd have plenty of backup; the two men were making sure the diner was filled with their people, posing as customers. The odds were in their favor, provided none of the traffickers got trigger-happy...

And as for him? Matt was supposed to stay here with Christina, far away from the action.

"It's okay," Emma said around a yawn. "I'm a mother and a nurse. Fatigue is pretty much my default setting."

He chuckled, wishing he had some caffeine to offer her. But their room didn't come with a coffee maker, and he didn't want to leave her to fetch her anything. With the meeting time drawing near, he wanted to spend every possible moment with her. Their time would come to an end soon enough.

She climbed out of bed and bent over her baby. Christina slept on the other mattress looking like a loaf of bread with her arms and legs curled up under her body. She'd woken a few times in the night, but Matt had managed to soothe her back to sleep before she could disturb Emma.

After satisfying herself that her daughter was fine, Emma headed into the bathroom. She emerged a few minutes later, her hair pulled back and dressed for the day.

"Are you ready?"

"As I'll ever be." But she didn't head for the door. Instead, she walked over to the desk and sat in the chair. She grabbed a piece of paper and wrote something on it, then handed it to him.

"What's this?" He kept his eyes on her, not liking her troubled expression.

She didn't meet his gaze. "Chris had a sister. I guess I should say *has*, because she's still alive. That's her contact information and address." She nodded at the paper in his hand. "If anything happens to me today…" She broke off, swallowed hard. "If something happens, promise me you'll take Christina to her."

"You don't need to worry about that—"

"Promise me." She looked up then, her brown eyes teary but filled with determination. Matt realized she needed to hear him say the words for her own peace of mind. It was the same with some of the men he'd served with in the army; before a big mission, they'd write letters home and entrust them to the care of others on base, with instructions to post them if the worst should happen. Matt hadn't ever done that. Maybe he was a little superstitious, but he didn't like to dwell on negative possibilities. Still, he understood that Emma, as a mother, would need to make sure her daughter was taken care of in case she couldn't be there.

"I will," he said, reaching out to grasp her hand. "Nothing's going to happen to you. But if it makes you feel better, I promise to take Christina to her aunt's if the need arises."

Emma nodded. "She doesn't know about any of this. But she'll do the right thing."

"She won't have to," Matt said. He needed Emma to believe him. She was about to walk into the lion's den. She needed to project confidence, or she might not make it back out again.

It won't come to that, he told himself. He trusted Dave and Skip, and by extension, their people. They would keep her safe.

Or answer to him.

"All right." Her tone was final—she was ready to get on with it. She stood and walked over to the bed, staring down at her daughter with so much love in her eyes Matt felt as though he could reach out and touch it.

"I don't want to wake her," she whispered. "But I have to kiss her goodbye."

She bent and pressed her lips to her sleeping baby's cheek. He heard her draw in a deep breath, then she straightened and walked toward the door, stopping only to pick up Christina's car seat. He'd made a decoy baby of sorts last night while Emma bathed. It wasn't sophisticated enough to fool anyone at close range, but hopefully it would buy Emma and her mother some time to get away from the men before Dave and Skip's people closed in.

Matt chased after her, catching her just outside the room. "Hey. Don't I get a goodbye, too?"

Her smile was brittle. "Of course." She put the

carrier on the floor and held up her arms, leaning in for a hug.

Matt drew her close, pressing his nose into her hair. He held her tight, trying to tell her without words how he felt. After a moment, she relaxed against him in a silent gesture of trust.

He pulled back, cupped her face with his hands, then leaned in to brush his lips against hers. An electric sizzle arced through him at the contact, but this wasn't a kiss of passion or arousal—it was a communion. She was hurting, and he lacked the words to help. So he offered her support in the only way left to him.

Emma's lips were stiff and unyielding, but after a second, she relaxed into his kiss. Her hands threaded through his hair, hesitant at first, then her touch grew stronger as the moment wore on.

She sighed against his mouth, a quiet, soft sound of surrender. Hearing it, Matt eased back, resting his forehead against hers as he stared into the brown depths of her eyes.

"I'll be waiting for you," he promised. "We have things to talk about once you're done."

Emma nodded, her tongue darting out across her lips. "Yes. That's true." She took a step back, her hands falling from his hair to glide down his arms and stop at his hands, which she gripped tightly. "Take care of her for me. She's my world."

He lifted one of her hands to his mouth, kissing the back of it. "You have my word."

With that, she pulled free, bending to pick up the carrier once more. He watched her walk down the hall and enter the elevator, taking his heart with her. Did she even know she carried it? Or was she oblivious to its presence?

He'd let her know soon enough. For now, he had a job to do.

He walked back into the room and checked on the baby. She had her eyes open and was blinking sleepily up at the ceiling. "Excellent timing, Christina." He was glad she'd woken up on her own—she was much less likely to be cranky now.

After a quick diaper change, he scooped her into his arms and headed for the door, stopping to grab her diaper bag along the way. After Emma had crawled into bed last night, he'd gone to the nearby big-box store and bought a car seat, which he'd installed in his truck. Matt had no intention of waiting in the hotel room, twiddling his thumbs while Emma walked into danger. It killed him a little bit to let Skip take her to the truck stop, despite knowing his friend was more than capable of handling things. He simply wasn't used to sitting on the sidelines while an operation went down. But he wasn't willing to risk Christina, either. So as a compromise, he was going to hunker down in the burger joint next door to the truck stop. If everything went to hell, he'd be close enough to help while still keeping the baby safe.

He dialed Dave after snapping the little one into her seat.

"Yeah?"

"Change of plan," Matt said shortly. "Take one

of your people out of the diner and send them to the burger joint next door."

"Now why would I want to do that?" Dave asked.

"Because I'll be waiting there with the baby. If things go south, I need to be able to leave Christina with someone so I can help Emma. Have them bring a gun for me, too."

Dave sighed. "I should have known you'd pull a stunt like this."

Matt cranked the engine of the truck and stepped on the gas. The meet was still a few hours away, but he had a bit of a drive ahead of him. "Are you going to help me, or what?"

"You know, I ought to make you charge into battle with a baby strapped to your chest, but I'm not going to do that to Miss Emma. I'll send someone over."

"Appreciate it," Matt said, merging onto the freeway.

"Though you should know, I don't appreciate your lack of confidence in my skills." Dave sounded a little piqued, and Matt realized he'd inadvertently stepped on his friend's toes.

"Sorry, man. It's got nothing to do with you. Put yourself in my shoes. Pretend it's your woman going into that diner. Tell me you wouldn't do the same."

"You're right," Dave allowed. "I'd call an audible like this, too."

"Everyone in position?" Matt asked.

"Mostly. They're filing in a few at a time so it doesn't seem too suspicious."

"Seen any advance scouts?" The traffickers were

cocky, but Matt didn't think they were stupid. Unless he missed his guess, they were sending people to the diner to check things out before bringing Emma's mother and brother there.

"A couple," Dave replied. "They've done a few quick drive-bys, but they don't seem to be paying too much attention to faces."

"That's good," Matt said. If the scouts weren't focused on the people in the diner, they wouldn't get suspicious when those same people were still sitting there during the meet.

"We've got this covered, LT."

"I know you do. Need me to pick up anything along the way?"

"I'd run naked down the highway for a hot cup of coffee right now."

Matt had to laugh at the absurd mental image Dave's words conjured. "I'm half-tempted to bring you one just to see that. But I don't want to give away your position." Dave was stretched out in the overgrown field near the truck stop, ghillie suit in place to help him blend in with the tall grass.

"Fair enough. But I'm definitely getting a cup when this is all over."

"Buddy, when this is over you won't have to settle for coffee. I'll buy you a stiff drink."

"Whiskey?" Dave suggested, his tone hopeful. "The good stuff, mind, not that cheap swill Skip likes to drink."

"Whatever you want," Matt promised.

"I'm going to hold you to that," Dave said. "Now get

to driving. I need to keep this line clear in case Skip needs to get in touch."

"Roger that," Matt replied. "See you soon."

"No," said Dave. "You won't. Master of disguise, remember?"

"How could I forget? Stay safe out there."

"Hooah," replied Dave, signing off with the army battle cry.

"Hooah," echoed Matt into the dial tone.

Christina gurgled a reply of her own, legs kicking in her seat. He smiled at her, though she couldn't see him. "Tell me about it," he said encouragingly.

She continued to babble as he drove, filling him with a sense of peace. He was still nervous about Emma and the traffickers, but somehow the sound of Christina's voice soothed his worries and gave him a reason to smile.

"We make a good team, baby girl."

"Da, da, da," she said.

His heart skipped a beat, even as he recognized she wasn't really calling him Da-da. She was simply testing out new syllables and had landed on this one for a change. Still, an odd sensation swirled in his chest—a mixture of pride and gratitude.

And love.

It was time he stopped denying it. He was in love with Emma, and Christina, too, for that matter. He wasn't sure how they were going to make things work, given the fact that they lived in El Paso and he lived several hours away in Alpine. But he was certain they would figure it out. They had to—he simply couldn't walk away from the two of them, not after everything they'd been through together. They'd had enough excitement to last three lifetimes; now Matt wanted to experience all the normal, boring moments with Emma and Christina. Doing the laundry, washing the dishes, cooking a big Saturday breakfast; it sounded wonderful to him.

And maybe someday, after they'd become a family together, Christina would call him Daddy for real.

Matt held on to that thought, tucking it safely away in his heart. He'd dwell on his dreams later. Right now, he couldn't afford to let his hopes for the future cloud the present.

He glanced over at the baby, still kicking away in her seat. He wasn't going to rest until he had both of his girls in his arms, safe and sound.

"Almost there," he muttered.

In more ways than one.

Skip cut the engine and turned to face her. "How are you holding up?"

Emma scanned the parking lot, a stone of worry forming in her stomach when she spotted the semitruck the traffickers had used before. "I'll manage," she said. She nodded toward the truck. "They're here already."

"Not to worry," Skip said. "Our people got here first. And you're not going out there unprotected." He rapped his knuckle against one of the panels of the bulletproof vest she wore under her jacket. Pessimistically, Emma knew it would offer little protection if the traffickers aimed for her head, but it was better than nothing.

Skip's voice broke into her thoughts. "Let's test this thing out one last time." He turned around, eyeing the car seat in the back with a degree of suspicion. "I can't believe LT actually put this thing together," he muttered.

"This thing" was the decoy Matt had created last night while she'd been in the bath. It was at its heart a motorized dinosaur toy Matt had bought—press a button, the creature walked. Matt had padded the legs and slipped a pair of Christina's pants over them, making it look more like a baby. He'd ripped the tail off so the overgrown lizard fit in the car seat, and somehow he'd disabled the voice so the creature no longer roared when the remote was used. As a final touch, Matt had draped a blanket over the front of the carrier, leaving only the legs visible. It was a contraption that would make Dr. Frankenstein proud, but Emma had no illusions about its ability to fool anyone for long.

Skip pressed the button on the remote, which was taped to the side of the carrier. The legs kicked in response, making it look like the "baby" was moving. Emma caught Skip's eye as he turned back around. He shrugged. "Should fool 'em for a minute, I suppose."

"If you say so."

"You remember the plan?"

She nodded, feeling curiously detached. She didn't dare hope this was going to work. But she had to at least try to save her mother. Her only consolation was that Christina was far away from all this, safe with Matt back in the hotel room.

"All right." Skip nodded, apparently satisfied with

her response. "Remember, we're with you. It's all going to be okay."

She heard his words, but they didn't give her the warm, fuzzy feeling she got when Matt told her the same thing. She wished he could be here as well—she'd feel so much better knowing he was close—but then again, she was grateful he'd stayed with her baby. There was no one else she trusted to protect her daughter.

Skip dropped his chin and spoke into the collar of his shirt. "Showtime," he said, apparently communicating with the rest of his team. Then he looked at Emma. "You're up, ma'am."

Emma climbed out of the car and started toward the diner, feeling eyes on her as she walked. Sunlight glinted off glass, and she glanced over to see a truck pulling into the parking lot of the burger joint next door. She frowned slightly. That looked like Matt's truck... but it couldn't be. Emma shook her head slightly and forced herself to keep going. She wanted him to be here so badly she was practically hallucinating him. Yet another reminder of how attached she'd grown to him over the past few days.

The bell attached to the diner door jingled as she walked inside. Motion caught her eye, and she turned to see a man waving at her from a corner table. She recognized his scar—he was one of the three men who'd chased her before. But the other seats at the table were empty. Where were her mother and brother?

She approached the table but didn't sit down. "Where's my mother?"

The man cocked his head to the side. "Where's Christina?" When she didn't reply, his expression darkened. "I hope, for your mother's sake, that you aren't having second thoughts."

Emma ground her molars together, hating this man and everything about him. "My baby is in the car. Did you honestly expect me to just hand her over to you without first knowing my mom is alive?"

"Fair enough," he said. He got to his feet, and Emma took a step back, not wanting to risk touching him. "What happened to the man who was with you earlier? The one you ran away with?"

"He's in the car with my daughter."

The man stared at her, his eyes narrowing with displeasure. "We told you to come alone."

Emma stood her ground. "I can go, if you prefer. I'm sure your boss will understand." She smiled, driving the insult home.

The look he gave her was pure malice. Emma was certain he would hurt her if he thought he could get away with it. "Get the baby," he said shortly. "Your friend stays in the car."

"Not until I see my mother."

He clenched his jaw so tightly she thought his teeth would break. "You'll have to come over to the truck to see her."

"Fine. Let's go." She wasn't going to be a meek, compliant sheep. She was going to make this difficult for them, every step of the way.

She could tell her reaction surprised him. Truth be told, she'd surprised herself. Matt had told her she was

strong enough to face these men, but she hadn't believed him. Now that she was here, though, she was
ready to take them on single-handedly to save her
mother.

Maybe he had been right after all...

They stepped out into the parking lot and headed
for the back corner, where the semitruck was parked.
Emma resisted the urge to stare at the nearby field—
according to Matt and Skip, she'd never find Dave, no
matter how hard she looked. She just had to trust that
he was there.

The man pulled a small two-way radio from his
belt and brought it to his mouth. "Get ready." Then he
led Emma to the trailer of the semitruck. She stopped
as they approached—the truck was parked so that the
gate faced the empty field. If she stepped behind it, no
one from the diner would be able to see her. He could
kill her and shove her body into the trailer with no one
but Dave the wiser.

The trafficker gave her a questioning glance, but
didn't try to force her to join him. He walked up to the
trailer and knocked three times on the gate. She heard
a metallic rumble as the gate was lifted, and a wedge
of light cut through the shadow cast by the trailer.

"You're going to have to get closer if you want to
see her."

Emma gave the man a wide berth, keeping him
in front of her as she skirted the edge of the trailer.
She craned her neck to see, then froze as she caught a
glimpse of the inside.

The interior of the trailer was padded with what looked like soundproofing material. That alone was enough to make her skin crawl, but what nearly sent her over the edge was the fact that it was all draped in heavy plastic. There wasn't a knife or a chain or a drill to be seen, and yet it was very clear this trailer was used for only one purpose: to torture people.

A small figure sat tied to a wooden chair in the middle of the torture chamber, head bent in defeat. Emma's heart leaped into her throat—was she still alive?

"Mom?"

At the sound of her voice, the woman lifted her head. "Emma?"

Relief washed over Emma even as her stomach turned at the sight of her mother's bruised and bloody face. "It's okay, Mom. I'm here to get you. I'm going to take you away from these men."

Her mother's expression of joy turned to one of horror. "No, baby. No. You can't give them Christina. Just leave me here. Go!" Her voice grew increasingly frantic and she began to strain against her bonds.

A man stepped forward from out of the shadows and stuffed a rag in her mother's mouth. "Stop it!" Emma yelled. "Leave her alone!"

She was so preoccupied with her mother she didn't notice that the man from the diner was now by her side. He grabbed her arm, his grip tight to the point of pain. "Shut up," he hissed, punctuating his words with a little shake. "Behave yourself, or I will make you wish you had."

Emma closed her mouth, though not out of fear for herself. She didn't want them to hurt her mom any more.

He pulled her away from the trailer, back out into the parking lot. "So. Now you know she is alive. Time to get the baby."

She tried to shake him off, but he wouldn't release her arm. She led him toward Skip's car, but he pulled her back before they got too close.

"This is not the car you were in before."

She wrenched her arm free, turning to glare at him. "No, it's not. We switched vehicles because we didn't want you to find us."

Was that a glimmer of respect in his eyes? "Smart."

"I'm so glad you approve," she snapped. "Now come on."

He grabbed her again before she could take a step. She opened her mouth to cry out, but the sound died in her throat as she felt something press into her side. *A gun*, she realized with a jolt of panic.

"Listen to me," he said softly. "We only want the baby. If your friend tries to get out of the car, if he tries to help you at all, I'm going to kill you and then shoot him between the eyes. You tell him not to be a hero today." When she didn't respond, he shook her again. "Tell him."

Emma made eye contact with Skip, who was leaning forward over the steering wheel. She made a production of shaking her head, and Skip nodded, relaxing back into his seat.

"Good girl," the man said. "Now we'll continue."

They marched over to the car. Emma opened the

back door and retrieved the carrier, being careful to keep the remote hidden by her body.

The man stood by the driver's-side window and gestured for Skip to roll it down. Skip opened it a crack.

"Drive off," he said. Skip began to protest, and the man showed him his gun. "Leave, now. Before I shoot you."

Skip gave her an apologetic look and cranked the engine. The man kept her there until Skip pulled out of the parking spot and turned onto the freeway access road.

Emma watched him go, disbelief and a sense of betrayal swirling in her chest. She knew she wasn't alone, but she couldn't believe Skip had up and left her like that, without a backward glance. A kernel of doubt formed in her mind. What if the others were like that, too? Were they still in the diner, or had they left already? And what about Dave? What if he was asleep out there in that field?

Her mind raced as they started to walk back to the trailer. The diner seemed like an awfully long way away, especially now that she was alone with this man, holding a fake baby in a car seat. He had a gun—it wouldn't take long to shoot her and her mother once he found out he'd been had. What could she do to even the odds?

"Where's my brother?" she blurted out. It wasn't much, as far as stalling tactics went, but it was better than nothing.

The man smirked. "I thought you didn't care about him."

She mulled that over for a second. "I don't. But I also don't want to see him hurt."

He snorted. "Trust me. He's not feeling any pain."

His words hit her like a slap to the face. Joseph was dead.

A thousand memories flooded her mind as her heart contracted painfully. Scenes from their childhood flashed before her eyes, and the sound of his voice echoed in her ears. Her nose burned as she fought the urge to cry.

The man glanced over, one brow raised. "Guess you care a little more than you thought."

Emma didn't respond. She took a deep breath and kept walking. As much as it pained her, she didn't have the luxury of mourning Joseph now. There would be time for that later.

If she survived.

She slowed her steps as they neared the semi. The man noticed, looking back with a frown. "Come on."

"No." Emma stopped, planting her feet in place. "I'm staying here. You bring my mother to me, and I'll hand you the baby."

He eyed the carrier with suspicion. Emma discreetly pushed the button on the remote, making the legs kick a few times.

"Fine," he muttered. "Whatever." He pulled his radio free from his belt and said something she couldn't make out. A few minutes later, Emma saw movement at the back of the trailer. Her mother walked into the parking lot, blinking at the sunlight. She was flanked by two men, but Emma only had eyes for her.

The truck engine roared to life, the semi nosing its way out of the parking spot.

"Does she know about Joseph?"

"Seeing as how he was killed in front of her, yeah." The trafficker's tone was casual, as if he inflicted this kind of cruelty on a daily basis.

In that moment, Emma could have killed him with her bare hands. Only her mother's precarious position kept her from wrapping her fingers around his throat and squeezing the life from him.

"You're a monster," she said, raising her voice to be heard above the noise of the truck, which had pulled closer to their position.

He turned to face her, his eyes cold and hard. "No. Just a survivor."

He lifted his arm, pointing the gun at her mother. Too late, Emma saw what she had missed before. The semitruck had pulled between them and the diner, obscuring them from view of the people seated within. They were going to kill her mother and probably her, then drive off with the baby carrier before anyone realized what had happened.

Acting on instinct, Emma gathered all her strength and swung the carrier at the man. She made contact with his shoulder, hitting his arm just as he fired.

One of the men flanking her mother jerked and dropped to the ground, apparently struck by the errant bullet. Emma didn't have time to worry about the other guard—she was still focused on the man in front of her.

He turned to her with an expression of murderous

rage. "You bitch!" he shouted. He tried to lift his arm again, this time to shoot her. She threw the carrier at him, hitting him solidly in the chest.

She didn't wait to see how he reacted. She pivoted on her heel and dived for her mother as a thunderous boom split the air next to her. She dragged her mom to the ground, noting with some surprise the other guard was now lying motionless on the cement.

There was another loud noise, followed by a pained cry. She glanced behind her to find the man from the diner on his knees, holding his stomach. His eyes were full of shock and pain as he dropped to the ground.

A roar filled the air as the driver gunned the engine and stepped on the gas. As the truck jerked forward, Emma saw people pouring out of the diner, all manner of weapons in their hands. The truck made for the exit, but a quick succession of pops was followed by a loud burst of air as several of the truck's tires blew out. The semi swerved onto the road, lurching drunkenly. She watched in amazement as Skip's car raced up from behind, running the big truck off the road before it could get very far.

Emma turned back to her mother, who was huddled on the ground, her thin shoulders shaking. "It's okay, Mom. It's going to be all right."

People surrounded them, their hands gentle as they helped her mother lie flat. "We're field medics, ma'am," said one of the men who was leaning over her. "We're going to take care of you until the ambulance arrives."

The circle of people closed around her mother, and

Emma stepped back to find a few people working on the man from the diner. She stepped over to lend a hand.

A quick glance at his injury told her he wasn't long for this world. Emma knelt and shook his shoulder. "Tell me about your boss," she said. He had to know he was going to die—maybe it would loosen his tongue, and the authorities could put an end to this organization.

He opened his eyes, staring up at her with undisguised hatred. "Why should I do that?" he wheezed. He coughed, then winced, closing his eyes again.

"This is your last chance to do something good," she said. "Why not try to earn a little forgiveness before you die?"

He cracked open his eyelids. "Maybe you're right," he said. His voice was so quiet she had to lean forward to hear. He craned his head up to meet her, and his mouth split into a terrible grin.

"See you in hell."

"Gun!"

She heard the shout even as the man brought his hand up, pressing his weapon into her stomach, just below the edge of the vest she wore. A thunderous roar of shots sounded, and the man's body jerked as a hail of bullets tore into him. His arm moved, but not enough. A hot knife of pain slid just under her ribs, knocking her back onto the ground.

Emma stared up at the sky, too dazed to move. Faces came into her field of vision, all of them frowning. People began to poke and prod at her, but she was rapidly growing numb to the sensations. Her vision grew hazy as darkness closed in. Just before it took her, Matt's face came into view. She frowned, tried to reach up to touch him. But the effort was too much, and she slipped away without a sound.

Chapter 15

The hospital waiting room was chilly and smelled so strongly of disinfectant it made the inside of Matt's nose burn. Christina was deeply unhappy—her eyes were swollen and red-rimmed from crying, though she was quiet at the moment. He offered her a pouch of applesauce, but she turned up her nose in refusal. She had to be hungry; it had been hours since he'd last fed her while they waited in the burger place. But the baby refused to eat and showed no interest in toys, either.

"Ma, ma, ma," she wailed. The little one wanted her mother, that much was clear. Her distress broke Matt's heart. He was willing to move heaven and earth to make her happy again, but the one thing he couldn't do right now was reunite her with the person who was her world.

He scooped her up and began to pace the empty waiting room. Dave and Skip, along with the members of their team, were still at the truck stop talking to the police, who'd arrived shortly after the ambulance. Matt hadn't bothered to stick around; he'd climbed into the back of the ambulance, carrying Christina in her car seat, refusing to leave Emma's side. The paramedics had initially resisted letting him and the baby come along, but they'd given in after Matt had made it clear he wasn't going anywhere.

Now Emma was in surgery, and he and Christina were relegated to this hospital purgatory while they waited for an update.

His mind was in high gear, flitting from one thought to another without really landing anywhere. He felt scattered, unsettled, pulled in a thousand different directions. Was Emma going to survive? If she didn't, what was he going to do? Emma had asked him to give Christina to her aunt, but could he follow through? He loved this baby—he wasn't sure he could stand to lose both her and her mother.

He paused before a monitor hung on the wall, reading the text on the screen. Emma was the only patient in surgery right now. He'd hoped for an update, but her status seemed to be stuck on "in progress."

Maybe that's okay, he thought. *She might already be done, and someone's just forgotten to punch it into the computer.* The operating room was probably a pretty busy place, and updating the monitors in the waiting room was likely low on the list of priorities. With any luck, Emma was being wheeled to recovery right now, still groggy from the anesthesia but on the road to recovery.

Or maybe her injury is worse than it looked. He'd only caught a glimpse of her side in the ambulance. From what he'd seen, the bullet had entered just below the bottom curve of her rib cage, on the right side. He racked his brain, trying to recall what organs were in that vicinity. *Stomach? No,* he realized with a creeping sense of dread. *It's the liver.*

His heart dropped and he cursed quietly. The liver was a pretty important part. Hopefully hers wasn't damaged beyond repair...

Without knowing it, Matt tightened his grip on Christina. She let out a yelp of protest, making him jump. She started to cry as he began to sway back and forth, sputtering apologies as he moved.

"She's scared, just like you."

Matt turned at the voice to find Emma's mother sitting in a wheelchair. A hospital orderly locked the wheels into place and straightened. "Can I get you anything before I go?"

"No, thank you, dear," she said. Her gaze never left Christina; she looked at the baby with a powerful hunger in her eyes that was obvious despite the bandage obscuring part of her left eye.

The orderly left the room, and Matt walked over to the woman. "Matt Thompson," he said, taking the chair next to her. "I helped your daughter look for Christina."

"I'm Maria," the older lady replied. She reached out to touch Christina's leg. "Are you all right, sweetheart?"

Christina turned to hide her face in his neck. Matt felt pleased but mildly embarrassed by her reaction. "I'm sorry," he said. "She's just really upset right now, and—"

Maria waved off his words. "It's fine. I don't look like myself, and the child has been through quite a lot recently." She studied him for a moment, her expression reminding him of Emma's scrutiny when they'd first met. "We all have," she murmured, her eyes welling with tears.

Matt's heart went out to the woman. Not only had she been slapped around by the traffickers, she'd been forced to watch them kill her son. "I'm so sorry for your loss," he said, wishing there was something else he could say to help ease her pain.

She smiled sadly, then nodded at him in acknowledgment. With a visible effort, she changed the subject.

"I'm glad to see Christina is so comfortable with you"

"Me, too," Matt said simply.

They sat in silence for a few moments. Christina gradually began to sneak glances at her grandmother, who pretended not to notice. Eventually, she reached out a chubby hand and placed it on Maria's arm.

"Can you hold her? Or will it hurt you?"

"I don't care if it does hurt. I want to hug my baby girl."

Matt carefully placed Christina on Maria's lap, smiling at their reunion. Then he turned his gaze back to the monitor, hoping to see an update…

"Do you love her?"

Matt glanced back at Maria, debating on how to respond. Part of him wanted to hedge and tell her he cared about Emma. After all, he hadn't said those three words to Emma yet, and shouldn't she be the first to know? But he took one look at Christina and knew he had to be honest. If the worst happened, if Emma were to die on the table… He wanted Maria to know that he loved her daughter, and her granddaughter. He wanted to be a part of their lives for as long as they would have him.

"Yes," he said simply.

"Emma?" Maria asked. "Or Christina?"

"Yes," he repeated.

She nodded, as if confirming some private suspicion. After a few minutes, Christina started babbling "da, da, da." He glanced over to find her reaching for him.

He scooped her up and held her close. His heart lightened a bit as she patted his chest. What was it about this baby that could brighten even his darkest days? "There's my girl," he said, smiling at her.

"Yes," murmured Maria. "I believe she is."

Her remark filled him with joy, but before he could respond, the door to the waiting room opened and the surgeon walked in.

Matt tried to read the woman's expression as she approached, but she had a mean poker face. She pulled up a chair and sat, leaning forward to brace her elbows on her knees.

"Emma's out of surgery," she said. "It was a complicated operation, but she did well. We had to remove parts of her liver, but there's enough left that it shouldn't affect her day-to-day life."

Matt felt something loosen in his chest, and for the first time since seeing Emma lying in the parking lot, he took a deep breath. "So she's going to be okay?"

The woman nodded. "If we don't see any complications in the coming days, I think she'll make a good recovery."

He frowned, not liking the sound of that. "Complications?"

The surgeon shrugged. "There are always risks after this type of operation. But we'll be monitoring Emma closely. She's an otherwise healthy woman. Try not to worry. Just focus on your daughter—let us take care of your wife."

Matt didn't bother to correct her as she rose and walked out of the waiting room. He turned to Maria with tears of relief in his eyes, only to find her crying, as well.

"She's going to be okay," he said, reaching for the older woman's hand.

She nodded, too overcome with emotion to speak.

Acting on instinct, Matt leaned forward and put his arm around her, hugging her gently as he cradled Christina against his chest. *So this is what it feels like.*

Maria pulled back a bit. "What did you say?"

He blushed, not realizing he'd spoken the words aloud. "I was just thinking this is what it feels like to have a family."

She smiled and patted his cheek. "All it takes is love."

And just like that, all of Matt's worries about the future faded into insignificance. The distance between Alpine and El Paso, their two jobs, their separate apartments—none of it really mattered. He loved Emma, and he loved Christina. That was all that was important. They would work the rest of it out, handling things as they came up. They were starting with a foundation of love. What more could they need?

"Have you told her yet?" Maria asked.

"Ah, no," he replied. "Not yet."

Maria merely arched an eyebrow. "I know," he said sheepishly, ducking his head. "But the time was never right."

"And now?"

"I'm not going to wait anymore," he promised. "I'm going to tell her soon."

"Good." Maria dabbed at her eyes. "After the events of the past few days, I need something happy in my life. Lord knows Emma deserves it, as well."

Yes, she does, he thought. And hopefully he was the man who could make her happy.

Three days later

Emma adjusted the angle of the hospital mattress, wincing slightly as the motion pulled at her stitches. She was still sore from the operation, but growing stronger by the day. The doctors said she might be able to leave in a couple of days, and she was already counting down the minutes.

Not that she was lonely. Her mother visited frequently, as did Matt and Christina. They were staying in a nearby hotel, and according to her mother, Matt was taking excellent care of her baby.

Emma wasn't surprised to hear it, but she was going crazy being away from her daughter for so long. Her spirits soared every time Matt brought her in for a visit, and her heart crashed back to earth every time they left. She knew a hospital was no place for an active baby, but that didn't stop her from missing her little one.

She appreciated all that Matt was doing for her— he'd basically put his life on hold to take care of her mother and Christina until Emma was released from the hospital. Still, a small part of her wished he would leave already. It felt like their goodbye was being prolonged, a long, slow stretch that was going to hurt all the more when it was finally over. She'd prefer to get through it quickly, like ripping off a bandage. The pain would still be there, but the acute sting would fade faster than this parting by inches.

Even though her personal life was in turmoil, Emma took comfort from the fact that the traffickers were being brought to justice. Detective Randall had sounded practically giddy when he'd called to let her know the status of the case. Dave and Skip and their people had lived up to Matt's esteem; they'd subdued all the traffickers at the diner and called in the authorities to make arrests. The police and FBI were having a field day questioning everyone, and apparently the mid-level manager in charge of things was cooperating in exchange for protection.

It made her angry to know the man who had overseen the killing of her brother and the torture of her mother might walk free. But hopefully the information he provided could help the police save other lives.

Joseph's face flashed through her mind. It didn't seem real that he was gone. She hadn't gotten to say goodbye. But really, what would she have told him? His recent actions had poisoned her feelings toward him. Logically, she knew she shouldn't throw away a lifetime of memories, but she wasn't sure how to process her brother's death. It was a complicated issue, one that would take her a long time to work through.

Her thoughts were interrupted by a perfunctory rap on her door. Matt poked his head into the room. "Morning," he said with a smile.

She smiled back, anxious to see Christina. "Hello."

He walked in and immediately passed the baby to her. Emma pressed her nose to her daughter's hair and inhaled deeply, the baby scent filling her lungs and bringing with it a sense of bliss. She kissed one petal-soft cheek, then rubbed her nose against Christina's, to her baby's delight.

Matt watched them from the chair, his pale blue eyes full of warmth. "She has a new trick," he said.

"Oh? What's that?"

"She's using the furniture to pull herself up, and she's now able to stand unassisted for several seconds at a time." He sounded like a proud father, as though she'd discovered the cure for cancer instead of her sense of balance.

"That is impressive!" She kissed Christina's other

cheek, feeling simultaneously joyful at her daughter's new milestone and sad because she had missed it.

Matt put his hand on her shoulder, squeezing gently. "Don't worry," he said softly. "I won't let her start walking yet. We'll wait for you."

She nodded, not knowing what to say. Christina reached for him, and he scooped her up easily. "Shall we take another tour of Mommy's room?" he asked. He began walking around, pointing out all the different things in her hospital room, from the IV pole to the telephone. Christina relaxed in his arms, enjoying his narration.

Emma watched them, her heart feeling torn. Matt was so good with her daughter, and it was clear her baby loved him. The longer he stayed, the more attached she was going to become. It wasn't fair of him to do that to her child. She'd been through enough in the last few weeks—his leaving was going to be one more blow to her, one she didn't deserve.

Matt caught her looking at them. Her thoughts must have shown on her face, because he paused in mid-sentence. "Everything okay?"

"What are you doing here?"

He frowned slightly, as if trying to assess her mental competence. "I'm giving Christina a tour of the room so she doesn't get bored. Do you want to rest now? We can come back later."

"No, that's not what I meant."

He tilted his head to the side. "Then what do you mean?"

"Why are you still here? My daughter loves you.

Every moment you spend with her is going to make it that much harder on her when you finally say goodbye. I appreciate what you're doing, but you've got to stop."

He walked over to the chair and sat again, bouncing Christina on his knee to keep her from protesting. "What if I don't want to stop?"

Now it was Emma's turn to frown. "I don't understand."

"You're worried about Christina's reaction to me saying goodbye. Well, what if I don't leave?"

"Don't leave?" she echoed dumbly. "You mean stay with us?"

He took a deep breath, nodded. "That's exactly what I mean."

Emma tried to puzzle out what he was saying, but she felt three steps behind. Maybe the pain meds were making her fuzzy.

Matt leaned forward, his expression earnest. "I've been meaning to tell you this, but there was never a good time. Hell, this probably isn't the best time, either, but I'm tired of waiting. I love you, Emma. And I want to be a part of your life. Yours and Christina's."

She felt a sudden rush of happiness at his words, but it fizzled out a heartbeat later. "You don't mean that," she said sadly.

"What?" Confusion swept over his face. "Why would you say that?"

"Fisher."

He froze at the little boy's name. "What does Fisher have to do with us?"

"You told me you left Jennifer because you couldn't

be a father to Fisher since he wasn't yours. Well, Christina isn't yours, either. What makes you think you want to be a father to her?"

He was quiet a moment. When he spoke, his tone was carefully neutral. "You think I left Jennifer because I didn't want to raise a child that wasn't mine by blood?"

"Didn't you?" Frustration lent an edge to her voice. Why was he arguing with her when she was only repeating what he'd told her?

"No. I left because she lied to me. I wasn't going to have a relationship with someone who would deceive me like that."

His words hit her like hailstones, each one cold and hard. She sat very still, absorbing this revelation.

Wondering why she hadn't realized it before.

How could she have been so blind?

Of course Matt wouldn't have wanted to stay with a cheater. Who would? She scanned back through her memories, reexamining every conversation they'd had that featured Fisher. Matt's love for the little boy had been clear every time. He hadn't wanted to leave the baby. But he couldn't stay with the boy's mother. So he'd had to walk away from them both.

Hot shame flooded Emma's system, making her skin flush. "Oh my God." She'd misjudged him so badly. She'd misinterpreted everything he'd told her about his past, and she'd let that misunderstanding cloud her feelings for him.

"I'm so sorry." She shook her head, unable to meet his eyes. "I don't know why I didn't see that before."

"You were worried about Christina," he said quietly.

He was trying to let her off the hook. It was better than she deserved. "That's true. But it's not an excuse. You've been nothing but good to me ever since we met. I shouldn't have questioned your character like that. Your actions have shown me who you really are—I shouldn't have ignored them."

"It's just a misunderstanding, Emma."

Tears filled her eyes and made her voice quake. "Yes, but don't you understand? I'm falling in love with you, too. Except I've been trying to stop, because I didn't think you'd want to be there for my baby. I should have listened to my heart instead of my head."

He placed Christina on her lap and moved to sit on the edge of her mattress. "Are you saying you've talked yourself out of loving me?"

She shook her head. "No. I tried, but it didn't work."

He reached up to wipe a tear from her cheek. "Then why are you crying?"

Emma thought about it for a second, realized she didn't know. She was simply filled with emotions that needed a release, and crying seemed as good a way as any to ease the pressure inside her. "I guess I just need to."

He chuckled, then leaned forward and brushed his lips against hers. "Then go ahead. But I'm going to be here to wipe away your tears."

She sniffed, nodded. They sat quietly together, Emma's hand stroking Christina's hair while Matt's hand caressed her arm.

Love. Just the word made her feel warm inside.

Matt loved her. He loved Christina.

She stared at the two of them, watching them through her lashes. One blond head, one brown. They looked nothing alike. But that didn't matter. Because when he looked at her baby, all she saw was love shining in his eyes.

"How are we going to make this work?" Practical considerations began to poke through her peaceful haze. "You work in Big Bend and live in Alpine, and we're in El Paso. That's too far away. We need to figure this out."

"We will," Matt said with a smile. "But first things first—you need to heal and get released from the hospital. Then we can start mapping out our future."

Emma nodded, seeing the wisdom of his plan. "I can do that."

"Good." He leaned in for another kiss, cradling Christina between them. "Because we've got a lot of decisions to make. Together."

"Together," she agreed, meeting his lips with her own.

It didn't get any better than that.

* * * * *

*Don't miss the previous volume in
Lara Lacombe's thrilling
Rangers of Big Bend miniseries:*

Ranger's Justice

*Available now from
Harlequin Romantic Suspense!*

ROMANTIC suspense

*Tessa Wilkes has trained to become a Special Forces
operator for her entire adult life...that is until she's
unceremoniously tossed out of the training pipeline.
But the gorgeous spec ops trainer Beau Lambert offers
her the chance of a lifetime: to become part of a highly
classified, all-female Special Forces team called
the Medusas.*

Read on for a sneak preview of the first book in
New York Times *bestselling author Cindy Dees's
brand-new Mission Medusa miniseries,*
Special Forces: The Recruit.

Hands gripped Tess's shoulders. Lifted her slowly to
her feet. Her unwilling gaze traveled up Beau's body,
taking in the washboard abs, the bulging pecs and broad
shoulders. A finger touched her chin, tilting her face up,
forcing her to look him in the eyes.

"We good?" Beau murmured.

Jeez. How to answer that? They would be great if he
would just kiss her and forget about the whole "don't
fall for me" thing. She ended up mumbling, "Um, yeah.
Sure. Fine."

"I don't know much about women, but I do know one
thing. When a woman says nothing's wrong, something's
always wrong. And when she says she's fine like you
just did, she's emphatically not fine. Talk to me. What's
going on?"

She winced. If only he wasn't so direct all the time. She knew better than to try to lie to a special operator— they all had training that included knowing how to lie and how to spot a lie. She opted for partial truth. "I want you, Beau. Right now."

"Post-mission adrenaline got you jacked up again?"

Actually, she'd been shockingly calm out there earlier. Which she was secretly pretty darned proud of. Tonight was the first time she'd ever shot a real bullet at a real human being. At the time, she'd been so focused on protecting Beau that it hadn't dawned on her what she'd done.

But now that he mentioned it, adrenaline was, indeed, screaming through her. And it was demanding an outlet in no uncertain terms.

"I feel as if I could run a marathon right about now," she confessed. She risked a glance up at him. "Or have epic sex with you. Your choice."

Don't miss
Special Forces: The Recruit *by Cindy Dees,*
available May 2019 wherever
Harlequin® Romantic Suspense books
and ebooks are sold.

www.Harlequin.com

Love Harlequin romance?

DISCOVER.

Be the first to find out about promotions, news and exclusive content!

Facebook.com/HarlequinBooks

Twitter.com/HarlequinBooks

Instagram.com/HarlequinBooks

Pinterest.com/HarlequinBooks

ReaderService.com

EXPLORE.

Sign up for the Harlequin e-newsletter and download a free book from any series at **TryHarlequin.com.**

CONNECT.

Join our Harlequin community to share your thoughts and connect with other romance readers! **Facebook.com/groups/HarlequinConnection**

HARLEQUIN®

ROMANCE WHEN YOU NEED IT

HSOCIAL2018

Reward the book lover in you!

Earn points on your purchase of new Harlequin books from participating retailers.

Turn your points into **FREE BOOKS** of your choice!

Join for FREE today at
www.HarlequinMyRewards.com.

Harlequin My Rewards is a free program (no fees) without any commitments or obligations.

MYR18